THE JADE SERPENT
THE COMPLETE CHINATOWN CASES
OF JIMMY WENTWORTH, VOLUME 2

BOOKS IN THE ARGOSY LIBRARY:

THE JADE SERPENT

THE COMPLETE CHINATOWN CASES OF JIMMY WENTWORTH, VOLUME 2

SIDNEY HERSCHEL SMALL

ILLUSTRATED BY
JOSEPH A. FARREN

COVER BY
LEJAREN HILLER

POPULAR PUBLICATIONS · 2024

TABLE OF CONTENTS

FANGED TERROR

Wentworth Felt Death Hanging Over Chinatown, for a Star Had Fallen and It Was Time for Kong Gai to Strike

1

JIMMY WENTWORTH WAS off duty and enjoying himself keenly. Across the candle-lit table of the San Francisco restaurant sat young Wang Chen-p'o, and between the gay Chinese and the detective sergeant of the Chinatown detail was Lucille Carrington. Chen-p'o and the girl were attempting to classify the other diners, a game at which Lucille was a match for the nimble-witted Oriental.

Several times each appealed to Wentworth, but Jimmy refused to make any decisions.

"All I've got to say is this," he said finally, grinning. "I notice that Lucille always picks the good-looking men to wonder about, and I'm going home mad pretty soon—"

"I don't blame her," Chen-p'o retorted. "Give the poor girl a little fun, Jimmy. That's the least compensation she ought to have for being willing to marry a flatfoot. If I were a girl, I wouldn't be seen with you, James."

Lucille laughed softly. "Are you going to be one of those jealous husbands, Jimmy?" she demanded.

Jimmy Wentworth smiled at the girl he had saved from Kong Gai, the King Cobra who directed every evil happening in Chinatown.

"Sure I am," he said.

"He'll probably beat you," Wang Chen-p'o decided.

"Every good husband beats his wife once," said Jimmy Wentworth, quoting from the Chinese.

The detective and girl looked at each other so long that Wang Chen-p'o turned, stared out of the window. From it he could see not only the black waters of the bay and the Pacific, where many a victim of Kong Gai's vengeance had been found floating, but also the yellow lights of China-town. Above the irregular tiled roofs young Wang Chen-p'o glanced at the vault of the sky, sprinkled with stars as bright as the artificial lights below.

He said suddenly, "Make a wish! I saw a star fall."

Lucille, happily, murmured, "I've made my wish. Have you made one, Jimmy? You mustn't tell it, or it won't come true."

"I'm pretty dumb," Jimmy Wentworth said. "I was thinking about falling stars. What it might mean in China."

Even Wang Chen-p'o, Chinese as he was for all his American education and manners, said with interest, "What about 'em, James? D'you mean Hollywood stars, or the other kind?"

"You should have read the Shan Hai Ching," Jimmy Wentworth retorted. "It tells all about stars. About the celestial dog, which assumes the form of a falling star. Which way did the star seem to be falling, Chen-p'o?"

"Right toward us. It was a bright one, Jimmy. Why?"

Jimmy Wentworth said, "Maybe it's lucky we're here in the States, instead of being in China. Why, a falling star, according to the Chinese, can destroy armies. Wherever one descends, there will be violence and death."

"How come?" asked Chen-p'o.

"THE CELESTIAL DOG is really a star demon," explained Wentworth. "It has a craving for human blood and... oh, the yarn isn't a good dinner-time story, Chen-p'o. If you

Wentworth's bullet ripped through the hatchetman's arm

want to hear it properly told, ask your honorable father. He knows it. He"—Jimmy wanted to change the subject—"isn't so filled up with geometry and college courses on the appreciation of art that he's forgotten his own mythology. He—"

"You lay off me," Chen-p'o said inelegantly. "I was going to pay for our dinner, but if you aren't nice to me I'll be darned if I will… say, Lucille, in a minute three men'll sit down at a table to your right. I'll bet you ten cents you can't tell me what they are."

Wentworth was glad that his Chinese friend had assisted him in starting conversation about something other than the celestial dog, which, as the Chinatown detective had said, was hardly pleasant hearing.

He, also, was able to see the three newcomers. Two of them were jovial and at ease; the third was obviously in command of the entertainment, and ordered loudly, complaining when the waiter insisted that no cocktails nor other liquor was available.

"Don't worry about it," reached the ears of the three. "We've all had plenty anyhow, Joe. This's a grand party, old man."

"My guess," said Lucille finally, "is that all three are from the country."

"Mine agrees for once," Chen-p'o told her. "Now, what's their business?"

"Small-town merchants, come to San Francisco to do their buying."

"Bets are off," chuckled the Chinese. "We're both in a dime. Or do you want to bet we're wrong?"

"Sure," said Jimmy Wentworth. "You're wrong."

Chen-p'o reached in his pocket and drew out a ten-cent piece, laying it on the table. "Put up or shut up."

Wentworth said, "I'll even give you odds," and laid a dollar on the cloth.

"You'll lose, Jimmy," warned Lucille. "And it'll serve you right for being so positive!"

"I'll give you one last chance to take back your bet," the detective grinned. "I hate to take your money on a sure thing. No? O.K. Here goes. Despite their clothing, and their choice of neckties, none of the men come from the country. They aren't at all impressed with this place, and they're ordering without any hesitation. If they'd been from the country, they would have asked for 'a shot' and done it timidly. Instead, they requested Gibson cocktails. I noticed when they entered that they seemed to know what to do with their hats. Put 'em right on the shelf, instead of hanging on to them, country-fashion, or looking for a check-room girl, city-fashion. That means they've been here before—"

"That isn't the bet," Wang Chen-p'o said hastily, already sensing defeat. "We aren't betting on where they come from, but what they are!"

"Easy, O unintelligent son of a respected father," laughed Jimmy. "This is in the nature of a party for the men. They aren't dressed up, hence the dinner is impromptu. They are in their everyday clothing. All three have bulges in their right-hand coat pockets. No, Chen-p'o; don't jump! They aren't gunmen—not in those clothes. There won't be anything more dangerous in the pockets than tools of their trade. The men appear to be unsuccessful general practitioners. Or veterinarians. I'd be inclined to say the latter. Now give me the dime!"

"Baloney," Chen-p'o said instantly. "That's a lot of hooey."

"Maybe you'll neigh like a horse, and act as if you had glanders," smiled the girl, enjoying the word war between the two. "Go ahead, Jimmy! I won't be embarrassed."

Wang Chen-p'o was delighted. "Disguise yourself as a horse, Jim," he demanded.

"You can find out more easily," Jimmy Wentworth suggested. "You won't need any disguise, Chen-p'o. Vets care for jackasses as well as horses, and—"

"Help yourself to the dime," Chen-p'o laughed. "I'm not convinced "—he turned slightly and looked at the three men—" but I won't argue with you. Not for a dime. My great brain won't work for less than a fifty-cent piece—"

2

WENTWORTH DID NOT add one other fact he had observed. The eyes of one of the men, the largest of the trio, seemed flecked with yellowish-red spots; the man's hands seemed never steady, and as he sat there he constantly moved the knives and forks back and forth. Discolored eyes. Uneasy hands. Loud manner. To Jimmy Wentworth all three marked the opium user.

He was listening to Lucille chatting gayly when the large man began to stare at them as if he had never seen anything like two men and a girl dining before. Abruptly, the newcomer stood up, and without a word of apology to his guests strode to Wentworth's table.

He addressed himself to Chen-p'o.

"Where I come from," he said, "Chinks don't eat where Americans eat."

Wentworth said soberly, "Well, sir, you'd better go back to the place you came from. Here, they do. The gentleman is my guest."

The large, red-eyed man looked at Wentworth, "Fool kid," he growled.

Wentworth didn't know if the man were under the influence of narcotics or merely drunk. He did know that Lucille was flushing hotly, and that his friend Chen-p'o was white with the insulting speech.

"Your friends are calling you," Wentworth suggested. "You'd better go back to them."

"I'll go," said the man, "when I get damned good and ready, and what do you think of that?"

"Very little," Jimmy said. He saw that several of the waiters were approaching, and decided not to add to the scene by saying anything more.

THE STRANGER STARED at Lucille. "You're too good-looking to hang around with Chinks," he said. "If you knew as much about 'em as I do… but I suppose you don't care who you go with, so long as he's got money—"

Wentworth was out of his seat. With practiced hands he had the larger man in firm grip, and, as the waiters rushed up, began to propel the insulting white man toward the door.

"I've got him," Wentworth said to the restaurant people.

In another moment he had hurried the protesting guest to the door, and flung him outside.

Behind him he could hear the laughing comments of the excited diners. With the insults of the man having thoroughly goaded him, Wentworth shoved the fellow so hard that the man stumbled and, under the gaudy lights, fell headlong. Wentworth decided rapidly to make sure that the man wasn't hurt. With that in mind he took a single step forward.

There was a stab of light, and the roar of a gun. Then, instantly, all became silent, both inside and outside of the restaurant.

3

JIMMY WENTWORTH WAS bending over the slain guest, having already fruitlessly looked for the assailant, before any one save Chen-p'o and Lucille emerged from the restaurant. When the proprietor took one glance, he slipped back to telephone the police, and, in addition, sent a waiter scurrying by a back door to find the officer on the beat.

The thought which one of the dead man's friends voiced was in every mind:

"You killed him!"

The sergeant of detectives turned, looked up, and said gravely, "He's dead, yes. Some one shot him, some one waiting out here." Wentworth did not add that it was entirely probable that the bullet was intended for himself. He was about to question the man's two friends, to ascertain if the whole thing were a plot, when a waiter said excitedly:

"Yeah. I saw him"—pointing to Wentworth—"pull a gun."

Knowing the worth of the testimony, Wentworth merely said, "You've got good eyes."

Nevertheless, the matter might become annoying. The newspapers would seize on the bare facts: Wentworth had beyond doubt resented insults, had thrown the man out of the place in anger. There had been a shot, and the man had been killed.

Lucille Carrington said quietly, "You didn't have a gun, did you, Jimmy?"

"He carries a gun most of the time," whispered some guest. "A gangster! And the girl's his woman!"

"Somebody," said the young Chinatown detective grimly, "is going to get himself disliked if he doesn't take care what he says."

The ring about the three, Wentworth, Wang Chen-p'o and Lucille, widened.

A man had been murdered—why? Wentworth stooped to begin his examination, when a burly guest shouted, "Leave the body alone, d'you hear?"

Other guests began to mutter angrily.

Wang Chen-p'o was smiling slightly. The situation amused him. His Oriental sense of humor at Jimmy's predicament was tickled.

JUST AS THE ring of excited men began to close in, with the intention of grabbing and holding the "murderer," the wagon's siren hooted, and in another moment the police automobile's brakes squealed as old Denny applied them. An officer and a detective leaped from the car.

Tracy had his hand on Wentworth's shoulder, roughly, before Jimmy looked up again; then Tracy saluted.

"You here, sergeant?" he asked. "We got the call—"

"I'm supposed to be the murderer," Jimmy Wentworth told him gravely. "Anyhow, the man's been killed, Tracy. By a good sized gun, too. He'd become offensive, and I threw him out. Then some one plugged him—"

"You did," growled one of the dead man's companions.

Indicating the waiter, he added, "This fellow saw the whole affair—"

"I don't see how he could have seen it," broke in another waiter. "He was helping me serve a pressed duck when we heard the shot."

"I looked up quick," said the flustered waiter. "I seen it, I tell you!"

"The door," said Wang Chen-p'o placidly, "closed automatically behind Sergeant Wentworth."

With all of this Jimmy was hardly concerned. Who had killed the man, and for what reason? Addressing the friend of the slain man who had spoken, he said, "What was the man's name, please?"

"Harold Cummings."

"His business?"

"Veterinarian. We're all veterinarians."

Swiftly Wentworth continued his questioning. He learned that Dr. Cummings had invited his two companions to dine at this expensive restaurant, explaining that he had been doing a very good business, and that his practice was picking up. This, according to Yates, the speaker, was unusual. Cummings had never been very successful. The men had stopped for several drinks on the way, and had ended at the restaurant in good spirits. Cummings had not seemed combative in the least until the liquor began to work on him.

"Who would want to kill him?" Jimmy demanded abruptly.

Carter, the other veterinarian, shrugged. "We don't know much about Cummings, personally. However, he couldn't afford wine nor women. He kept pretty much to himself."

"No bad habits?" Wentworth persisted.

Yates looked away. Carter coughed. "I rather not say, sergeant," he muttered.

Jimmy Wentworth said to the diners, "Won't you all go and finish your dinners, if this hasn't wrecked your appetites?"

As the guests filed back to the restaurant, opinion was divided. A good many still believed firmly that the detective had himself killed Cummings, and was now covering his trail by a lot of words.

"Now," Wentworth said simply, smiling at Lucille to tell her that there was no cause for worry, "I'll help you out, gentlemen. Cummings used narcotics, didn't he?"

Yates shrugged. "People said he did," he admitted. "I don't know it for a fact, sergeant. He did act strangely at times."

"Where'd he get his dope?"

"No idea," Dr. Yates grunted. "Never told me. Might have made out prescriptions for himself and had 'em filled."

"We can check that," broke in Detective Tracy.

JIMMY WENTWORTH WONDERED where the trail would lead. He said, "Hop to it, Joe. It's important. Or it might be, depending upon what you learn. Go look through all his Treasury Department books, and have some one go over his old stubs. Now... here comes O'Kane. And he's got somebody!"

Officer O'Kane hurried toward the little group, towing a captive.

Saluting, he said, "I come as fast as I could, sergeant. On th' way I sees this rat, and thinks I, bring him along. So here he is!"

Wentworth said promptly, "Hello, Toad Wilson! I thought you were in L.A. on parole. What you doing up here?"

The captive snarled, "Gettin' so a feller can't take a walk without a big Mick grabbin' him. I got p'mission from th' parole office t' come to Frisco."

"Got a job here?" Jimmy demanded.

"Yeah. An' workin' at it!"

"Sure," Wentworth said genially.

"Making enough money so you can hit the pipe, too, Toad?"

The captive blinked.

"Say," he blustered, "whyn't you mind yer business, Big Dick?"

"I am," Jimmy told him. To Tracy, loudly, "Frisk him, Joe."

Nothing of interest was found on the man.

"Glad you've gone honest," Wentworth said then. "Good-by and good luck, Toad. Better leave the hop alone, boy."

"Lettin' me go?" blinked Hop-toad.

"You're free as the wind!"

4

AS THE UNEASY ex-convict shuffled away, Wentworth spoke hastily to his fellow detective.

"I'll see to checking Cummings's books. You tail Toad Wilson. If you can find where he flops, that'll help. Call Dunand whenever you get a chance. We'll get relief to you, and another man, when you can tell the captain where to send him. This may mean something. Keep him in sight, Joe!"

"Right, sergeant."

Tracy slid away, following the shuffling figure of the ex-convict—who was, in Wentworth's sober reasoning, connected by three possible threads to the murder. Firstly, Wilson was in the vicinity. Secondly, Wilson was an opium addict as well as a two-time loser for second-degree burglary. Thirdly—

"What makes you feel he's guilty?" asked Lucille, both curious and also sorry for the former San Quentin inmate.

Aloud, in answer to the question, Jimmy voiced his third reason: "He said, 'Lettin' me go?' and was surprised instead of merely being pleased."

While the questioning had been going on, Officer Mulready, from the automobile, had been systematically doing his job. He came out of the shrubbery at last, his flash in one hand, a weapon in the other.

"Department Colt, sergeant," he said, handing the weapon to Wentworth.

One shell had been ejected from a filled clip. The muzzle of the automatic retained the odor of burned powder.

Looking at the number, the Chinatown detective said, "George Mannion's gun. The Chinese got him in February. We'll just say it was a police revolver, Mulready, in case we're asked."

"Yes, sergeant."

"And if the newspaper boys say anything, Mulready, all you know is that it was a police gun! Don't forget!"

"No, sir. A police gun it is, sure enough. And—"

"It might have been *my* gun," Jimmy Wentworth said softly.

"It might, sergeant, if th' numbers were different! Many's the time I saw old George polish that gat! Why—"

"Forget George Bannion and the gat," Wentworth said smilingly. "You've done a mighty good bit of work finding it, Mulready."

" 'Tis surprised I am that it was thrown away!"

"Since we've got the law making a parole violator of any paroled convict found carrying a gun, Mulready, a man like Wilson—half full of hop—would throw the gun away, no matter what his orders might have been." Crisply, "Please stay here with Cummings's body until the dead wagon comes, officer."

Wang Chen-p'o remarked, "My appetite, handed down to me by bloodthirsty ancestors, is as good as ever, James. I want the rest of my dinner! I know I owe you money, Jimmy. You're a good guesser."

"I—I don't think I'm very hungry any more," Lucille

said, shuddering. Bravely, she added, "But I'll have some coffee, anyhow, Jimmy."

"Wish I could," Wentworth said regretfully. "It's going to be some time before I get a decent meal! Be sure and slip down to headquarters later tonight, Wang. And take Lucille home after dinner."

"Where are you going?" Lucille demanded.

"Don't tell any one," Jimmy grinned, "and then they can have the fun of reading it in the papers. James Wentworth, patrolman, is going to be arrested for the murder of a man named Cummings. I can feel it in my bones, Lucille!"

"But, Jimmy—"

"And you might as well get used to having your picture in the paper, as the wife of a cop," Jimmy went on, smiling broadly. "The whole story'll come out, dear. When you're interviewed, tell what happened, but don't say anything about whatever took place outside of the restaurant! Just say there was an argument, and that's all you know. And don't mention anything about my being a detective, although that will be kept under cover by Captain Dunand. The papers have got to be good, and print what we tell 'em, or they won't get any story at all this time. We'll be in position to bargain."

"Jimmy! It sounds so ridiculous. You've got to explain." In the same breath the girl added, "I don't understand."

"Neither does he," said Wang Chen-p'o maliciously. "Why, if somebody told Jimmy that the moon was made of green cheese, he'd go up right away and have a look-see. An inquiring nature—"

"Up in the sky," said Jimmy Wentworth slowly, "a star

fell. The star demon is known, by the Chinese, to bring violence. Death. Was Cummings's death the one foretold? Or is this a sign from the gods that we must try to avert evil? Perhaps this is the time I'll really find Kong Gai! He'll think I'm out of the way."

"I still don't understand."

"Cummings was killed. He was a narcotics addict. He was shot by another opium smoker, with the gun that some Chinese took away from a dead patrolman. Why? I've got to learn, dear. It's my job."

"An inquiring nature," said Chen-p'o, "is, as I tried to say before, a most fatal gift. Good luck, Jimmy. I'll see you at headquarters. And if Lucille poses for her picture, as the woman in the case, or the star witness, or something, I'll see that she isn't posed like a debutante in the rotogravures—"

"How is that?" the courageous girl smiled, her hand going into Wentworth's.

"All leg," chuckled Wang Chen-p'o.

5

AT TWO THIRTY the following morning, when honest Chinese were asleep behind their shuttered windows, a custom-built touring car meandered in a crooked course along Chinatown's main thoroughfare. The Oriental district appeared as silent and deserted as Peking in the days Jimmy Wentworth was a boy in that city, when at night the Inner and Outer Cities were closed to one another by the Great Gates, which were only opened after midnight by sleepy Manchu guards for ten minutes, so that gorgeous red-and-blue trapped carts, drawn by sleek mules, might speed to the Imperial Palace for the Daybreak Audience with the Throne.

In all Chinatown there seemed nothing alive save this one automobile, obviously guided by an intoxicated driver, and with equally drunken companions singing in gleeful chorus.

As the custom-built car purred forward in unsteady course, a sudden twist of the wheel brought a front tire over the curb, so that the front of the car was half on the sidewalk, just before the curio shop of P'ien Ching. One of the men in the rear seat shouted blissfully at the driver; another began to sing more loudly than before.

The rear door of the machine was opened, while the driver roared his motor—apparently bound to do everything possible to attract attention and wake peaceful sleepers—and, noiselessly, swiftly, a dark figure slipped out, stooped and, protected in all directions save southward, moved like a black shadow to the door of the curio shop. This opened, and the figure disappeared into blackness.

Without seeming to hurry, two black-clad Chinese approached from the north, from the heart of Chinatown. Without seeming to stop, the two hatchetmen looked the riotous party over, and continued on their way. Without seeming to turn, the two Chinese observed that when the car continued on its way there were the same four drunken white men in the big devil-machine.

JIMMY WENTWORTH, UNOBSERVED, was already in a room on the second floor of P'ien Ching's building. His ruse had worked. The hatchetmen passed on and into the dark shadows of Chinatown, unaware that the custom-built car had contained five men, one of whom had been the patrolman of the district, known only to Kong Gai as being actually a sergeant of detectives.

P'ien Ching, a slender old Chinese, was frightened when he stood beside Wentworth in the empty, dark room on the street face of the building; frightened, and showing his fear.

"Do not worry," Wentworth said quietly, in singsong Cantonese. "You know that Wang Yu trusts me, and that young Wang Chen-p'o, his son, made the arrangements. Do you suppose they would do anything which might bring danger to you and your family?"

"To capture this Evil One named Kong Gai," said P'ien Ching, "the honorable Wang, head of our house, would set fire to the relics of his ancestors."

"And you?" Wentworth asked curiously.

"I am an old man, and not afraid to die," said the curio shop owner. "I have children and grandchildren. I do not want them to feel Kong Gai's vengeance!"

"They will be protected, honorable P'ien Ching. No one will know that I have hidden here."

"You will be missed, and then the search commences! Kong Gai's spies and hatchetmen will report every possibility, and in a day or two the highbinders will knock at my door. You may escape, but my family will be punished."

"Wait," Wentworth assured him. "You will see. There will be no search. All has been carefully prepared."

And in the morning, when the news began to circulate through Chinatown, P'ien Ching saw that the white man had spoken the truth.

Down at headquarters, however, Captain Dunand was being given an uneasy time. The newspapers, told that there might be more to the "accidental death" of Cummings than his being shot by a department officer, were willing to print what was furnished by the captain of detectives. In their zeal to "get in right" with the police, the stories were tempered. That in the Bulletin was about the same as the others:

POLICEMAN KILLS VETERINARIAN
ALLEGED INSULT AVENGED IN FATAL
QUARREL

Resenting what he considered an insult to Miss Lucille Carrington, Patrolman James Wentworth last night shot Dr. Harold Cummings to death in the Castle Café. According to eyewitnesses....

After a fairly accurate account of what had taken place,

the newspapers all ended with the statement that charges would be preferred against Wentworth, and that pending the investigation being conducted by Captain Dunand, the offending officer was being held incommunicado.

WITHIN A HALF hour of the appearance of the morning papers four elderly Chinese arrived at headquarters. With them were two white men, both of whom Dunand recognized. A.W. Morrison, San Francisco's leading criminal attorney, and Blanding Graydon, attorney for the Six Companies, the great tong organization.

"For the first time in years," said the head of the Six Companies, "we have an officer in Chinatown who has tried to bring us peace. Even the children love him, captain. Therefore the Six Companies have decided to come to his defense. Mr. Morrison will have charge of the case, and Mr. Graydon is here to arrange for bail, no matter what amount is set, sir."

Here was a complication neither Wentworth nor Dunand had expected.

The gray-haired captain of detectives, for all his uneasiness, began to smile, and as soon as his face moved from its grim mask, the head of the Six Companies smiled also.

The venerable, learned Chinese wiped the smile from Dunand's face by saying, "So that is it, captain?"

"That is what?" blustered Dunand, knowing that the canny Chinese knew.

"The very walls have ears," said the Chinese. "We are not needed, are we? Not our money, nor our men of the law. It is well, captain. If you should by chance see Mr. Wentworth, will you tell him a star fell yesterday evening, and that there is fear in Chinatown?"

Dunand no longer hesitated.

"He saw the star fall," he admitted quietly. "You're right, sir. This charge is meaningless. Can you give me an idea what is feared?"

The Six Companies man shrugged. "Death," he said laconically. "The terrible death brought by the blazing Red Dog of the skies. In what form no man knows. But we think we can tell who will be the carrier of death… No, captain, do not say the evil name of the Deadly One!"

"Then there *is* something up," Dunand growled.

Again the Chinese shrugged.

"Do not ask us what," he said wearily. "We do not know. But death is intended for the Evil One's enemies. It has been intimated that the King Cobra waited for a sign from the gods, and the falling star was the sign. It has always been the sign in the past. And"—keenly—"so the policeman who pats children on the head, and assists old men across the street, knows of all this?"

"It was told him," Dunand countered briefly.

"Then he is a wise man, having listened," said the Six Companies man. "We will go now, captain. We came to help the man who befriends Chinese, and we are glad that all is well with him."

The white attorneys were listening without understanding. Morrison said, "Can Wentworth be cleared of the shooting, captain? If necessary I'll defend him, or we can pull a few wires—"

"We don't need to do either," Dunand said frankly. "Keep this to yourselves, or Wentworth's life won't be worth a dime, gentlemen, but he didn't have any more to do with killing this man Cummings than you did."

6

AFTER THAT, ALONE again, the gray-haired captain of detectives wondered if he had talked too much for Wentworth's success. At least he had given no intimation of his sergeant's whereabouts.

While the Six Companies men were in Dunand's office, Jimmy Wentworth was watching the teeming street below. On a little teakwood stand beside him was a kettle of boiling water, a bowl of tea leaves, another of rice, a third of spiced plum jam—the fruit picked from the trees in Kansu province and crushed to a pulp by Chinese women—his breakfast. Seated Chinese-fashion, he ate as he watched the horde of busy Chinese, through which tourists, interested and gay, made their way. He saw what they missed. A man in black, entering stores, and emerging a moment later. A hatchetman collecting tribute. A woman with a shawl, black and green silk, half over her face: a leper woman. He must get her out of the district as soon as he came out of his hiding place. Two men speaking friendlily together—one a hatchetman of the Suey Sings, the other a rival tong murderer. Each had his hands concealed in his sleeves. Each held a weapon. But nothing took place.

Now and again Officer Simpson, assigned during Wentworth's absence, marched his beat, watching alertly, but seeing none of the things which meant so much to Wentworth.

Quietly, later, Wentworth read over the report smuggled into the curio shop; Wang Chen-p'o, as agreed upon, wrote:

"Nothing new. No sign of anything. Write you to-night again. Did you know you were important, James? The Six Companies tried to bail you out, but you are still in jail. They have expressed sorrow publicly that nothing can be done about it. As we say in Chinese, '*Yau yan wa ho'nan hok.*'"

Which, Jimmy knew, meant, "It is very hard to wait."

Was he making a mistake, hiding like this, on the long chance that it might mean a chance to catch Kong Gai? Would the Evil One, reckless now, and eager to consummate his plans, whatever they might be, during Wentworth's absence, leave a loophole which might prove Kong Gai's destruction?

Wentworth, eyes always on the street below, tried to piece his facts together and make something of them.

Dr. Cummings, a veterinarian, had been shot to death. Cummings had been a narcotics addict. The report from headquarters, after investigation of the Department of Justice files, showed that Cummings did not write his own prescriptions for opium, therefore the veterinarian, to get the drug, must have patronized some one who was in the employ of Kong Gai.

Toad Wilson, also a dope user, had shot Cummings beyond much doubt. Toad had left a good job in Los Angeles to come to San Francisco, and, according to Mulready, was living in a decent apartment house and seemed well supplied with money. There was no proof that Toad was selling drugs, and every proof that he wasn't. However, a search of the apartment, when Wilson was out to breakfast, showed that the man had a good supply of opium there.

Both of these facts had been communicated to Wentworth by means of notes taken to the curio shop below.

Cummings was a narcotics user; so was Hop-toad Wilson. It meant something, Jimmy believed, when combined with the thing Cummings had said in the restaurant: "If you knew Chinks as well as I do…"

It meant something… but what?

AND THEN WENTWORTH'S keen brain began to put two and two together, and get the proper answer! At first it seemed so fantastic that it was utterly impossible, and yet Wentworth, time and again, had solved Chinese crimes on little better clews. Here is what he had, as twilight slowly came again to Chinatown, to keep him company in the growing dark:

Cummings was a veterinarian. In a city, most of a vet's practice was with dogs and cats. Cummings had made money suddenly—more money than he needed to buy his drugs. How? And, after the money had been paid Cummings, the veterinarian had been shot down shortly after, by another man, an ex-convict of unsavory reputation, who was also a user of opium. Why? What had Harold Cummings done, for which payment had been made, which caused some one to desire the white man's death?

That was the initial problem to solve. No matter how Wentworth sought to follow the puzzle to a solution, it seemed to wind closer and closer about Kong Gai's evil body. Kong Gai, the controller of the illicit opium trade of Chinatown.

What could Kong Gai want of a veterinarian? Did Cummings's profession enter, in any way, into this crime? That was another problem of possibly vital importance. Would this lying in wait solve it?

The great bell of the old brick cathedral struck the hour, and a light began to burn yellowly under the sign on the tower:

Son, Observe the Time
And Flee from Evil.

Jimmy Wentworth saw the familiar words without reading them, and then he gazed perplexedly past the cathedral and into the sky above.

All this affair had commenced with the appearance of the fiery star demon, the falling star, last night. The terrible Dog Star, foretelling horrible death to mankind. Dog Star... Red Dog of Heaven... veterinarian!

Wentworth said, "No!" aloud. Then, whispering to himself, he voiced his growing amazed thoughts. "It's impossible! It couldn't happen. It wouldn't work. Mad dog! What a way to clear one's path of enemies!" Again he said, "It wouldn't work. A mad dog runs in a straight line, and snaps at anybody or anything in his way. No! I'm just trying so hard to solve this thing that I'm going batty. Why—" The last word died away, and Jimmy Wentworth sat bolt upright.

From somewhere below, northward, there sounded a hoarse, fearful bark, followed by a series of weird, uncanny, sinister throaty howls... the sound of a dog attacked by the furious madness! As Wentworth listened, blood turning cold, the unearthly howl arose again, nearer and more awful.

7

WENTWORTH WAS ON his feet, gun out. The Chinese, recognizing the fatal howl, began to mill about in terror. Shrill cries came to the detective sergeant's ears. Younger Chinese shrieked in fear only of a mad dog, but the elder Chinese gasped out, "Red Dog of Heaven!" and "Star Demon!" and seemed unable to move. Groans of despair rose high above the storm of sound, punctuated again by the terrifying mad howl of the beast.

Cautious no longer, Jimmy Wentworth threw wide his window. As he saw the fanged terror rushing down the street he raised his gun. Then, gun leveled, he stopped. Running northward was Officer Simpson, gun in hand, breaking his way through the horde of Asiatics.

One instant longer Wentworth looked at the afflicted animal. What he saw made him cold as ice.

Snapping furiously, a great mongrel, with bloodshot eyes and mouth dripping saliva, tore down the crowded street. Once the mad dog paused and heedlessly chewed its own foreleg. Then, howling terrifically, it continued its deadly race. Again and again it sprang at some Chinese. Sometimes it leaped at shadows, sometimes at visions visible only to its mad brain.

Then Simpson's blue-clad arm rose as the waiting officer managed to get a clear shot. The gun roared mercifully.

The mad dog leaped high and then fell to the pavement. No second bullet of mercy was necessary.

Wentworth, colder than before, saw what was taking place in the street below. Here and there black-clad hatchetmen were moving through the groups of excited Chinese, and going about a peculiar business. There were a full half dozen of these men—lean Cantonese with the prison-like pallor of the professional killer on their faces.

What these hatchetmen were doing seemed at first glance to be of no importance. Coming up behind some respectable merchant, or official of the Six Companies, they would touch the back of his neck gently with something that flashed under the lighted street standards, and then instantly follow this motion by brushing the skin with what appeared to be a handkerchief.

So this was what the opium-smoking veterinarian had taught some one… taught some one who could only be Kong Gai! The hot blood in Jimmy Wentworth's veins turned to ice, and it was a full minute before he was able to rush from the room.

Chinatown had never seen him in plain-clothes. Kong Gai, and Kong Gai's men, were certain that he was securely locked up in the Hall of Justice, awaiting a trial for murder. Even if he were discovered, Wentworth knew that he must risk detection. The search for Kong Gai, for the time at least, was over. He dared not wait.

P'IEN CHING, DESPITE the smiles of his grandchildren, was bowed down before a paunched image in his shop. Wentworth, in passing, and without apology, seized the old Chinese's broad-brimmed black slouch hat and pulled it down over his own face; then he hurried into the street.

As he closed the door behind him he saw, directly before him, a venerable merchant, high in the councils of the Companies, who had stood firmly for law and order and against the sinister influence of Kong Gai. Up to the merchant shuffled a black-clad Chinese, and deftly touched the back of the Companies man with the point of a tiny, very keen knife. So cleverly was this done—and so excited the merchant—that not the slightest pain was felt.

From his sleeve the hatchetman drew a wad of cotton, torn from the padding of a Chinese winter jacket. The hatchetman's own hand was gloved with shining material, rubber. Kong Gai's highbinder raised the cotton toward the tiny spot of blood on the merchant's neck, and then Wentworth's fist crashed against the side of the Asiatic's jaw. Down went the Chinese, striking against Chinese legs as he fell.

So dense was the group of people, so excited their minds, that only one person saw the hatchetman drop—a second of the deadly King Cobra servants. Swiftly the other hatchetman moved through the throng, who were all engaged in discussing what might happen because the white policeman had shot the devil-sent Red Dog to afflict people with madness. How lucky it was, they said, that the dog had only bitten a few in his mad course!

Straight toward Jimmy Wentworth the deadly hatchetman weaved his course, his beady black eyes never leaving the detective's figure. Wentworth saw him coming. He marked also how Officer Simpson was nearing him, on his way to the nearest call-box, to have the dog's body removed for examination, and to report what had happened.

When the hatchetman, hands in sleeves, was no more

than three feet away, Wentworth deliberately turned his back. Out slipped the hatchetman's heavy assassin's blade; up went his arm. In another instant Wentworth would have been slashed from neck to shoulder in the long, circular blow of the Chinese killer.

The knife went up, and, timing his action to the split-second, Wentworth whirled around. He took no chances this time, swinging the heavy butt of his gun full in the hatchetman's face.

The Chinese staggered back. Officer Simpson cried, "What's this? Stop it, I tell you!"

Confident that the hatchetman's pain would cover what he said, and that the other Chinese were incurious and interested only in the appearance of the fatal Red Terror of the Skies, Wentworth said, "Cuff him, Simpson! Quick! He's got cotton on him. So's the other Chinese I knocked down. Get it. Pick it up with a handkerchief! I'll call headquarters. Look out for trouble!"

Simpson said, "What th' hell—"

WENTWORTH HAD NO intention of returning to P'ien Ching's curio shop. To do so would only call down the vengeance of Kong Gai on the old man. Instead, he slipped hastily into another store, owned by a Six Companies man; the shop was empty. Every one was in the street, discussing the strange event.

Jimmy called the Hall of Justice. He said less than a dozen swift words: "Riot car! Box 217D! Wentworth calling!"

Then he hastened back to the doorway and, gun in hand, watched Simpson's blue-clad figure tower above the smaller Chinese.

Simpson had cuffed the second of the hatchetmen, whose face was bleeding. The other was out of sight. Wentworth couldn't tell if the fellow was still unconscious on the pavement, or if he had slunk away. But he could tell that other hatchetmen were worming through the crowd toward Simpson, who was dragging his captive nearer the call-box.

The Chinese now realized that something which none understood was going on, and, Oriental fashion, did the thing Jimmy hoped they would do. They backed away from the white officer, leaving a broad space about him—a space into which there now entered a lean, black-clad figure… another… a third… all shuffling nearer the tall patrolman at the call-box.

Simpson had the box open, and the telephone off the hook, when some Chinese shouted—in Cantonese, which did Simpson no good—" Beware, O man keeping peace! Look out! Knives!"

With far less compunction than he would have felt at shooting the poor maddened beast, Wentworth's arm came up. His bullet ripped through the hatchetman's striking arm as it flashed up behind Simpson's unsuspecting back.

For a moment the other hatchetmen held their attack, peering about to see from whence the unexpected shot had come instead of leaping on the patrolman. Before they were able to slash Simpson down as he stood at the call-box, the riot car came roaring down the street, and the men from headquarters circled about Simpson. By sheer good luck one more of the hatchetmen was made captive; the fellow had forgotten, in his amazement, to hide his knife.

Of the half dozen black-clad assassins Wentworth had

seen from the window high above the street, three had been made captive... no! Four! Up from the pavement staggered the first man Wentworth had hit with his fist, and Detective Henderson, as a matter of principle and because the fellow was black-clad and lean and had an evil face, arrested him also. Four out of six!

8

JIMMY WENTWORTH SLID along against the building walls, one block, two, three, and then hurried down toward the Hall of Justice.

He found Captain Dunand in his office, fuming because he did not know what the riot call might have meant.

"Made a mess of it, chief," Jimmy Wentworth said, standing before the gray-haired captain of detectives' desk. "Things happened; I couldn't stay where I was. No catching Kong Gai this time."

"Slower, boy! What happened?" Wentworth explained swiftly.

"Hmm," Dunand muttered. "Made a mess of it, eh? Only caught four of the men? Only prevented the deaths of the finest Chinese in the district? Say, young fellow, what do you want, anyhow?"

"To catch Kong Gai!"

"Wait," Dunand suggested soberly. "You two will meet face to face again. I want you to get him, lad, but... what a fiend he is!"

While they were talking, the riot car returned, and Detective Henderson, together with his prisoners, came to Dunand's office also.

"No speakee English," Henderson said disgustedly. "I tried 'em out while we come back in the wagon. They were tryin' to get Simpson, chief. With knives. We all saw it. What'll I book 'em for? Attempted assault?"

"Attempted murder," Jimmy Wentworth said. "That's the charge, until we see what happens. It may prove to be straight first degree murder."

"O.K., sergeant," said Henderson. He could stand it no longer. "What happened, Jimmy?" he demanded.

"Did Simpson give you the cotton wad?"

"Sure. Said something about not touchin' it—"

"Unless I'm all wet," Detective Sergeant Wentworth said soberly, "that cotton is impregnated with rabic saliva, from the mad dog Simpson shot. If the saliva from a rabid animal gets on a cut, or a tear, or even a crack in the skin, it'll cause hydrophobia… and Henderson, when I was a kid in China, I saw a man who'd been bitten by a mad dog. The man goes mad sometimes. He'll attack any one near him… and he himself is apt to die."

Henderson, shivering, said: "But… I don't get all this yet! Do you mean to say that—"

"Exactly," Wentworth said quietly. "The mad dog represented a sign from heaven to the superstitious Chinese. Hatchetmen slipped around in the crowd, and touched the back of respectable merchants' necks with the saliva, after making a painless cut with an extremely sharp knife. When these men sickened and died, it would look like a visitation of the gods, or people would suppose they might have actually been bitten. The back of the neck is near the brain, of course; the infection would travel swiftly and surely.

"And," grimly, "the man behind all this is Kong Gai! That's why I fear him, and hate him!"

At the name of King Cobra, the Venomous One of

Chinatown, one of the handcuffed Chinese snarled a few words to a companion.

In the same crackling Cantonese, Wentworth said, "You are mistaken, O killer! You are not the great men of death you suppose. Those who were bitten, or poisoned from the dog's spittle on your cotton, will all recover. We, the foolish white men, will show them the way to regain health."

"Deport 'em," growled Dunand. "Back to China, eh?"

"That's the best way to get rid of them," Jimmy Wentworth agreed. Thoughtfully, he added, "Better bring in Toad Wilson now. He can be charged with whatever degree murder you want, chief. After Dr. Cummings—as the price of getting opium, and for money as well—had told Kong Gai how to use rabid dogs to kill men, Kong Gai had Wilson put Cummings out of the way. As an added touch, Cummings was murdered with the same gun that was used to kill one of the force… and Toad, full of hop, threw the gun away instead of hanging on to it.

"I… well, I just happened to be in the restaurant."

"If you hadn't," said Dunand sharply, "you'd have been on your beat, and the mad dog would have torn down the street, and you'd have shot it… and that would have been all. You wouldn't have seen the other things happen. When the poison worked, we'd have had a dozen, or fifty, or a hundred deaths in Chinatown! And you told me you'd made a mess of things!"

"I'd hate to see him when he's working good, chief," Henderson said.

"We've got to get together and give the newspapers a story," Dunand told Wentworth. "They've played fair with us. How'll we manage it?"

"Henderson gets the credit," Wentworth decided. "My name doesn't appear. Nor do we mention any arrest except Toad Wilson's, and the fact that I'm cleared. Wilson we charge with murder. We'll tell him we're saying he's exposed Kong Gai, and then Toad won't ever want to get out of prison! He must know what the Evil One's revenge would be. Anyhow, Wilson is a two-time loser already. He'll plead guilty to manslaughter to escape the rope, and that's three times and out. Or, in! In Folsom for life. And now, if you don't need me—"

"Need you? What for? All you do is mess up our cases on us!" Dunand's keen eyes were twinkling. "You've only been workin' two nights and a day; What now?"

"Got to finish a dinner we started last night," Jimmy grinned. "And give two people a good cussing, chief."

"That tells me a lot!"

"Lucille, sir. And Chen-p'o. I'm going to give 'em both the devil. Wang promised to see that Lucille's photographs for the newspapers didn't show too much—er—well, I saw the Bulletin's picture, and it—"

"That's the way the newspaper boys always take pictures," Dunand laughed. His eyes bored into Jimmy's as he added, "You're a real detective, lad, but you don't know anythin' about women! Say nothing about th' legs, Jimmy! Take my advice!"

"You understand all about the ladies, don't you, chief?"

Dunand laughed outright. "I've only been married thirty-one years," he said. His hand went friendlily to the young detective sergeant's shoulder. "Run along," he told Jimmy Wentworth. " 'Tis only once you're young, boy."

YELLOW VENOM

*Into the Heart of Chinatown to Strike
a Blow at Kong Gai, the Evil One,
Creep Two Strange Hatchetmen*

1

THE ROOM OF the apartment house standing high on San Francisco's hills into which Jimmy Wentworth stepped was filled with the heavy air of death. The Chinatown detective felt that he had been allowed to enter under protest, and this made him watchful and alert.

Although sunlight streamed in through the windows, lighting a bowl of yellow jasmine flowers on a table, Wentworth would have known that death was in the room, even without Captain Dunand's telephoned information. There was death in the silence, in the constrained attitude of the two men and one woman who stood waiting for him to speak.

They did not need to be advised as to Wentworth's purpose. He was in his blue patrolman's uniform. A little earlier his only duty had been to settle a dispute between a fish dealer and his clerk regarding the payment of wages, part of which was in cash, part in shark's fin, cuttlefish, dried oysters stuffed in fishmaw, and blue-gray edible seaweed. Now he had stepped across a threshold where he might have need of all his wits.

Jimmy Wentworth said quietly, to the man who had ungraciously opened the door, "I've been ordered here, sir."

"You aren't needed," the man snapped. "I'm Carter Langley, Gordon Langley's brother."

The detective's gun
roared twice

All Captain Dunand had told Wentworth was that a man named Gordon Langley had died, and that some one had called for the police. Since the request had come to headquarters a moment before Wentworth rang in from Box 27C, just three blocks away, on the southern edge of Chinatown, Dunand had ordered him to leave his beat and see what the trouble might be. In this way valuable time could be saved. If necessary, men from the Hall of Justice could take the case over, should Wentworth report that it was advisable.

Wondering just what Carter Langley's nervous attitude

really meant, Wentworth said flatly, "Somebody called for the police. That's why I came."

The woman pointed her finger at the other man in the room.

"You did, doctor," she cried. "That's why you slipped outside! To telephone the police! Now you'll say it was your duty, and Gordon's name will be blackened, and it will all be in the newspapers—"

She was becoming hysterical.

"You called us, doctor?" Jimmy Wentworth said quickly.

Dr. Stevens said defiantly, "Yes, officer. I did." To Mrs. Langley he added, "It is to keep Gordon's name from any stain that I summoned the police, Marcia. Remember, I was Gordon's friend—"

"A hell of a friend," cut in Carter Langley grimly. "If you hadn't started him when he was sick, he wouldn't have ever—"

"I tell you he didn't," snapped Dr. Stevens.

"Don't lie!"

"You're excited, Carter."

Mrs. Langley whispered, "Oh, Carter... don't fight. Please. With Gordon in the next room... dead."

WENTWORTH LOOKED PAST the angry man, at the closed door. In a moment he would see what remained of Gordon Langley. Already, from the hasty words, he knew that Langley's brother accused Dr. Stevens of starting the dead man in the use of drugs. That was perfectly clear. However, if Gordon Langley had died from an overdose, why would the doctor himself have requested the police? It didn't make sense. Out of the east window, Jimmy Wentworth could see the curved roofs and bright tiles of

Chinatown, elbowing against the red brick spire of the old cathedral. A thin wail of sound, where a singsong girl was entertaining some fat and wealthy merchant, came to his ears. Drugs might mean Chinatown... opium might mean Kong Gai. Was he again on the trail of the King Cobra, the Evil One? And who was the dead man, Gordon Langley, anyhow?

Enough time had been wasted. Wentworth said abruptly, "I'm sorry to trouble you, Mr. Langley. I take it that your brother has died. Firstly, please give me his exact name."

"I'll give it to the proper authority," Carter Langley growled. "Not to the first rookie cop who comes barging in."

"I'm afraid I must insist that you tell me," Jimmy Wentworth suggested. He, also, was growing angry at Carter Langley's attitude, although he was as quiet as ever. "You see, sir, I've been detailed to this case—"

"Who do you think you are?" asked Langley unpleasantly. "The chief himself? Or perhaps Detective Sergeant Wentworth?"

"I'm Wentworth," Jimmy said softly.

FOR A LONG moment the man stared at him; even Mrs. Gordon Langley stopped her sobbing.

Wentworth said swiftly, "Please answer my questions. I know that your brother's name was Gordon. I've heard enough to indicate that he may have used drugs. I must know how he died, and why Dr. Stevens sent for the police. Will you tell me, or must I have you all taken to headquarters?"

Dr. Stevens said quietly, "Gordon Langley did not use drugs, sergeant. As his physician, I can vouch for that, irrespective of the evidence. That is why I requested the police... again, irrespective of the evidence!"

"You can imagine what this means to me," Mrs. Langley choked. "How the newspapers will play this up! My poor Gordon! I can see the terrible headlines already. Immigration official killed by... opium. It's awful, sergeant. Can't you see that it be kept quiet, please?"

Jimmy Wentworth said, "A Federal investigator, Mrs Langley?"

"Yes. Gordon was leaving to-morrow for the border. To catch some Chinese, he said, who were to be smuggled over the line."

Unconsciously, Wentworth's brain recorded the image of Kong Gai, murderer, poisoner, thief, who eluded every trap set for him by the police. There might be something to this case, something which did not appear on the surface. He was very glad now that Captain Dunand had sent him to look about and report. The obvious thing had been that Carter Langley might have profited by his brother's death. However, even before this instant, Wentworth had decided that the truculent Langley was merely distressed, outraged, and angry at Dr. Stevens. He was positive of this now, and had no intention of even questioning Carter Langley.

Time to have a look at the dead man!

"Please come with me, doctor," Wentworth said soberly, and walked toward the closed door leading from the living room.

"I'll come along," Carter Langley decided.

Wentworth didn't want more arguments: "You'll stay where you are," he said.

Eye met eye.

"Very well," the older man said slowly. "I only thought I might be of assistance… answer questions—"

Jimmy Wentworth almost said, "You had your chance." Instead, but with a grim undertone to his words, he said only, "Thanks. I only want Dr. Stevens."

2

GORDON LANGLEY'S BODY lay on the bed. He was in pyjamas. Since the other twin bed had not been disturbed, it seemed probable that Gordon Langley had returned to the apartment during the morning... returned to die horribly.

Wentworth stepped between the beds. He bent over and touched the dead man's hand gently, inquiringly. It was only slightly cold. The eyes were glazed, the eyeballs shrunken, but the jaw was not yet rigid.

"Death occurred just about the time you called us?" Jimmy asked.

"Yes, sergeant. Within two or three minutes. Langley has been dead less than a half hour."

"Tell me what happened."

Although Jimmy Wentworth listened closely, his eyes roved about the room while the physician spoke.

"Mrs. Langley summoned me at about ten o'clock, sergeant. Langley had been in high spirits at breakfast. He ate heartily, smoked a cigarette, and left for the immigration office as usual. An hour or so later, approximately nine thirty, he came back, complaining of headache and pain in his eyes. He said to Mrs. Langley that he had the illusion of seeing double.

"At first he refused to go to bed, but suddenly became

very sleepy. He seemed unwilling, or unable, to speak clearly. When he finally complained of a pain in his chest, Mrs. Langley sent for me."

"You were able to come at once?"

"I was in my office, and came immediately. I have known Gordon Langley ever since we were boys. I found a rapid, shallow pulse, no reflexes, shallow and very difficult breathing. While I was preparing to go to work—while I was listening to what Mrs. Langley had to say, which of course was extremely important in determining what to do, Langley, without warning symptoms, settled into a coma from which it was impossible to arouse him."

"Everything pointing toward opium!"

"Everything, sergeant. It appeared so obvious a case that I lost no time in following the established treatment—"

"Explain, doctor. Omit nothing."

"I administered permanganate immediately. Being without a stomach tube, I injected hypochlorate to induce vomiting. Smelling salts and strong coffee failed to arouse Langley. I used a heart stimulant—"

"Strychnine?"

"No! Something warned me against using a poison, sergeant. Even while I was engaged in attempting to save Langley's life, I must have suspected something. In place of strychnine, I used amyl nitrite; pearls of it crushed in a handkerchief and held under Langley's nose. Needless to say, even this failed. Langley died as I was trying artificial respiration."

"If you were to state the cause of death, doctor, from the symptoms you would say 'Excessive use of opium.'"

The physician flushed, and then said, "May I speak plainly?"

JIMMY WENTWORTH FOUND himself liking the earnest doctor. He said gravely, "You can. And it will be between us two, Dr. Stevens. I want to know how Gordon Langley died. If accidental, if even suicide, I'll step aside. Murder is different. Go ahead and have your say."

Stevens stared down at the dead man, and then said, "I believe you. Suicide? Gordon Langley's life has been an open book. Accidental? No man was ever more careful. Murder? He had no enemies. You heard his brother berate me for prescribing a narcotic some years ago. Langley, at the time, suffered from neuralgia. His brother is merely one of those men who object to tobacco, liquor, narcotics… anything! To say that Gordon Langley used drugs is ridiculous!"

"Just the same, he's dead," Jimmy Wentworth said soberly.

"Yes. I said I'd speak plainly, sergeant. It is my opinion that he was murdered, and that is why I called the police."

Wentworth said softly: "A postmortem will tell the story, doctor. Unless—"

"Unless," Stevens snapped, "Langley was killed by an opium poison. What will show then? Nothing, sergeant! A pathologist cannot determine the presence of opium or morphine after death. There are no positive signs. But, Wentworth, I will stake my reputation on one small fact, against all the other apparently positive proof, one little fact, depending on my own word only."

"And that is—"

"Gordon Langley's eyes were widely dilated just preceding death! And the eyes of a dying man from opium are—"

"Contracted," Wentworth said instantly. "That's great, doctor! You have given us something to work on, something to substantiate your belief that this may be murder." Wentworth made up his mind swiftly, and then said, "Where's the telephone here?"

IN THE HALL, with the buzz of voices in his ears as the Langleys questioned Dr. Stevens, he called Captain Dunand.

"Will you send up a couple of men, chief?" he asked. "Yes… might be murder. The place should be searched. I'll send one of 'em back to headquarters, to make analyses of food from here. And there'll be a post-mortem… and an argument. What? No, not a notion yet. Just that it looks curious."

Before returning to the living room, Wentworth slipped back to the body. With practiced hands he searched Langley's clothing; handkerchief, wallet, money, ticket to Vancouver, fountain pen. No papers of interest at all. In the buttonhole on the coat lapel was a tiny spray of yellow jasmine.

Mrs. Langley had broken down when Wentworth returned. Carter Langley's face was pale with rage.

"Look here, Wentworth," he said, "I'm not going to permit an autopsy, and you can make up your mind to that."

Jimmy's patience and courtesy was exhausted. "I didn't ask you for permission," he said mildly enough. Then his face grew stern. "From your behavior, Mr. Langley, I am afraid it may be my duty to arrest you—"

"What! Me? Good heavens, sergeant!"

"You're attempting to impede the progress of this investigation, and you act like a guilty man."

"I... why... I'm only trying to protect Gordon's memory..."

"Then," said the Chinatown detective grimly, "act like a brother! Don't suspect Gordon Langley of drug-using. Think as I'm thinking—that an honest man has been killed in the execution of his duty!"

"Do you believe that?" Mrs. Langley breathed. "If you can only prove it!"

"I'm going to prove it," said Jimmy Wentworth. "That is, if you will help me. I need your help, Mrs. Langley."

"Anything, sergeant!"

"Good. Now, your husband was going to Canada, to prevent Chinese being smuggled across the line. Did he say anything about this to you?"

"Only that he was going away. Gordon was always secretive about his work."

"Thank you. When was he going?"

"To-morrow morning."

"Who knew he was going, Mrs. Langley?"

"I knew; Carter knew. Carter wanted him to bring back a British-made overcoat from Vancouver, but for some reason Gordon only laughed, and didn't promise."

Wentworth's eyes brightened.

"Who is his superior at the Immigration Office, Mrs. Langley?"

"Mr. Post. However, Gordon seldom explained to Mr. Post where he was going. The Immigration Department try to keep everything secret. He may have only said that he was leaving town, and would get men for the capture of the Chinese at Seattle."

Wentworth asked, "Who were Mr. Langley's friends among San Francisco Chinese?"

The woman smiled sadly.

"He had friends, yes," she admitted, "but I didn't know them. They never came here. Sometimes Gordon made their stay at the Immigration Station on Angel Island more pleasant, and then afterward they'd send him little presents... like this bunch of jasmine on the table."

"Who sent the flowers?"

Mrs. Langley shrugged. "Some Chinese Gordon must have befriended. They came last night, together with a package of jasmine tea. Gordon insisted on drinking some of the tea for breakfast, but it was too highly scented for me—"

CONCEALING HIS ELATION, Jimmy Wentworth said softly, "Believe me when I tell you we are on the trail of your husband's murderer, Mrs. Langley. May I have the package of tea?"

"You think—"

"It's too soon to think," Wentworth told her. "But your husband drank the tea, and you didn't... and you are still alive."

"Jasmine!" Dr. Stevens muttered. "Jasmine!"

"In the old days in China," Wentworth said to the startled doctor, "the favorites of the Emperor were poisoned with an infusion of jasmine petals. I don't know the name of the poison—"

"Gelsemium! Or gelsemine. Yellow jasmine! It causes death by paralysis of the respiratory nerves... acts like opium, sergeant! A sixth of a grain will cause death. The treatment is the same as for opium poisoning, except that…"

The honest doctor covered his face with his hands.

"What's the matter?" all three asked him.

"Back of my mind must have been that damnable opium idea," Stevens groaned. "I didn't give morphine for that reason. If I had… Gordon might be alive. It is the real antidote. And I didn't use it!"

"How could you have known?" Mrs. Langley asked. "You did your best, Walter. And you alone believed in Gordon." Her head went high as she faced Detective Sergeant Wentworth. "Find who killed my husband," she begged.

"I think I know who was back of the killing," Jimmy Wentworth said. "And it is safe to say that Gordon Langley was killed in the performance of his duty. You can be proud, Mrs. Langley."

"I am. Gordon would have asked no better way to die."

3

THE BELL RANG. Carter Langley admitted Wilson, Mulcahey and Oliphant from headquarters. Wentworth gave his orders rapidly. Oliphant was to return to the Hall of Justice with the package of jasmine-scented tea for analysis. Mulcahey was to remain on duty at the apartment, and was told to let no one, on any pretext, come inside.

Best of all was the presence of Wilson, and with him Wentworth laid his next plan. The two detectives went over it carefully, and at last Wentworth was satisfied.

"You're taking a chance, sarge," Wilson said briefly.

"Not with you on the job. Anyhow, it's worth trying."

"I'll do my darnedest, Jimmy," said the older man.

Carter Langley broke in: "Aren't you going to telegraph Vancouver, Wentworth? It seems to me—"

"We'll do all that later," Jimmy Wentworth said vaguely.

Dr. Stevens had slipped from the room; he returned with a flushed face. "I've investigated," he said abruptly. "A post-mortem is not necessary, sergeant. I am willing to testify that Gordon Langley met his death from gelsemium… and, in another half hour, or less, no investigation would discover any poison at all!"

"Which would mean that every one would suppose Langley met his death from opium," Wentworth said. "Thank you, doctor."

"I remembered that gelsemium vanishes within an hour after death."

"Good. Ready, Wilson?"

"Ready, sergeant."

"Let's go."

While the Langleys and Dr. Stevens stared at them, the two detectives left the apartment of death. After the wide-eyed elevator boy had taken them to the main floor, Wentworth and Wilson walked along the wall to the entrance. For several minutes, keeping in concealment, they observed the opposite buildings.

In a level voice Wilson said, "My guess is third story, fourth window from the right, Jim. It's open six inches—enough to look out. The blind is drawn almost to the bottom. Or it might be the half open window on the seventh floor."

"Too high for a decent shot. How about the grating above the delivery entrance of the other apartment house, George?"

"Don't think so. Anybody passing would ruin the shot. I'll keep my eye on it anyhow. There might be two of 'em, lad."

"Or none," Jimmy Wentworth admitted. "I think it's the window on the third story. The blind on the window next to it is halfway up; that looks funny."

"Good luck, Jimmy!"

"Good hunting, George," the young Chinatown detective grinned. "Well, here goes nothing."

Jimmy Wentworth, whistling, stepped through the door.

Pressed, hidden against the side of the wall, George Wilson followed his sergeant. Wilson's gun was out, his hand was steady. His keen eyes flicked from window to delivery door and back again.

Into the sunlight walked Jimmy Wentworth.

Before he had taken five steps, Wilson's gun roared twice. Wentworth went for his own weapon, and then the other detective cried, "Got him! He's… here he comes!"

WENTWORTH'S OWN AUTOMATIC was out now, its steely barrel leaping toward the third story window even before he fully recognized what his fellow detective meant by his words. At once the Chinatown detective backed into the protective shadow of the apartment. There was no other shout, nor anything to be seen except excited residents, mostly women, shoving up windows and poking heads out to see what was taking place. One of these blew furiously on a police whistle.

On the ledge of the third story window hung a limp, black-clad figure. While the two detectives waited, cautiously watchful, the body in dark clothing began to slip, and justified Wilson's shout of "Here he comes!" by falling to the street with a horrible noiseless impact.

"He raised the window to get a better shot," said George Wilson, finest marksman of the force. "I couldn't miss such a target, sarge. Got him just as he was bringing his rifle to his shoulder."

"Let's go have a look at him."

"Careful, Jimmy!" Wilson pleaded. "You've said yourself that these highbinders always travel in pairs. I don't see his partner."

Wentworth's knowledge of the ways of the Chinese hatchetmen caused him to say, "If he fired from the shoulder, and not from the hip, he isn't a Chinese, George."

Jimmy was not mistaken. The dead man was no Oriental. He was dressed in black prison serge, and his face was gray with death. His hair, cut round in the back, indicated the San Quentin convict barbers. A paroled or discharged prisoner.

Above them, Mulcahey was shouting from the Langleys' window:

"Is it us you're needin', Jimmy Wentworth? Is anything wrong with you down there?"

"Everything is O.K. now," Wentworth called back. "Phone for the wagon, Pat." Jimmy wished that Mulcahey hadn't used his name. However, the important thing was having learned that the Langley apartment was being watched—watched by a gunman, an ex-convict, who was marked on the chest with a tiny, freshly tattooed emblem. A king cobra, hood outstretched, ready to strike. The sign of the deadly Chinese, Kong Gai, the venomous Evil One of Chinatown.

4

JIMMY WENTWORTH ENTERED Captain Dunand's office after finishing his patrol of Chinatown. He unbuckled his heavy black belt with a feeling of relief. Now he could really bear down on the Langley case.

"It's time you reported," growled the gray-haired captain of detectives. "You know what one of the news hounds is intimating? He says, 'We got information that Langley was a hop-head, and that you're coverin' it for his family.' How about it, Jim?"

"What did you tell him, chief?" Wentworth countered.

"Told him if he or his paper has any information relative to the death of Gordon Langley that it is their duty to present it to the proper authority. Which is us. That shut him up, boy! He thinks he's got an exclusive story, but we won't verify it for him, and that makes him sore. It's a good thing he hasn't talked to Dr. Williamson."

Williamson was the department chemist.

"This is one time," said Jimmy quietly, "where the infallible Williamson has missed something—beyond his knowledge, chief."

"What's that?"

As clearly as if he had been present at the autopsy, Wentworth outlined the chemist's report. At the end he said, "And there has been found nothing abnormal in the post-mortem appearances, from which William-son suspects opium poisoning. He has found every other characteristic opium sign—blood fluid, lungs congested, heart clots on both sides of the heart, body livid. But, chief, each of these signs might come from another drug. It is called gelsemine, and it's the extract of the pretty jasmine flower. It leaves no sign; it's deadly, and if Williamson will examine the packet of tea I had sent down, he'll find the deadly drug in the leaves! Somebody wanted it believed that Gordon Langley died from natural causes. If—"

"Opium isn't a natural cause."

"No, unless a man used the narcotic regularly, sir. That is what Kong Gai hoped every one would think."

"Hmm. It doesn't make sense. What are you driving at, Jim?"

THE YOUNG DETECTIVE sergeant helped himself to one of Captain Dunand's cigarettes, a long-tubed Imperialles, such as many Native Sons smoked in the old Vigilante days. He said earnestly, "Chief, I'm driving at this: Kong Gai is behind this death. That is proved by the ex-con George Wilson shot. I'll wager when you looked up his record he was a D.U."

"That's right. He had seven months added for having morphine shipped into the pen. In the handle of a shaving brush. He used dope, sure."

"And when he came out of Quentin, he got in touch with Kong Gai, naturally. To get a headful of hop. Kong Gai had him watch the Langley apartment, to see what happened. And probably told him about me. When he saw me... bang!"

"You and Wilson managed that pretty well, Jimmy."

"Thanks. Now, Kong Gai's reason for wanting Langley out of the way is all tangled up with Langley's Immigration Office work—"

"If it is," said the gray-haired captain of detectives, "he'll get the surprise of his life! The Immigration Department has already wired Seattle. The northern border will be watched from end to end. Any Chink that's smuggled in will have a tough time getting past the cordon! There won't be any wholesale smuggling done, you can rest assured."

Jimmy Wentworth began to smile. "That'll give the Immigration officers a lot of healthy exercise," he said. "The Canadian border is pretty long, chief."

"Maybe. Every road will be watched. All available men on the Mexican border have been ordered, today, to fly north so as to be on the job—"

Wentworth looked at the end of the cigarette, and then said earnestly, "In the last half hour, sir, I've done some investigating. In Chinatown. And, with the department's help, and with young Wang Chen-p'o's assistance, outside also. Will you call up Immigration headquarters, sir, and ask them to reverse their orders?"

"What do you mean?"

"Tell 'em," Jimmy said crisply, "to have the Mexican border watched, and forget about Canada!"

CAPTAIN DUNAND STARED at his sergeant. Once he made a noise in his throat, and then he lifted the telephone from the desk.

"Colonel Hotchkiss?" he said finally. "Sergeant Wentworth has something to say to you about the Langley case." With that he handed the instrument to Wentworth, as if saying that he washed his hands of the matter.

Grinning broadly, the young Chinatown detective said into the transmitter: "I understand you are acting to prevent Chinese being smuggled across the Canadian border to-morrow, colonel."

"Correct, sergeant. Please say nothing about it."

"No, sir. However, you won't catch any Chinese."

Hotchkiss's deep voice boomed, "We'll get 'em, sergeant!"

"Not along the Canadian border. If you send your men there, Gordon Langley will have died in vain. Send your men along the Mexican line, colonel."

"Perhaps you didn't know that Langley had already bought his transportation to Vancouver?"

"Yes," Jimmy said soberly. "I knew that, sir. I also know how secretive he has always been, which is probably why he was so successful in preventing other smugglings. And, colonel, I've learned a few other things. With the help of a young Chinese, who has assisted the department before, I've learned that Langley always bought transportation somewhere… and always went somewhere else! His true destination was never the place for which he bought his ticket!"

"Eh?" Hotchkiss ejaculated. "I never knew that!"

"In Chinatown," said Wentworth, "there aren't many things we white men do that the Asiatics don't know. I've verified this information, colonel. The Santa Fe have wired San Diego, sir, and on March 22, after Langley had bought a ticket to Walla Walla, Washington, he boarded a Santa Fe train and paid fare to the southern end of the railroad. On June 6, after having purchased a ticket to Spokane, and engaged a berth in his own name, he actually went to Dallas, Texas. On July 11—"

"Enough," Hotchkiss begged. "Hold the line just a moment, sergeant. I want to countermand my orders! I believe you!"

While Wentworth waited, Captain Dunand said contentedly, "Good work, Jimmy! So that's why I missed some of the boys to-day? Hangin' around th' railroad companies, were they? No wonder you were sure about Mexico being the smuggling den!"

"Didn't have time to give you all the dope, chief," Jimmy explained. "And you have said a good many times that you wanted results, and not clews—"

"You can't put men in jail on clews," said the gray-haired chief. "I've said it, and I say it again. Action is what we want in this department!"

"And the man who killed Gordon Langley! If I can only… Oh, hello, colonel… no, there isn't anything else I have to tell you. You don't know about any one ever having threatened Langley?"

"No, sergeant. If such a thing happened, he said nothing about it. He really was a very silent man. By the way, do you put any credence in the story that he smoked opium?"

"No. It isn't true. Who told you about it, sir?"

"An anonymous letter. It hinted that we ought not employ men who were addicted to narcotics."

"Was there a drawing of a snake at the end of the letter?" Wentworth demanded.

"No. There wasn't any signature."

There was nothing more Wentworth needed to learn; he said politely, "Thank you very much, colonel," and replaced the telephone on Dunand's desk.

"WELL, THAT'S THAT," Dunand grunted. "I'll bet the

Bulletin reporter's city editor got another of those unsigned letters, Jimmy. It's a great thing that you were able to find out that Langley had been poisoned by this jasmine stuff."

"I didn't discover it. Dr. Stevens was suspicious. If Langley's eyes had looked differently when he was dying, every single fact would have pointed toward opium—even Langley's secretiveness. That's another sign of the narcotic user. Now... I've got a little walk to take, chief."

Captain Dunand looked at his watch.

"I wouldn't mind a walk before dinner myself, lad," he announced. "The missus said something about a baked ham, Jimmy. With lima beans. There'll be apple pie and cream. A walk will give us an appetite! Will you come home with me?"

Wentworth said, "I'd like to, captain, but—"

"But you're going to dinner with Lucille Carrington?"

Months before, the Chinatown detective had torn the Carrington girl from the coils of Kong Gai; she kept in hiding, as Captain Dunand knew, lest Kong Gai's vengeance might again seek her out. Not even the head of the department knew where the white girl lived.

"No," Jimmy said, grinning. "I wish I were, chief! But... well... I may be longer than I think, taking this walk. I'd like to have dinner with Mrs. Dunand. If you go with me, and we're late... No, I'd better go alone, sir."

Captain Dunand's face did not move a muscle.

"What a liar you are, Jimmy Wentworth," he said jovially. "You're on the track of something. You think it might be dangerous. Boy, a good many crooks have had a crack at my old tough hide! I'm going with you! Only, tell me where, Jimmy, and also why!"

Orders were orders.

His face alight, Wentworth said keenly, "I had one clew to follow, sir; one tangible clew. The box of jasmine-scented tea. Here's what happened:

"The tea was of a grade far superior to that sold to tourists. It was first-chop Formosa tea, marvelously scented. The leaves were all the pointed young growth, without stems, rank outside leaves, or buds. It was a sun-dried tea, such as the Emperors formerly drank.

"Kong Gai would have been wiser, chief, if he had sent common tea as a present to Langley! But, like all crooks, yellow, black or white, he didn't want to lose face by purchasing anything except the best. I had an idea that the jasmine-scented tea would not be the sort Kong Gai would drink himself; he's Cantonese, you know. They prefer a brick tea.

"So, with Wang Chen-p'o's help, we began checking. First-chop Formosa tea does not grow on bushes… that is, except in the Taiyal country in Formosa. If the tea had been smuggled in, nothing could be done. However, it was part of a regular shipment, assigned to seven Chinese merchants here. This information came from the Customs officials—"

"I could use a few more dicks like you," muttered Captain Dunand.

"—and Wang Chen-p'o then went to work. He learned every purchase made from the seven merchants. There were only six in the last month. Jasmine tea comes high! Five packages went to reputable merchants. The sixth went to Sun Gi'i Woong, and I've had my eye on him for a long time!

"The son of the merchant who sold the tea took it to Woong. Woong immediately left his shop, and walked part way up the street with the other Chinese... and, chief, step by step, inch by inch, Wang Chen-p'o traced Woong's path! I tell you, nothing is missed in Chinatown!"

Captain Dunand again picked up the telephone. To his wife he said, "Young Jimmy Wentworth is comin' for dinner. Eh? Yes, I'll tell him. If we're a bit late, will it be all right?"

Smiling broadly, the gray-haired captain of detectives said to Wentworth, "She says it's about time you came again, Jimmy, and that if you don't bring a good appetite she won't give you a weddin' present. She won't put the ham on till we come." In a placid voice, "No sense sayin' we... mightn't come, eh, Jimmy?"

"No sense," agreed Jimmy Wentworth.

5

A HALF HOUR later, two black-clad figures slipped from the side door of the grim Hall of Justice. The heavier, shorter man walked with a decided limp; the younger man was erect. Both faces were shielded, concealed, by limp, black slouch hats. Under the brim, the countenances of both men appeared yellowish, Chinese. A scraggly thin beard—no more than a dozen gray hairs—trickled over the older man's chin.

The taller of the two men walked with shuffling gait, feet parallel. Chinese-fashion. The other man's limp made it impossible to determine the manner in which his feet touched the pavement.

For a long time Detective Sergeant Wentworth had been prepared for just such a day—a day when it looked as if Kong Gai's den had been discovered.

Speaking Cantonese like a resident of that Chinese city, Wentworth had no fear of detection save by close examination. He must depend upon his wits to prevent anything like that. Captain Dunand, disguised as a grandfather-tongman—one who had killed his twenty-nine men—would have no need to speak at all. The younger "hatchetman" would, properly, do whatever talking was necessary.

"Keep your hat on, and your head down," Jimmy Wentworth cautioned as they stepped into the sunlight. "That's all you've got to do, chief. Don't try to even look up, no matter what happens. Your eyes are blue, you know, and there's no way to change 'em Now—"

"Wait a minute," Dunand grumbled. "That bandage on my knee hurts like the devil, lad! I limp like I was born this way! Anyhow, the traffic signal's against us—"

"Great," Jimmy said, fighting down a desire to grin. "We'll cross right now."

"But—"

"From now on, I do the talking, remember," said Jimmy briskly. "Not a word out of you, oh Wing Yo'u, grandfather of eagles and son of the clouds!"

"Bah," growled the gray-haired captain.

Nevertheless he shuffled limpingly after Wentworth, heading into the traffic of Kearny Street and toward the hills of Chinatown.

A WHISTLE BLARED. Officer Jenson left his post and walked angrily toward them. In the silence, as all traffic was halted, could be heard the nasal cries of Chinese children at their lessons, and, hardly more musical, the blare of a mechanical piano as the Barbary Coast tuned up for the evening.

"And where," demanded Officer 7011, "do you think you're going?"

Wentworth, perfectly aware that several Chinese on the opposite side of the street were listening, said shrilly, *"Ngo p'a'ngo tong cho lu lok!"*

Which meant merely, "I am afraid I have lost my way."

"Yeah," said Officer Jenson. "Sure. I like 'em fried myself. And turned over."

A truck driver, homeward bound, laughed loudly.

Given an audience, the traffic officer made the most of it. "Boola boola itchy baloney," he said. "That means, 'if you don't watchem red light I put you in jail, sabbe?' Now... get along, get along. And make it fast."

As the pair scurried across the street, Dunand muttered, "In the back he jabbed me, th' flat-foot! I'll 'watchem red light' him! To-morrow he goes out where a red light would be excitement. I'll put him out like a light, believe me! Jabbin' me in the back... and likes 'em fried! I'll fry him! I'll—"

"Shut up," said Jimmy Wentworth. "And keep shut."

His captain made a noise in his throat, but that was all.

What Wentworth hoped for happened. One of the watching Chinese sidled up, saying, *"Chi'u kola!* What is the trouble, oh, brother?"

"Is it forbidden," Wentworth said in singsong Cantonese, shrilly, "to cross a street with an honorable grandfather?"

"It is all a matter of lights," said the Chinese. "The ways of the white man are very hard to understand. Whom do you seek? Perhaps I can help—"

All this, Jimmy knew, was proper, up to the place where the other offered to be of assistance. That, according to Chinese custom, was not only unnecessary, but highly improper. He observed also that the other Chinese left the scene, as if not caring to remain near their countryman. Therefore, the "friendly" Chinese must certainly be a spy or hatchetman, despite his jovial expression and Occidental clothing. Good enough!

"THE AUGUST GRANDFATHER," said Jimmy carefully,

"goes to the temple of the Seven Extremely Pleasant Sins. Why, I do not know. I was appointed to bring him from the south. It has been a long way, brother."

The Chinese lost interest. Many Chinese came to San Francisco for a similar purpose. And so he said only, "The way to the temple is easy to find, brother," and walked away.

Climbing the first steep street, Wentworth said softly, "Spy, chief. If he were suspicious, he'd have given a signal, or walked with or ahead of us. We've passed the first inspection."

"I—"

"No talking," Jimmy grinned.

Side by side the two detectives walked slowly up the street. It was the hour for food. Strange smells and odors reached Captain Dunand's nostrils: odors which Wentworth recognized instantly. Glazed duck, being fried in bean-oil to which bits of green sugar-cane had been added. Dumplings, containing slices of squid, boiled in red-colored water. Fermenting rice-sprouts and pork sizzling in the cooking-pots. The hour of relaxation, when men rested after the day's work; rested, and ate and smoked. The acrid fumes of forbidden *ng ki po*, potent Chinese liquor, seeped into the narrow, darkening side street.

Here and there children, already fed, ducked out of the way as the "honorable elder grandfather" in black walked painfully up the hill. Captain Dunand had no need to make believe he was advancing with effort. Wentworth had tied the bandage expertly and tightly.

A man raced out of an eating shop, followed by an irate Chinese brandishing a knife. Wentworth clutched his companion's arms, whispering swiftly, "Nothing, chief. The beef was tough. That's all."

"I—"

"Ssh!"

A black-clad hatchetman sauntered up to them a second time, "Is it far from the southland, brothers?" he asked in passing.

"Far," said Jimmy Wentworth. "We seek the temple of the Seven Extremely Pleasant Sins. None have told us where to find it—"

"This is not a country town," the hatchetman said, and went his way.

"Word's out," Wentworth said grimly. "We're not under suspicion. But we're being watched. Remember what I said! When I cough—that's the signal."

"If—"

"Pipe down," Jimmy Wentworth snapped.

6

ALONG THE SIDE street they went until they reached Dupont. There still a third man in black approached them. This time all that was said was, "The temple is one block north, one block east."

And, a half block from the temple, was the place into which Jimmy Wentworth intended to break! Had word reached there—word which would put Kong Gai on guard, if the villainous Chinese was actually hidden in the abandoned shop where the package of jasmine tea had been delivered, where Kong Gai had poisoned it with the deadly extract? Or were the spies being merely alert? Either way, there was no backing out! If Dunand and Wentworth did not go toward the temple at the next corner, both would be shot down. If they did, would they find Kong Gai prepared? Then Mrs. Dunand would wait in vain for her husband!

Otherwise they had a chance of nabbing the fiendish King Cobra, the first real chance since Jimmy Wentworth started along the bloody trail of the Evil One.

As they turned up the hill again, a block farther north, the captain of detectives was fully realizing why a frontal attack, in force, would have been a complete failure. Nothing could get past such an intricate and delicately operating spy system. Why, Kong Gai probably knew every time the riot squad left the Hall of Justice! But there were other stations besides headquarters. As Dunand limped along, he wondered if Jimmy's simple plan would really work.

Ahead now was the gaudy, vermilion-painted front of the Chinese temple. Since it was the Hour of Food, the little cracked bell rang ceaselessly, as a hungry servant of the temple kept pounding it with a brazen hammer. Inside, the priests went hungry, while common men fed. Later they would eat also, sparingly, of millet and rice.

Halfway up the hill Wentworth paused, as if doubtful, or weary.

Paused directly before the blank door of an empty shop. From across the street, as he had hoped, two black-clad men sidled swiftly. Each had his right hand in his left sleeve—holding a knife or gun.

"What is wrong, oh brother?" asked one of the Chinese.

"We seek the temple of the Seven Sins," Jimmy Wentworth said clearly, almost loudly. "My honorable grandfather, who is very tired, has already killed thirty men, and comes to pray that the last of their deaths not be accounted to him. Twenty-nine he should have killed, as is written, and not thirty. He is very sad. He fears that the gods will be angered at him, and—"

A CONCEALED PANEL in the blank door opened noiselessly and a sharp voice commanded, "Bring in the man who has killed thirty men! There is a Someone who might wish to inquire as to his methods of killing."

The door opened and the two "Chinese" stepped inside.

Whatever happened now would be a matter of minutes. Jimmy Wentworth's heart began to pound. He could feel the blood pulsing in his veins, and throbbing in his neck.

So far everything had gone like clockwork, but what would happen next?

Oriental fashion, their guide, or guard, walked ahead. As the two detectives passed through door after door, in total darkness, Wentworth marked each of the doors with a bit of chalk.

The fifth door opened into a room dimly lighted. One rape-seed oil lamp burned on its teakwood stand. There was not a single object in the room save a gigantic screen, ornamented with a silvery king cobra painted on the middle panel.

A clear voice asked, after a moment's pause:

"*Ni kiu mat' meng... a?* What are your names?"

"The honorable grandfather is Wong Yo'u," Jimmy Wentworth said in singsong Cantonese. "I am of no importance."

"The grandfather goes to the temple of the Seven Sins, having killed too many men?"

"Even so, August One," answered the Chinatown detective.

Was Kong Gai behind the screen? Kong Gai, murderer, thief, fiend; Kong Gai, the deadly influence behind every sinister happening in the Oriental district; Kong Gai, who had directed the death of Gordon Langley. Although Wentworth stood seemingly at ease, hat on, head down, as is proper when facing a man of higher caste, he was tingling in every nerve. In another minute... in seconds, perhaps....

"Remove your head covering," said the clear voice. "I would gaze upon the man who has killed thirty men. Perhaps I may even hire his bloody hand."

WENTWORTH'S ALERT EARS caught a fragment of sound. Dunand, of course, understood not a word of what was transpiring. It came to young Jimmy Wentworth that the chances of ever dining again were mighty remote. Just the same, now was the time to eliminate the devilish Kong Gai, no matter what the result. And so, while appearing to clear his throat, he muttered to Captain Dunand, "Now!" and leaped forward to the attack.

Before he could reach the screen, before Dunand's gun was out, lights flashed up in the room, making it blindingly white. Voices screamed warnings in wild alarm. There was the reek of gun-smoke, without sound of discharged weapons. From somewhere high in a wall a knife flashed toward Wentworth's head.

Down went the cobra screen before Jimmy's onslaught. Dunand's gun roared instantly, knocking over the man-sized image seated on a teakwood stool.

"He's gone," Dunand roared. "After him, Jim!"

The room went black as the pit.

For a moment Wentworth tried to find a crevice in the wall, through which Kong Gai might have escaped. Then he whispered urgently, "Back to back, chief! Fire at anything you hear!"

How slow the time went! Had his plan gone wrong? If so, two bodies would soon be floating on their way toward the Pacific, and there would be a mystery for some other detective to work on.

Wentworth could hear little ratlike noises here and there in the room. Once, in the blackness, there was a loud clang—a trapdoor being dropped. Had they been standing over it, that would have been the end. Dunand's gun cracked again, and a Chinese's scream filled the room with horrible sound.

"Got him," the gray-haired detective said grimly.

A voice—not the clear voice of Kong Gai—cried, "Rush them, brothers of the knife! When I give the word, rush!"

The word was never given.

BLUE FLAME DARTED into the room, and, at almost the same instant, picked men from headquarters, having melted the lock with their torch, leaped into the chamber. For only a moment there was conflict, and then the Chinese—all save the dead and wounded—faded away, through secret panels in the wall.

From end to end of the building the detectives searched, but found never a sign of Kong Gai.

Again the villainous King Cobra had fled.

"If I had fired earlier," Captain Dunand mourned, "I might have hit him—"

"Look," Jimmy Wentworth said, showing Dunand the toppled figure of the Snake God. "We never had a chance to get him to-day, chief."

Kong Gai had never been in the room at all, as was proven by the apparatus concealed in the image, and the telephone wire running from the Snake God through the floor. Kong Gai, safe elsewhere, had merely looked into the room, and by means of a telephonic amplifier had made his voice come from behind the cobra-painted screen.

"Anyhow," said the gray-haired captain of detectives, "I've worked me up a good appetite, Jimmy, and I think we've thrown a little fear into our Oriental friend."

For answer a knife flashed into the floor between the two men!

And the clear voice of Kong Gai cried gayly, "Wait, oh white fools! My day is coming!"

Again the old building, with its secret panels and concealed passages, was searched, but a second time nothing was found. Not until the detectives demolished the walls did they discover the narrow chamber in which Kong Gai must have been, and which he left by an underground tunnel, destroying it after departing!

When the two men were in Captain Dunand's house, the captain said, "Not a bad day's work, Jimmy, even if Kong Gai thinks his day is coming. We have two of 'em wounded, and the yellow stains on the big Chink's fingers, plus the poison you found on him, ought to swing him for Langley's death. That was accident, Jimmy, but we can use a break once in a while. That was great work, lad."

"I'm anxious to hear what happens to-morrow down on the Mexican border. That's the important thing."

"Not now it isn't," said Captain Dunand. "Right now, dinner is the main thing."

At noon the next day, Detective Sergeant Wentworth, again arrayed in his blue patrolman's uniform, was approached on his beat by a party of tourists.

He gave the impression of listening to their questions, but in his ears was the shout of a newsboy.

"Extra! All 'bout the big fight down in Mexico! Hundred Chinamen captured! Two dead! Smugglin' plot foiled! Extra! Extra!"

So Kong Gai's plot to bring Chinese hatchetmen, highbinders, gunmen, into the States had been thwarted; Gordon Langley, brave and silent man, had not died in vain.

"Officer," demanded the man of the party, "aren't there any interesting dangerous places for us to see?"

"No, sir," said Jimmy Wentworth courteously. "There are the Chinese temples, and the shops, and the restaurants—"

"He's only a policeman," sniffed one of the ladies. "He wouldn't know!"

The male tourist said, "Thanks, anyhow, officer. You're pretty young. New to the force, eh?"

"Yes, sir," said Detective Sergeant Wentworth, smilingly. He was still grinning to himself as he marched along his beat, his lithe, blue-clad body swinging tirelessly over the pavement.

FIREFLIES OF DEATH

Chinatown Blamed the Evil Devils
for the Murders, but the Only Devil
Wentworth Believed in Was Kong Gai

1

THE HEADLESS CHINESE

SEARING, STIFLING HEAT poured into the office of the Inland-California Hotel, the quivering yellow heat of mid-August, which ripens grain and fruit in the broad valley, and makes all white men hunt for shelter and shade. The blinds were drawn. A fan hummed. Nevertheless the room was like a furnace.

The portly manager, at his desk, appeared completely miserable, wilted, and unhappy, as if the terrific heat added an intolerable burden to other troubles. He was in shirt sleeves. As he glanced unwillingly up, the presence of a younger man, obviously cool and comfortable, must have provoked him. But habit forced him to ask:

"What can I do for you, sir?"

In the hotel man's mind was the thought that this immaculate young fellow had nothing to make him hot, weary, and uneasy. Why, this man was the guest who had driven up from San Francisco an hour or so ago in a roadster, and entered the lobby whistling contentedly, a sound which—today of all days—had severely taxed the manager. A kid out of college, whose father paid the bills, coming in to Collins's office because there weren't enough bath towels, or something just as senseless. Collins's wide shoulders sagged.

And then the smiling, cool young man said quietly, "You can tell me when, where, and how the headless Chinese's body was found, please."

Collins swung around in his chair. "I knew the papers'd get it," he muttered. "It couldn't be kept under cover, even if Joe Murphy promised." In a louder voice he insisted, "I can't tell you anything. You've got to see Chief Murphy."

The dejected manager was more unhappy than ever. If the San Francisco newspapers exploited this strange crime—and Collins could only think that the young fellow standing beside his desk was a reporter—mighty little business would come to the hotel for a long time. It would be ruinous, for the guests already registered would check out at once. Fearful of saying anything at all, Collins finally added: "I'm very busy this afternoon. You go see Murphy."

"It's too hot to go looking for him," Collins's visitor smiled. "All I want to know is—"

"I can't say a word," the hotel man mumbled. He wondered what would happen if he asked the young fellow to keep the affair of the headless Chinese quiet. Now that he had a chance to look the youngster over, Collins didn't believe that a bribe would do any good.

While the manager examined the hotel's unwelcome guest, the guest was examining him also, and Collins became nervous under the scrutiny. Then the young man said amiably, "Murphy isn't in the City Hall. I've telephoned there. Anyhow"—slipping his hand into his pocket, and after withdrawing it, showing what was in

Wentworth fired when the
hatchetman was almost on him

the palm to Collins—"you can save everybody a lot of time
by telling me whatever you can."

COLLINS'S EYES OPENED wide. He stared at the immaculate guest, and then he ejaculated, "You're a dick—a detective?" His eyes wandered back to the shield. "A sergeant of
detectives from San Francisco?"

Jimmy Wentworth grinned. "I'll get older," he said.
"Chief Murphy asked the head of the bureau to send somebody up here, and I'm the goat. Now, let's get down to cases.
Tell me what you can about the dead Chinese. I don't want
to waste time looking for Murphy."

"You been here less than an hour, and you knew a man
was murdered here! You haven't been in touch with Joe
Murphy. Only one man in the hotel, besides myself, knows
about it. He's the man who found the body. I've sent him
home; he was almost nutty. Poor old Wing, murdered!
Why, detective, Wing wouldn't hurt a fly! He'd worked for

us a long time." Perplexedly, Collins went on, "His body was only discovered a little while ago—"

"Sometime after twelve o'clock," Jimmy Wentworth said. "And of course you haven't been able to find the head."

Collins cried excitedly, "How do you know all these facts? It's been kept secret—"

"I stopped at a couple of fruit stands along the highway," Jimmy Wentworth explained. "Bought fruit wherever Chinese operated the stands. In one of 'em, just outside of town, the Chinese were all worked up. I listened and picked up a word or two."

"You understand Chinese, detective?"

"The language, yes," Jimmy Wentworth admitted grimly. "Nobody understands the people."

"How'd you know we found the body just after twelve?"

"Because it's probable he was murdered at twelve."

"Good Lord! How'd you know that?"

"The *Tai Sang Kan Ying P'ien*—that's the book telling the best way to raise trouble, Mr. Collins—recommends noon as the most propitious time for a certain class of murder. Now let me ask you a few questions. Firstly, where was this Wing's body found?"

"Jammed in a clothes hamper in Room 433. The same clothes hamper in which he had been collecting sheets and towels for the different rooms."

"Was it a pretty bad mess?"

His voice very low, Collins said, "No. That's the funny part. There was little blood anywhere." Wiping perspiration from his face, he said, "Even the sheets and towels had hardly any blood on them, detective."

This time Jimmy Wentworth's face showed excitement.

He knew of no Chinese custom where murderers drained the blood from a victim's body; that was something the underworld devils were supposed to do, not men. The case showed interest and promise, it might really come to some excitement. He said alertly:

"That's strange. A new one on me. Have you been able to determine in which room Wing was murdered? The exact place?"

"We haven't found blood anywhere, if that's what you mean. Chief Murphy and one of his men looked, but didn't have any luck."

With the San Francisco Chinatown detective prompting him, Collins was able to reconstruct what had apparently taken place.

WING HAD BEEN going about his duties as usual, collecting soiled linen on the fourth floor of the hotel. The last person to see him alive was Oscar Swanson, the porter, who had been carrying a guest's bags along the fourth floor corridor. Swanson had seen Wing enter Room 434 with his pass key. Room 434 was an outside room, facing on an alley, while Room 433, in which the body of the unfortunate Chinese servant was discovered, was just across the hall, and on a light well.

Wing had been pushing his clothes hamper, a wicker affair larger than the Chinese, before him, and singing to himself in a monotone, just as he always did. The Chinese had been slightly downcast for a few days, and then had been allowed to sleep at the hotel. Since then he had seemed to cheer up.

A little later—sometime just after twelve o'clock noon—a telephone call had come for Wing, and Oscar had been sent to find him. The porter tried Room 434, and found the towels all gone. He crossed the hall to 433, and at once saw Wing's dead arm hanging out of the clothes hamper. Oscar phlegmatically went to the wicker basket, but when he saw Wing's stump of a neck inside the hamper, he rushed with the story to Collins.

Chief Murphy had been summoned immediately. The incoming telephone call could not be traced. The girl at the switchboard was unable to say if a white man or an Oriental had asked for the old Chinese.

Jimmy Wentworth, without much effort, was able to guess just about what had happened. Some one had climbed up to Room 433, and had waited there to kill Wing Ch'i; had murdered him—how, Jimmy did not know as yet—and then cut off his head. Just how the old servant had been killed he would learn shortly.

The whole affair was another link in the curious chain which had caused the perplexed Chief Murphy to send to San Francisco for some detective experienced in dealing with Chinese.

But why was the body bloodless? Wentworth knew Chinese methods of murder, and this was not one of them. It looked to him rather like a campaign of terror, as if some one, for some reason, wanted it to appear as if the devils had slain Wing, and had taken his blood.

Why, also, had the old servant been done to death?

And, again, why had the hotel been told that Wing had been murdered? Wentworth knew that this had been the purpose of the mysterious telephone call.

The Chinatown detective was beginning to feel that Chief Murphy, in asking for aid, was not being stampeded by public opinion, but acting in a sensible manner. Only a man acquainted with the ways and crimes and customs of the Asiatics would have even a "Chinaman's chance" of working out this crime.

A dead Chinese, his head cut off, his body bloodless. What did it mean?

Jimmy Wentworth was no longer cool. His earlier intention, to look up the town chief of police, he discarded. The hotel people could try to get Murphy by telephone. This was going to be a real case, involving more than rumor and a dead servant.

"Look here," he said to Collins. "Try and get the chief for me. I'm going to take a look-see around town. When you get Murphy, have him come to my room at five. I'll be back then. And… can you tell me anything about what's been going on? All I know is what my own chief said—that a lot of queer things have been taking place."

"I'd better let Murphy tell you," begged Collins. "This— this just about caps the climax! Joe's told me a little, but he'd better tell you himself. He warned me not to say a word."

"I haven't seen anything in the newspapers, nor heard anything at headquarters," Jimmy Wentworth said. "We try to keep in touch. Tong troubles in the interior cities sometimes spread to San Francisco—"

"Is that what you think this is, detective?"

"I don't know. It isn't the way hatchetmen kill. It isn't the way Chinese kill at all. Until I talk to Murphy… somebody's coming to see you. Perhaps it's Murphy himself."

"A big man?"

"No. Little fellow. Gray suit."

"The local reporter," Collins moaned. "He's wormed it out of Joe."

"How much has been in your local paper so far?" Wentworth was trying to learn if this reporter had a source of news which might prove valuable, or if Chief Murphy was being pumped, in which case he himself must avoid talking to the chief.

"Nothing," said the hotel man. "But there hasn't been a murder before. Although there've been some funny accidents; Henry McIntyre, a lawyer, and a good one, was found dead beside his machine a couple of days ago… shh!… here comes the reporter."

"Don't tell him who I am," Wentworth urged.

THE SCRAWNY LITTLE reporter slid into Collins's baking office. "What's new, Bill?" he asked.

"You can get the names of the arrivals at the desk!"

"How about departures, Bill?"

"You don't print 'em, do you?"

"We do if the departing gent is a stiff, Bill. Yes, William, we still print murders."

Wentworth, at the door, said soberly, "What? Has somebody been killed? Right in the hotel here?"

"Run along, mister," the reporter told him. "I'm a busy man."

"Sorry to have bothered you," Jimmy Wentworth grinned as he left the office. He hoped Collins would be able to ward off the reporter, but doubted it. To have remained himself and tried to help out the unhappy hotel manager would have been dangerous. Wentworth wanted to work alone.

In the lobby, a sudden notion came to Jimmy Wentworth. He went to the telephone desk and gave the girl at the switchboard Captain Dunand's private number at headquarters, and, when the connection was made, went into the booth. Notwithstanding the improbability of any leak, Jimmy took no chance:

"This's Jim," he said when he heard Dunand's crisp voice. "Yes, it's pretty warm up here. I've been around the bank, but I can't get the information you want about the newspapers." Jimmy grinned as he thought of impetuous Captain Dunand, at the other end of the wire, wondering what all this nonsense was leading up to. "I thought, perhaps, you could get better information in San Francisco. Where the *true* ownership of the newspapers"—Wentworth emphasized the word—"really is. Keep your—negotiations—quiet, of course."

He could almost see the gray-haired captain of detectives scowl into the telephone, and then he heard his wise old chief say, "Very good, Jim. I'll do the best I can. If possible, the negotiations will be kept quiet."

Which meant that Dunand understood what his detective was driving at—to try and keep what it was Wentworth wanted kept out of the town newspapers. Wentworth in doing this was merely backing up Chief Murphy's attempt to maintain silence. Until he saw the chief, he did not clearly understand why secrecy was desired, although there must be some good reason for it.

Then Dunand said, "How is everything, Jim?"

"Hot, sir."

"Well, don't get burned… sunburned."

"Not if I can help it," said Jimmy Wentworth as he hung up the receiver.

2

—

DEVILS!

HE DID NOT glance at the switchboard girl to see if she had been listening to the conversation, not withstanding that he felt that there was a leak somewhere. For a young man wishing to avoid heat, Jimmy Wentworth should never have left the hotel lobby. However, he passed through the revolving doors, and walked straight to where his roadster was parked in the blistering sun. It was high time that he take a look about, if only to see how the land lay. This would prove invaluable to understand locations before talking with Chief Murphy.

The engine, as hot as when Jimmy Wentworth had raced through the broad valley on his drive from San Francisco, started with a roar. Jimmy throttled it down. The principal street was almost deserted as Wentworth drove slowly along. The air against his face seemed to wither his skin. Not even China, during the dry famine season, had been much hotter. If there had been layers of thick dust, and creaking Peking carts, and beggars whining for a bowl of water beside the road, Jimmy would have believed that he was again in China.

The prosperous town simmered in this blistering weather which ripened the fruit in the foothills, fruit which was dried and canned in plants east of the town. Over one yellow brick bank a flag hung listlessly. As the well-kept stores and shops changed to pool rooms and ex-saloons masquerading as soft drink parlors, Wentworth's casual air vanished. He knew that he must be approaching Chinatown.

On the next corner he saw, on the window of a grocery store, the name of the proprietor: Chen Chung Lo. Wentworth smoothly swung the roadster down the side street. His guesses were right. He was in the town's Asiatic district, and it was a larger one than he had expected. On both sides of the street were signs in Chinese.

What surprised Wentworth was that every store along the street had its shutters in place. Why had the thrifty Chinese, who minded heat not at all, shut up shop? Wentworth's head worked rapidly. This was no Chinese holiday. He was positive of that. Something, obviously, had terrified the Chinese. The headless, bloodless body of Wing Ch'i? Why not?

At the next laundry Wentworth stopped the car, deciding that it would be perfectly safe to see what was up. The shutters were tightly in place, the door closed. The wood of the door seemed to have been cracked and splintered. At the height of the young detective's throat were two round holes, bored clear through the wood. Alert now, Wentworth's nostrils drew in air, and his keen eyes caught a twin spiral of grayish smoke emerging from each of the holes, smoke which smelled very sweet. Incense! Jimmy Wentworth was even able to identify the variety of perfume being burned—the peculiar odor of Sun and

Moon Incense, of which good spirits are very fond; but which keeps away devils.

It was entirely possible that some one in the Chinese district had died in a near-by house, and fortunate spirits were being attracted by the incense to guard the Orientals from devils. It was also possible that every one had gone to the Chinese cemetery and locked up their shops against their return. But there was a third possibility. The Chinese might be guarding against the supposed underworld fiend who had drained the blood of the Chinese servant, Wing Ch'i.

Wentworth didn't like it.

HE BANGED ON the door. Instantly some one inside began to cry out, and bells began to ring furiously. Not one bell, but a dozen. Under the tumult, some one seemed to be arguing, and at length a concealed panel in the door, high up, was slid back, and a thin voice squeaked:

"*Ho la li sin!* What you want?"

"I want my brother's laundry," Wentworth said loudly. "What's the idea? Have you lost it? He's tired of waiting."

"*Tak ming yat ha' chan' lo,*" a Chinese whined. "Tell him to come back to-morrow afternoon."

Jimmy Wentworth intended to get inside the laundry, where he had managed to invent a logical excuse to speak with the Chinese, and where they could not guess his identity. If he stopped at another place, after visiting the laundry, he would be immediately under suspicion.

"My brother wants his shirts," he shouted. "Come across with them!"

An old cracked voice said, "Let him in, oh cowards!" and

some Chinese retorted that the dying did not need to fear death and devils.

So there was something involving devils in the wind! These Chinese were badly frightened.

While Wentworth waited for a decision to be made inside, he was examining with caution the scratches on the door. They seemed to have been made by some gigantic claw, raking down the wood. The two holes were above the splintering scratches. One was larger than the other. Wentworth's thumb would have fitted into the larger hole, his forefinger into the smaller. Was this what had terrified the Chinese? Were there similar devil-marks on the other doors of Chinatown, made during the night when devils roam about?

Jimmy Wentworth, knowing tongmen and hatchetmen, believed in human fiends, but not in unearthly ones. So this was what his job was to be—to track down whoever was terrorising the Chinese!

He called out, "If I don't get shirts, I'll go call a cop!"

The door was at last unbolted, and Jimmy Wentworth managed to slip through the small opening, then it was locked behind him instantly.

The simple laundry apparatus was idle, and there was no steam from the tubs. A dozen Chinese squatted on the bare wood floor. In a corner were baskets and sheets filled with soiled clothing. Only one old man—the oldest Oriental Wentworth had ever seen—was smoking his long bamboo pipe. Wentworth saw that the ancient Chinese was blind.

"No can do laundly," a Chinese said to the detective. "You come mebbe-so to-mollah." He pointed to the heap of unwashed clothes. "No can do to-day."

As if he expected the visitor to understand, the wrinkled old man said in Cantonese, "These fools are afraid of shadows, of games and fantasies, oh white man! If I were younger, I would beat these sons and grandsons of mine. But I am old. The Wind of the Closing Gates of Sunshine blows on me. I cannot walk. I cannot see. Accept nevertheless my apologies for these children of mine who fear greatly what they do not understand."

In the same language one of the Chinese shrilled, "It is fortunate that the white man cannot know what you say, oh grandfather!"

Wentworth would have given anything to have asked the old man, in Cantonese, just what the others feared. He knew the patriarch would not be allowed to reply. Devils were certainly involved—the devils, according to the Chinese, who had made the horrible scratches on the door.

The detective said, as if very angry, "Well, if you haven't got my brother's stuff, I'll wait until to-morrow. But I want 'em then, remember!" This would give him a chance to return, if there were any reason to do it.

"Can do," several of the Chinese promised. Wentworth knew they did not mean it. They wanted to get rid of him. "You come to-mollah. Or mo' bettah, nex' day."

They seemed in a fearful hurry to get rid of him. Were they afraid that the "devil" might be angered because of the presence of the white man?

"Don't forget," Jimmy Wentworth growled as he turned.

The door was opened for him. When the Chinese saw some one standing beside Jimmy Wentworth's roadster, they fairly pushed the white man through the door, and

slammed it hastily behind him. Instantly the din of bells—
which frighten goblins—began anew.

AS HE STARTED grimly toward the automobile, Wentworth thought, "If you think you'll learn anything about
me by looking at that license, Mr. Inquisitive Chinese,
you're all wet."

The driver's license, fastened to the steering column, was
in the name of R.A. McPherson, the same name Wentworth had used in registering at the hotel. The address of
the "owner" was given on the license as being in a city in
the southern part of the State.

The detective was ready as he stepped up to the machine.
He whistled as he approached, instead of slipping up and
surprising the man who had been looking inside the driving compartment. He had no intention of alarming the
Oriental. Wentworth did not want a knife drawn, nor a
fight, in the empty street. If that happened his usefulness
would be at an end. And it looked as if it was going to be
an interesting case, chasing devils!

"Say, what d'you want in my car?" he demanded when
the Chinese turned and saw him.

The Asiatic bobbed his head. "I like-see velly fine
aut'mobile. Him b'long you?"

"Sure it belongs to me. And, say, if you think I like to
come chasing down here after some shirts my brother left
before he went away, you're crazy. You got anything to do
with this laundry here?"

The Chinese shook his head, and then said, "Too bad."
He stared at Wentworth deliberately, insolently, as if mark-
ing the white man for remembrance. "I velly solly."

"Like hell you're sorry," Wentworth grumbled, as if

angered at all Chinese. To himself he added, "Maybe you'll know me again when you see me, Mr. Chino with the light eyes, but that goes double. And you're a half-caste. And what's more, I wouldn't trust you any further than I could bust you on the nose, either."

The Chinese kept his foot on the running-board. "I like li'l ride in fine aut'mobile," he giggled. "Mebbe-so come some day I like buy. You sell aut'mobile fo' 'Merican comp'ny?"

So the Oriental wanted to know who he was?

"I'll give you a ride as far as my hotel," Wentworth suggested. "You likee?"

"Mo' bettah we take nice li'l ride in country. See flowers and birds. I show you. An' I know fine place fo' whisky dlink!"

Wentworth felt that every eye in this Chinatown was on him. Who was the half-caste with the pale eyes? Was he the person back of the mysterious things the Chinese feared? It was beginning to look like it. If such were the case, Wentworth felt it would be sensible to see what the man was up to, but the idea of a ride in the country with such a companion did not appeal to the detective. Too much like trying a poison to see what might happen.

"Got no time," Jimmy Wentworth said, as if he wished it were possible. "You can come as far as my hotel if you want."

"Can do!"

The Chinese with the pale gray eyes stepped—too easily and familiarly—into the seat. As Wentworth settled himself behind the steering wheel, he knew that the half-caste was attempting to ascertain whether or not the white man carried a gun. Wentworth waited until the searching hand, very cleverly, slipped toward his side, and then, swift as light, Jimmy seized the half-caste's wrist.

"What you trying to do?" he demanded, his grip like iron.

For one long moment the Eurasian's eyes bored balefully, malevolently, into the white man's. Then he smirked.

"I 'fraid I fall out. I hold on. You no like?"

"No," Jimmy Wentworth told him. He let go the other's wrist, as if satisfied with the explanation. "Get out of my machine," he commanded.

A second time the man with the pale eyes looked as if ready to draw a knife, and a second time he finally giggled. Then he said, "Sure. I go. Velly fine aut'mobile." In Chinese, almost inaudibly, he whispered, "But wait, oh rich and arrogant white ape without a tail! Some day no one will dare speak to me as you have spoken." Even while he protested so bitterly, his thin lips, utterly Chinese, retained their smile.

Wentworth watched him in the rear vision mirror until the car reached the end of the street. The Eurasian had turned and walked away. Wentworth did not see which store or house, if any, he entered.

As Jimmy drove up to the hotel, he was grinning to himself. The man with the light gray eyes, the Eurasian, had not learned a thing, except that a man named McPherson was a customer of the laundry, rightfully attempting to get clothing which should have been delivered.

Jimmy Wentworth had beaten the half-caste at his own game. He had discovered more than the other. He knew that the prying Eurasian was capable of speaking good

English, the man had said "flower" instead of "floweh," although he had said "bettah" instead of "better." And although the sly Oriental had not learned if "McPherson" was armed, Wentworth had done his own investigating with more success! He knew, from one discerning touch made while first shifting gears, that a heavy assassin's knife nestled under the Eurasian's arm on the left side, where hatchetmen invariably carry their weapon.

The Chinese was certainly mixed up in the campaign of terrorism, and it was up to Wentworth to find out why. The headless, bloodless body was intended to frighten the Chinese—and Chief Murphy ought to be able to tell him the reason. Then Jimmy Wentworth would be able to make his deductions and lay his plans to thwart the reign of terror.

He was positive of one other thing: the Eurasian might assume a hundred disguises, but he could never change the pale color of his eyes. Jimmy Wentworth would always know him.

3

THE RACKET

CHIEF MURPHY WAS a troubled man; Wentworth could see anxiety written deeply in every line of the chief's face. Nor did the appearance of the young Chinatown detective cheer Joseph Murphy very much. He had asked the San Francisco police for bread, and it looked like to him as though they had given him a stone—had sent up a youngster when he needed a tough, experienced man. He was disappointed in the quiet young fellow dressed in gray flannels.

Wentworth merely said, "I'm from the detective bureau, chief. Dunand sent me up, you know."

"It's a terrible hot day," Murphy said. "Th' boys in th' canneries tell me they got to work fast to keep th' peaches from spoilin'. They got a crew of workers comin', maybe. I dunno. This is pretty tough on 'em."

"You've got to tell me more than that, chief," Jimmy Wentworth suggested. "Remember that all I know is that a hotel servant has been murdered, and that you have an idea an attorney named McIntyre may have been murdered also."

"Yeah," said the chief. "I think so, but nobody else does. It looked like an accident. Car went off a small bridge.

But there've been many funny things goin' on. That's why I asked for help." In a weary voice he said, "I was in the department a long time ago. I wish I was back there right now, on a nice, quiet beat!"

"Let's hear about it."

The chief nodded. "It started a few days ago, detective. Th' first tip on trouble come from Hank McIntyre himself. He said, 'Chief, th' Chinks is all scared, although I dunno why.' I says, 'Maybe hoodlums is botherin' 'em. I'll keep a sharp eye on Chinatown, Hank.' Henry said he didn't think it was a gang of toughs, but that th' Chinks was bothered about somethin' like devils tryin' to eat 'em. I dunno.

"Henry was th' lawyer for a lot of Chinamen. An' that night, after Hank come to me, his car went off th' bridge. We found him with his neck broke. An'… come closer, detective!… although out of symp'thy for Henry's widow me an' the coroner kept it quiet, there was two holes in Henry's body… an'… not a drop of blood in him!"

Jimmy Wentworth lit a cigarette, and then said soberly, "Go ahead, chief. What else?"

"As I says, we kept it quiet. Next mornin', somebody telephones th' afternoon newspaper an' says, 'Better investigate McIntyre's death. He was murdered. Look into it an' you'll get a damn' big story.' Which meant that I have that rotten little Taylow Dowd hangin' around, snoopin' an' hintin'. But he don't get anywhere. The coroner sits tight, an' I sit tight. Now he's got me where I live, with this headless body of old Wing. I'll get a swell roastin'. I tried to keep it quiet, for Bill's hotel and th' town's reputation, and to give you a chance to work on th' case.

"Now it'll be all over th' front page—"

WENTWORTH TOOK A yellow envelope from his pocket, and handed the telegram to the miserable chief.

Reading aloud, Murphy's face became perplexed. " 'Matter attended to at bank here. No publicity for the present. O.M. Rogers.'" Scratching his head, the chief demanded, "It don't make sense. An' who is this guy Rogers?"

"Just a name. I phoned Captain Dunand, asking him to keep this all out of the newspapers here if possible. He worked it through some bank, which must have pulled the necessary wires. You see, chief, somebody wants this in the papers, and that's a good reason for us to keep it out if we can. And I'm going to learn who is doing all the fancy news broadcasting!"

The chief's desolate countenance brightened.

"Now," Jimmy Wentworth continued, "let's get at what has been frightening the Chinese. Like doors being scratched."

The old chief stared at him. "You seen it, huh? Well, detective, there's been a yowlin' all night, something terrible t' hear, an' a procession to th' Chink's graveyard, an' bells ringin' an' firecrackers goin' off. Th' Chinks is scared. I asked my laundryman what was th' matter, but he wouldn't talk. Said I couldn't help 'em none. Said... well, that blood'll be drunk! Yes, sir, he told me that. Not a Chink is workin'... an' th' canneries need 'em bad right now—"

"So that's it?" Jimmy Wentworth said softly.

"That's what?"

"Why they are being terrorized—frightened by devils."

"Is it? I dunno. But I know this: th' fruit's goin' to spoil before it's canned. All on account of a lot of Chinks!"

Nodding, Jimmy Wentworth, decided against asking whether or not any one had demanded money from the canners, in return for which the Chinese would be pacified and willing to work again. He knew the dodge: it was done in China to get gold from the silk-filature owners. It was necessary for the young detective to save the fruit crop from destruction, but it was also his duty to bring the murderers back of the plot to justice.

In a sharp voice Wentworth asked, "D'you know a well dressed Chinese who looks something like a white man? My height, thin, and with gray eyes?"

"George Lee? Sure. He went to school here, an' went away to college. He's a fine boy. Know him?"

"I hope to know him better. What does he do?"

"I dunno. George's too lazy to work. Or maybe too educated. He must have a share in th' lottery business. I never heard of George Lee workin', but he always has plenty of money." Aware that he was off the track, Murphy continued, "Now, about th' murder here in th' hotel. Got any clews?"

"I've looked around, chief. Whoever killed Wing slid down from the roof to Room 433 and hid under the bed. The rope mark is clear on the cornice, and the place where the killer lay under the bed shows on the carpet. What happened to Wing's head? I can't say yet. Why was the body drained of blood, as McIntyre's was? To make it appear as if something inhuman, something not of the world, had done the deed. A devil. The most evil demons are supposed to live on blood."

"Yeah… but who *done* it?"

Jimmy Wentworth said, "Mightn't it be—whoever is back of keeping the Chinese away from the canneries?"

There was a rap on the door before Murphy could reply. Wentworth called, "Come in!"

The boy from the lobby handed Wentworth an envelope addressed to "Mr. McPherson, Inland-California Hotel," in printed letters.

"Got a friend here?" Murphy asked.

"Looks like it," Jimmy agreed. He asked the boy, "Where'd this come from?"

"A kid brought it, sir." The hotel boy added that the letter had been handed in at the desk, and that there was nothing unusual about the deliverer. If the child had been Chinese, Wentworth knew that the hotel boy would have mentioned it.

Jimmy Wentworth opened the letter. In it was a five dollar bill, and a note: "Can not find wash. We pay $5. Wo Sing Laundry."

WHEN THE HOTEL boy had left the room, Wentworth handed the crude message to Murphy, saying, "Good of 'em, isn't it? Of course I never had any shirts at the laundry." He went on quietly, "The time seems to have come to have a little talk with Mr. George Lee, who has plenty of money, can't speak good English, and carries a knife like a hatchetman."

"He's th' last man to be mixed up in this," Murphy protested. "He's a educated Chink. He don't believe in no nonsense like ghosts and drinkin' blood."

Jimmy Wentworth said, "Do you believe in ghosts, chief?"

"I do not. But th' Chinks is different. It wasn't no ghost that killed Henry McIntyre, nor Wing, neither."

A strange voice asked, from the door which Jimmy Wentworth had not locked behind the hotel boy, "Well, then, who was it?"

The two men looked up and saw the thin reporter.

"Who was what?" Murphy growled. "And don't you knock when you come into a gent's room, Dowd?"

"Usually," the reporter drawled. "Not always. It depends on whether the gent is… a gent, if you get what I mean, chief."

Jimmy Wentworth stopped Murphy's outburst by saying, "It's pretty tough, isn't it, Dowd? Makes you mad, doesn't it?"

"Yeah… and it's going to make a good story, too. Our chief of police calls in a city dick, and the two of 'em lock themselves up in a room so the ghosts don't get 'em. A good story."

"Why don't you print it?" Jimmy Wentworth suggested calmly.

The reporter snapped, "I'm going to print it, Mr. Fresh Dick! I'm just waiting for developments."

Wentworth leaned forward in his chair. "So you know I'm a detective? Which means you managed to get my call to the city traced, and which means also that the switchboard girl'll be out of a job, and never get another with any telephone company."

"Go on, be nasty," the reporter snapped. "When it's all over, Mr. Wise Dick from Frisco, I'll find a way to ride you that you won't like."

"Is this the way you usually get news, buddy?"

The reporter sensed something friendly in the young detective's question. "Try getting news in this town any other way," he blurted. "Say, the coroner's office denies having a stiff even after the funeral. And if you asked Murphy what time it was, he'd have 'nothing to say!'"

"Where I come from," Jimmy Wentworth said soberly, "we play ball. You want this yarn. That suits me. But I don't want it printed yet. It's a good wire service story, too, good for a column, and perhaps a by-line. But the A.P. and the U.P. won't take an inch from you, because you can't quote anybody. Now, Dowd, you lay off Murphy, and I'll give you a break on the story the moment we've got the murderers—"

"What murderers?"

"Well, as a start, Dowd, we want whoever has been tipping your paper about what has been going on."

"We can't violate confidences."

"So you know who is doing the tipping, don't you?"

The reporter helped himself to Wentworth's cigarettes. Then, slowly, he said, "And a big fathead I am, not to realize that whoever was tipping me knew too damn much about the whole business! I'm a bigger ham than Murph! Say, detective, this releases me from my promise of silence, doesn't it? He told me a wild yarn about 'overhearing' what was up, and I fell for it.

"Give me a break on the story before you let the city papers in on it, and I'll tell you who said Henry McIntyre was murdered."

"Probably a half-caste with pale eyes, named George Lee," said Jimmy Wentworth.

"How'd you know?" Dowd gasped.

"Lee went to college, he speaks good English. Whoever 'overheard' must have understood Chinese also."

Mournfully, the reporter said, "I didn't tell you, which means you don't need to give me the break on the yarn—"

"I'm willing to play ball," said Jimmy Wentworth. "Here's your job, Dowd. Go to the canneries, and see—I'm coming clean with you, boy!—see if any one has been trying to hold them up for a substantial amount of cash."

"I know 'em. They haven't said anything about it to me."

"Go ask. And don't let your chum George Lee know you've seen me, whatever you do. I want to keep healthy, Dowd. If you get another tip from him, let me have it fast."

Dowd took a final puff on his cigarette.

"George Lee told me, just a little while ago, that I'd be doing the town a service by having you go away before you went off a bridge the way Henry McIntyre did. I didn't want to tell you this until I learned your business, detective. George said, word for word, 'This man McPherson is trying to cause trouble, according to what I hear. If he is really on business, he will leave town to-night. Otherwise he may get more than he bargained for.'"

"I'm staying," Jimmy Wentworth grinned. "I like bargains."

"You better give me your name, in case you get—in case there's a story."

"Wentworth," Jimmy said. "Sergeant of detectives, San Francisco."

Dowd's jaw dropped. Chief Murphy stared at the immaculate young man in flannels. At last the reporter muttered, "And I thought you were a smart-alec rookie! No wonder the Chinks haven't got you worried. Detective

Sergeant Wentworth! Boy, what a story this'll be, no matter which way it busts!"

"Thanks," grinned Jimmy Wentworth. "I hope I tell it to you, and that you don't write it about me. I'm like you, I want to stay healthy as long as I can, and I don't want to get killed to get my name in the paper!"

4

FROM KONG GAI

WHEN THE SUN went down, the streets of the cannery town became alive, and only the Oriental district remained black and silent. Through the principal street great trucks were driven, piled high with boxes of peaches for the canneries. The foothill fruit ranches were sending down the finest of their crops, contracted for long in advance. If the ripe peaches were not cooked in sirup and canned as they arrived, thousands of dollars would be lost.

Jimmy Wentworth knew this. Dowd had given him a report from one of the cannery managers, although the Chinatown detective had figured out, step by step, what was back of the deaths and sinister happenings. Through Dowd he had learned that although arrangements had been made to bring in outside labor, the local Chinese had finally agreed to come to work shortly after midnight, and that the difficulty had been fixed up.

"How much did it cost the cannery people?" Jimmy Wentworth demanded.

"Plenty," Dowd informed him. "If it had been just a small holdup, or a raise in wages, they'd have stood for it. Now, they say they'll be lucky to break even."

"How were the arrangements made—the racket payment?"

"By phone from San Francisco."

"Where's the payment to be made? Who gets the money? When?"

"The cannery outfit wouldn't tell me. They're afraid the deal might fall through if it received any publicity."

Wentworth had been ordered to this town to do two things: learn what was wrong with the Chinese, and ascertain what was back of it. In addition, he had two murders to solve, and he thought he could do it. The headless body of Wing Ch'i, the drained body of the white attorney....

Seated in a big chair in his room, Jimmy Wentworth let his mind go back many years, to the tales and stories he had learned in China. He recalled at last the sleepless nights, after his Chinese *amah* had told him about dead men who walked the earth, living on blood. Yes, that was the particular kind of devils the Chinese feared, just as he had suspected.

Jimmy Wentworth was not puzzled about the attempt to have all of the details of the gruesome murders in the newspapers. Not only would this keep other Chinese laborers from coming to the town, to replace those already frightened, but it would make it possible to repeat the performance elsewhere by associating the vampire-devil with fruit canning.

McIntyre had been the lawyer for some of the Chinese. McIntyre must have learned what was up and the Chinese killed him. Wing, innocent old Oriental, had been murdered in the midst of white men, to show the power of the deadly ghost, and perhaps also to show the power of the influences behind the racket.

This seemed obvious to Wentworth.

Just how would it be possible to allay the fears of the Chinese, to get them back to work this very midnight? What could bring them from their houses, where they had been cowering behind locked doors? It would of course be something supernatural, and by finding whoever directed the performance, Wentworth would either get the criminals, or be close to their tracks.

Midnight! After midnight they would return to work! Jimmy Wentworth puzzled desperately over this. Then he said aloud, "Of course! The hour when the dead walk from their graves! It'll happen at the Chinese cemetery!"

It was growing darker outside, the moon had not yet risen out of the Sierras. The dull roar of the fruit trucks had never stopped. They seemed an endless procession, bringing in the perishable merchandise. In the east there was a faint glow, and a pall of smoke, as the furnaces of the canneries heated the giant caldrons of sirup up for the ripe peaches, which the Chinese laborers were to prepare. Day and night this work would continue, until the crop was safely in millions of cans.

Jimmy Wentworth settled back more deeply in his chair. At midnight the Chinese would be at the graveyard, to see the evil spirit exorcised from ever returning to earth. How this would happen Jimmy Wentworth did not know. It was the one missing link in the chain of his deductions. But he would be there to find out—he, the chief, and enough men to circle the graveyard.

WHEN A TAP at the door finally roused him, he was ready

for action. He had taken off his coat, and with his customary caution had placed his holster and gun under it, out of sight, but within easy reach.

However, even if he had intended securing it, there was no time for a servant in whites came into his room, carrying a tray.

"Ice-wateh," said the Chinese servant pleasantly. He was stooped, as if old, with head down and lined face. "I put him on table." As if in further explanation, he said, "Numbah-one boss, he say I bling. Mebbe-so you like cold dlink."

Wentworth, after one apparently incurious glance, said tonelessly, "Put it on the table. Here's a dime, boy."

The servant held out his hand.

Jimmy Wentworth seized it like a flash, and there was one quick flurry, after which the Oriental was thrown to the floor. The Chinese's knife was out, but Wentworth's gun covered him.

"Mr. Lee?" Jimmy Wentworth grinned. "Those funny-colored eyes of yours are a handicap, aren't they? Well, now that you're here, what do you want?"

The half-caste remained silent, his face a combination of fear and hatred.

"Talk," Wentworth suggested. "I haven't a lot of time to waste."

"I work in the hotel," the Eurasian said slowly, in faultless English. "I—"

"I said talk, not lie," Wentworth snapped. "Who sent you here, Lee?"

Instant fear sprang into the half-caste's pale eyes, wiping away every other expression.

A light came to Wentworth. The power behind this racket was in San Francisco; George Lee was in terror at the mere mention of the super-criminal. Lee had been reporting events to the city, and had told about "McPherson," which meant that he had been ordered to find out more about the visitor, and, if necessary, remove him. Lee had failed, and was in deadly fright. This meant only one thing to Wentworth; Kong Gai was the brains behind the affair! Kong Gai, with whom he had so often crossed swords. Kong Gai, the Evil One, spreading out his snake-like influence to wherever money could be made in unlawful, profitable ways.

Lee said shakily, "I came—to warn you—"

"Warn me? Say, Lee, all I want is to do a little business in this town, and get some shirts of my brother's… warn me? What for?"

The Chinese's eyes betrayed him.

Wentworth swung about. His gun roared. A Chinese had swung in through the window, like a yellow ape. Wentworth's swift shot missed; he fired again when the man was almost on him, and then whirled. Lee's knife was already in the air. Had the half-caste been all Chinese, Wentworth would have been a dead man. But the Eurasian, coward at heart, had hesitated one instant before driving his assassin's blade into the white man's back.

The Chinatown detective's fist crashed up. He wanted Lee alive. Wentworth was faster than the half-caste. The heavy blade clattered to the floor, and George Lee over it.

The Eurasian screamed, "Father! Father of Snakes and of me! I was faithful, oh Father Kong Gai!"

Blood welled along the carpet. In some strange way, the half-caste had fallen on his own knife.

The Chinese who had climbed through the window, Lee's accomplice, or perhaps a hatchetman assigned to see that the cowardly half-caste did his work well, was dead. Wentworth's second bullet had finished him.

QUICKLY THE DETECTIVE went to work to save Lee's life. Whether the long blade had pierced the half-caste's lung, Jimmy Wentworth did not know, although no bubbly froth appeared at the Eurasian's lips. As soon as he dared, Wentworth went to the telephone, telling the girl to call Chief Murphy, and get a doctor.

"Yes, sir," she said. "Is everything all right? We heard a noise—a shot—"

"Go ahead and tell your boy friend Dowd about it," Wentworth said, and hung up. His gun was in his hand again as the door opened, and the hotel manager rushed in. When Collins saw the shambles on the floor he was horrified.

"More dead men," he wailed. "Everybody in the hotel's heard the shooting! What happened, detective?"

"Only one is dead," Jimmy told him. "The other may be dying. Know him?"

"George Lee! Everybody knows George. A smart boy—"

"With a smart father," agreed Wentworth. "Maybe we'll keep him alive long enough to hang him." Unconsciously, Jimmy shivered. If George Lee were really Kong Gai's son, the King Cobra of Chinatown would go after the white detective in earnest! "He was suspicious of me," Wentworth said. "I've phoned for a doctor already."

"There's people in the hall. What'll I tell them?"

"Laugh about it. Say I had a nightmare and thought there was a burglar in the room."

The moment he was alone, Wentworth bent over the dead hatchetman. Expertly he sought the fellow's silken coin sack, finding it tied by a string about the highbinder's neck. In it were ten bills, totalling a hundred dollars, and around the currency a slip of paper, on which was written in Chinese:

"Payment for sending the miserable soul of Wing Ch'i to the underworld."

Under the Chinese characters was drawn a crude picture of a king cobra, hood spread to strike, Kong Gai's mark.

Wentworth said, "I'll get you some day, Kong Gai," and, wanting a look at the half-caste before the doctor arrived, repeated his search. He found a wallet well filled with money, a few letters without interest, and a tiny bottle, glass, with a glass stopper. It was wrapped in a heavy piece of brocaded silk, on which was a snake embroidered in gold thread.

The bottle made Jimmy Wentworth instinctively glance toward the pitcher of ice-water. That would be the half-caste's way to do murder. Jimmy thrust his finger into the chill liquid, and tasted it. It appeared innocent, although the extreme coldness might keep any taste from being noticed. Besides, Wentworth knew that the Chinese employed poisons without taste or odor.

He next opened the tiny vial of colorless liquid, and sniffed cautiously, first trying to blow fumes with his hand toward his nostrils. Again, no odor. The poison—Wentworth supposed it must be poison—might be so deadly that a single drop on his tongue would produce sickness, if not actual death. Jimmy Wentworth saw no reason to test the liquid by tasting, but out of curiosity he placed a few drops on his palm, and rubbed them gently to see if the contents of the vial were acid, or an oil.

Then, although the doctor was knocking at the door, Wentworth's eyes did not raise from his hand. The electric light in the room was lit, but the inside of the detective's palm glowed and shimmered with a strange, unearthly light.

"So that's how they're going to pacify the Chinese laborers." Wentworth whispered in elation. "The fireflies of death! The sign from the gods that all is again well!" Wentworth had heard of the magic fireflies from heaven; it was a part of Chinese folklore.

For a moment he was afraid that possibly only George Lee had the remarkable phosphorescent liquid, and then common sense assured him that one man alone could never accomplish what was necessary—paint the wings of hundreds of insects, bees, or flies, with the liquid. Besides, the vial was two-thirds empty. Much of the liquid had already been used.

"Got them," Jimmy Wentworth thought grimly. "Thank heaven for a good memory. Now I know just the moment to act."

What performance the Chinese racketeers would go through the detective did not know, but the end of the scene at the graveyard would be the liberation of the false fireflies. Wentworth knew that his deductions were logical, and exactly the way the Asiatics would proceed. It was clear to him. The Chinese, frightened by uncanny means, must of course be soothed in the same way.

Where did the fireflies of death appear? Only at the place of burial. When? At midnight. Everything dovetailed.

THE DOCTOR WAS finishing his bandaging, after having told Wentworth that the half-caste would live, when Chief Murphy hurried into the room, out of breath.

"What's goin' on?" he rumbled. "Say, you can't come here an' kill everybody in sight. George Lee hurt! Say, George's a law-abiding citizen—he's tipped me off to a couple of gamblin' joints—"

"Where they haven't come across with their protection money for hatchetmen," Wentworth said. "This man Lee is—"

The sound of his name caused the Eurasian's pale eyes to open. When he saw Murphy standing over him, he said weakly, "I was trying—to do—this man—a favor. I wanted—to tell him—that somebody was going to try—and kill him. Just like it happened. Man came through window. Chief, take me to—a hospital—"

"You bet, George!" To Wentworth Chief Murphy growled, "Go on back to the city. You've done enough damage."

"Take Lee to a hospital, and he'll be out of it before you will," Jimmy Wentworth said sharply.

"Don't let—Wentworth—tell you—what to do," Lee pleaded.

Jimmy was about to speak, but when he saw the chief's eyes begin to show doubt, he remained silent. Murphy himself said slowly, "George, I got to ask you a question. How do you know this feller's name isn't McPherson?"

Wentworth smiled. That was it!

"I better take you to jail," the chief went on heavily. "We'll make you comfortable there, George. I gotta do it. You knew this man was Wentworth."

None of the half-caste's arguments, nor, at the end, tears, could move the chief from his decision.

5

THE HOUR OF THE DEAD

AS THE NIGHT wore on, empty fruit trucks returned toward the orchards. Most of these took the eastern highway, some few went on other roads. One truck rumbled out toward and past the Chinese cemetery, and, when it was out of sight behind a clump of trees, stopped for a moment. The driver did not get down, but focused any watching eye by lighting a cigarette, so that the flash of the match would draw attention away from the rear of the truck.

Quickly, silently, armed white men—Murphy's officers, and a dozen deputies—climbed out of the truck and sought the shelter of the black trees. Well off the road, they sat on the dry grass, waiting. In a low voice one of them complained, "I darn' near busted my spine when we hit that bump on the bridge," and another said, "That's what maybe happened to Hank McIntyre. Goin' too fast over the bridge." He added that it should be repaired, fixed somehow.

"Fixed me eye," growled a third. "It felt like a timber to me. Say, d'you think th' Chinks are wise?"

"Shut up," their leader ordered. "And no cigarettes, boys. We're near the graveyard, and there's a moon."

Toward the cemetery a roadster was rushing now, Jimmy

Wentworth's. There was no other way to get to the burying ground, save by going miles to an intersection, and there was not time enough for that. Eleven thirty was the deadline of the Hour of the Dead. Wentworth had learned this by telephoning Wang Chen-p'o, his friend in Chinatown. Eleven thirty, when the dead come alive—the unholy dead! Chief Murphy sat beside the detective sergeant, frankly skeptical.

"All you got to go on is that you say th' Chinks won't go back to work until they ain't afraid," he said. "Say, if people hear I spent th' night lookin' for murderers in a Chinee graveyard, I might's well turn in my star."

Jimmy's foot pressed harder on the gas.

"How come we ain't passed no Chinks, if there's goin' to be a meetin' at th' cemetery?"

"They won't get there an instant before eleven thirty. Take my word for it, chief."

"Well… maybe. Drive slower, sarge! That's the bridge where Henry McIntyre got his."

"Right. Keep your eyes peeled. If any one tries to stop us, hang on, because I'll run him down."

Curious to see if a dark shape would rise from the shadow of the concrete bridge, Wentworth did slow the car. His alert eyes watched for obstructions, but he saw nothing except—now that he was close—a shadow or two thrown by the bridge itself. One of the shadows suddenly became what it really was, a heavy timber lying on the floor of the bridge. Wentworth's foot pressed down on the foot brake; Chief Murphy, not knowing what was happening, lifted his gun. There was a bump, and, at the same instant, a sharp metallic crack. Wentworth's foot jammed on the brake, his hand went to the emergency. The roadster swerved sharply, and then stopped.

Jimmy Wentworth's own gun was out, but no one rushed them. He said quietly, "That's how they got McIntyre."

The two men worked to push the useless car to the creek-bottom, under the bridge. When the roadster was concealed, Murphy said, "Why'n't you hold on to the wheel, sarge, and push her that way? You're all dirty as it is."

"Because somebody's fooled with the steering appara- tus, and it went haywire when we hit the timber. George Lee may have done it when I was in the laundry. It took a good bump to finish the job. That's what the gang did with McIntyre's car. If he hadn't known something was up, and come out to the cemetery to see, he would be alive to-day, perhaps."

Murphy said, "We figured maybe th' steel crystallized on Hank's car."

"Let's start walking, chief. We haven't any time to waste." **SIDE BY SIDE**, the two officers hurried through the fields toward the trees where the others waited. Once Murphy muttered, "Th' dirty murderin' Chinee," and Wentworth said, "A half-caste hasn't got nerve enough to do the kill- ing himself. You can be sure that Lee thought out the way to murder McIntyre—"

"Did Lee… you know… take out McIntyre's… blood?"

"No. You'll find out about that pretty soon. Let's get going, chief."

When they arrived a deputy asked, "What happened? Never knew you liked to walk except for a glass of beer, Murphy."

"This's no joke," the chief said severely. "You boys take orders from Sergeant Wentworth."

"You fellows all know the lay of the land," Jimmy Wentworth told them. "We keep out of sight until I give the word, which will be when we see smoke rise. Then we advance toward the cemetery in a half circle. When those of you at the end of the lines are past the smoke, begin to close in, so we surround the graveyard. Then go forward on your bellies as fast as you dare. If you see Chinese, stop, and stay where you are. No noise! When you hear the chief's whistle, rush to the smoke."

"How do we know who to grab, sergeant?"

"I'll do that," Jimmy Wentworth said. "If you see any fancy work being done with knives, use your own judgment. It's a bright night; don't kill any inoffensive Chinese. Just get to me as quickly as you can. That's where the fun will be. If anyone tries to escape, you can tell pretty well whether to grab him or not. That's all."

Down the road, a silver ribbon in the moonlight, Wentworth and the officers could see dark shapes straggling toward the cemetery. All watched the pale, moonlit sky. It was a full half hour later before a thin column of smoke began to ascend.

"Good luck, fellows," Wentworth said, and, with the words, left the trees. The deputies and officers swung out efficiently in a long line, and the half circle began to take shape. Wentworth and the chief were in the middle. Slowly, carefully, the line of men neared the smoke column. The road itself was empty now.

One by one the white men dropped to their knees, continuing to wriggle forward. Wentworth and Murphy were the last to go to the earth. Always forward they moved, until at last Wentworth, who raised his head from time to time, whispered, "Over to that rock, chief. That's fine. Now you can see."

The chief said, when he looked, "Holy saints!"

"It's just the Ta Ch'ing, chief. The dragon of hell. He lives under sacred altars, and if an irreverent remark is made, his tail stays there, but his body will uncoil and roll after whoever curses the gods. This is just the start! It's going to be some performance! You'll see sights to-night few white men ever even heard about. Now do you believe what I told you about Chinese devils?"

"I never seen nothing like this in all me life!"

IT WAS INDEED a sight to make white men wonder. A thick, black vapor of incense rose from a flat spot in the middle of the graveyard, where a fire burned, and into which a tall, angular Chinese in yellow silk robes threw handfuls of sacred powder. Around the fire were ranged terrible naked figures of awful gods, some with heads like crows, others with the bodies of tigers and faces of women. Near the yellow-clad priest were five or six Asiatics in ordinary clothing, men whose faces were as grim and expressionless as the images. Hatchetmen. Wentworth recognized one as a fellow he had seen in Chinatown in San Francisco—one of Kong Gai's men, he knew now.

The man Jimmy Wentworth recognized held a black rooster under his arm. Another of the highbinders had a ferocious red chow—the fiery dog of violence—on a short leash.

Ringed about the actors in the drama were the inhabitants of the town's Chinese district, men, women, children, wide-eyed and gray with fear. When the detective was able to see clearly through a lane in the shifting Orientals, he caught a glimpse of what he expected to see—an open grave.

His deductions had been correct!

Without warning, the yellow-robed Chinese threw a handful of something into the fire, and it blazed high and red, making the scene wilder than before. Next he spat in eight directions: to heaven, to vapor, fire, thunder, wind, water, mountains, earth. When the yellow-robe began a harangue to keep all demons from the grave, old Murphy whispered:

"Is he a Chinee priest, now?"

"A renegade," Wentworth replied.

Shrilly, the yellow-robe began to shout, "At last we have found the devil who must be satisfied with blood! Oh devil, leave us alone. Let us work again and be happy. Now we will give you your last food on earth." The renegade priest took the black cock from the hatchetman, and with one flash of the knife severed its head. Blood gushed forth, and the yellow robe let it spurt into the open grave.

While the audience trembled, the master of ceremonies grasped the red chow's leash and dragged the animal to him.

The powerful red chow snarled at the priest. As the yellow-robe dragged him nearer, to slash his throat, the animal, instead of holding back, leaped forward. The priest cried out in pain as the chow bit deeply. He dropped the leash, and like a red comet the dog dashed out of the circle.

Some one cried, in Cantonese, "What does that mean, O Priest?"

"It means," Jimmy Wentworth whispered, "that the gods do not look with favor on the performance. *Now* he's got to talk!"

"Oh, my brothers," Feng Shan cried, holding his bleeding hand under his yellow robe, "it is a favorable sign. It tells us that the devil not only cannot remain on earth, but will also be kept out of hell! He will float with the wind, nowhere! Now we will slay this devil, who murdered Wing Ch'i and drank his blood, the devil who is afraid of no one, not even white men, for he drank a white man's blood also. I saw it, oh, my brothers! My spirit was there at the bridge."

As he let that sink in, Wentworth said softly to the chief. "That's great. He's admitted he knew why McIntyre was killed, and you'll be able to satisfy any white jury of his guilt."

AT A WORD from the yellow-robed Feng Shan, the hatchetmen slid into the grave. In a moment they thrust a wooden coffin up beside the fire. The cover was ripped off without hesitation. Then Feng Shan reached under his robe, and took out a white man's hat and a Chinese's token-bag.

"Hank's hat," Murphy rumbled. "He always wore one like that—"

Saying loudly, "Here are objects from the men you killed, oh, undecayed Lower Soul," the priest dropped hat and token-bag into the coffin. While the Chinese gasped and tried to pray, and children whimpered and hid their faces, Feng Shan and two of the hatchetmen raised the coffin so all could see what was inside.

It was the body, unmutilated, of some dead Chinese. The face seemed livid, as if alive, and between the folded arms of the corpse was the head of Wing Ch'i, dry and bloodless.

The Chinese fell to their knees at the sight of this apparition with hollow eye-sockets and blood-red cheeks. Feng Shan seemed to have a fight to wrest the head of the hotel servant from the body. At last he dropped it into the sacred fire. "Ascend to heaven," he shouted, "and ask the gods, Wing Ch'i, to show us that this devil vampire will walk the earth no more. Show us a sign, oh, gods!"

Wentworth said, "Just one second now, chief!"

From somewhere behind the fire, tiny bits of phosphorescent lights began to rise, to dart and sway and move about like fireflies.

The Chinese gave a great shout of gratitude that covered, except to the waiting white men, the blast of Murphy's whistle.

Jimmy Wentworth, gun drawn, raced ahead of the older chief toward the fire.

He tore his way through a horde of Chinese and shoved his gun in the renegade priest's face.

"Ni hai! ngo ke' fan hai lok loi'lo," Wentworth snapped. "You are my prisoner. Don't move!"

Even as the amazed yellow-robe said, *Ni mo k'un*—you cannot arrest me," he was motioning to the hatchetmen to attack.

A knife caught red light from the fire as it was lifted behind Wentworth's back. Chief Murphy's gun roared, and the highbinder fell into the open grave. Before the other Chinese assassins could do any damage, the officers of the law were upon them, bearing them to the earth and handcuffing them all.

The inhabitants of Chinatown, no less amazed than the plotters, could only jabber. One of them whimpered to Murphy, "Why you do so? Pliest good man. He stop allo Chinaboy be killed. Why-so you come?"

"Tell them," Jimmy Wentworth said to the yellow-robe, "that you are no priest at all, and that your robes are stolen."

The man in the yellow silk spat in Wentworth's face.

Jimmy wiped the venom away, and then said, "The man of two bloods, the half-caste son of Kong Gai, could not stand torture, Feng Shan. He has spoken, and his words will hang you."

"What do you know of the Great and Evil Kong Gai?" the renegade breathed. And then he must have known the answer to his question, for he snarled, "So! You are the white man who is Kong Gai's enemy! Wentworth! *Hai!* Some day your eyes will be pulled out, and your skin flayed—"

"You will not see it," Jimmy Wentworth promised. "You will be in jail, waiting for a walk up the thirteen stairs for having murdered Henry McIntyre. You kept his hat to place in the vampire's coffin, but what have you done with the bit of metal which must be taken from every murdered man? Search him, boys!"

The attorney's ring was found in Feng Shan's token-bag. Wentworth's knowledge of Chinese customs had not failed him.

"And that'll crack his neck," Murphy said solemnly. Then he cried to the Chinese, "Go home! You men, hurry and go to work!"

In Cantonese, Jimmy Wentworth shouted, "This priest who is no priest was to have been given gold when you returned to work. All this"—he waved his hand over the coffin—"was to frighten you. Return to work, my friends."

"Wing Ch'i was my cousin's husband," a Chinese shrieked.

"The white lawyer was my friend," screamed another. "Vengeance!"

"There will be vengeance," Jimmy Wentworth said quietly.

After Feng Shan and his hatchetmen had been taken to town and locked in jail, and Jimmy had assured Murphy that he had only used his knowledge of the Orient to solve the crimes, he called Captain Dunand.

"I was waiting to hear from you," the captain of detectives said. "You all right, boy?"

"Got 'em all."

"Fine work. You've stopped something. Other canners have been approached, and threatened with a similar racket. That's ended. And it is why Kong Gai and his crew wanted it all in the newspapers, so they wouldn't need to go to the trouble of doing more killing. The newspaper reports would be proof to show the canners… and the Chinese as well. That Kong Gai is a fiend, Jimmy—"

"So you admit Kong Gai was back of it, chief?"

"It seems you've done something to a son of his. Got a letter from him a few minutes ago, promising all he's going to do to you."

"A Chinese up here made the same promise," Jimmy said calmly.

"What about him?"

"He's in jail," said Wentworth. "They're going to hang him."

THE COBRA STRIKES

Two Lives Hung on Wentworth's Move—
and He Couldn't Move Because Kong Gai
Had Hidden His Murder Trail Too Well

1

ABDUCTION AND MURDER

AT EXACTLY TWENTY minutes past eight, on Friday morning, the custom-built car belonging to the Roger Peckhams was driven sedately out of the garage and brought around to the front of the banker's great house. Mr. Peckham was at his breakfast and the newspapers. Mrs. Peckham, according to her usual habit during the early San Francisco summer, had already departed for the golf club in her roadster.

The two Peckham children, Lois and Dorothy, came from the house just as Dennis O'Toole, the chauffeur, stepped from the automobile to hold open the rear door. On any other morning, after the children were driven to school he would have returned to take Mr. Peckham to the bank. Friday was O'Toole's day off. His one duty, after conveying the children to school, was to drive the car to a foreign mechanic for special servicing. After that the day belonged to him.

Touching his cap, Dennis said, "A fine day, Miss Lois. A grand day, Miss Dorothy. An' school soon over f'r th' rest of th' week. No wonder it's smilin' ye are to-day."

"Good morning, Denny," the girls chorused.

The old chauffeur was humming under his breath as he

closed the door behind the children. And why shouldn't he
smile? Mr. Peckham might be fussy about things like being
on time, but he was the grand man to work for. Hadn't he
helped Denny finance a garage for young Michael in a
live country town—where Denny would go for the day,
after the car was delivered safely down town? Wasn't the
sun shining brightly, and hadn't Denny eaten largely of
oatmeal and corned beef hash and eggs, washed down
with several cups of fragrant coffee, the same as Mr. Peck-

Jimmy's gun fired as
he leaped for shelter

ham himself, with all his millions, was drinking now? And in old Denny's breast pocket were the two fine perfectos Peckham always gave him on Friday mornings along with his wages.

O'Toole turned the purring custom-built car into the park, using the same entrance he always took. He wondered if the chattering children behind him smelled the perfume in the air. To be sure, Mr. Peckham had him drive through the park in order to lessen traffic hazards, and also because it was thereby possible for O'Toole, by watching speedometer and clock, to return to the house on the dot. Nevertheless, Mr. Peckham was the grand man to work for. Loyal old Denny did not mind his employer being fussy about time.

The park, at this early hour, was as deserted as a country lane. Sunshine dappled the macadam where light filtered through the bordering trees. No city morning could possibly have been more peaceful.

Denny guided the car gently around the next long curve in the parkway. He saw, drawn to the side of the road, a machine of the same make and color as Mrs. Peckham's, with an automobile association towing car beside it. O'Toole mechanically slowed down and drove closer. He did not disengage his gears nor stop, but only drew alongside to be positive that Mrs. Peckham had not met with an accident. In his mind was the fact that his master did not like accidents, and Mrs. Peckham might have tried to keep one from him.

THE AUTOMOBILE THROTTLED down to a crawl, slipped along until it was opposite the disabled roadster. At that moment a man leaped from the rear of the towing car and to the running board of the custom-built machine. A gun was in Denny's startled face. The man's left hand jerked the hand brake and the car stopped instantly without a sound. With the practice of years, automatically, Denny's left foot slipped the clutch; while his hand moved the shifting post to neutral.

"Don't move!" the man with a gray cap pulled down over his eyes snarled. "One wriggle and I'll send you to hell."

" 'Tis no way to talk, what wit' me young leddies in the

car," Denny protested mildly. He was not a bit afraid. "Me few dollars ye c'n have, an' welcome. 'Tis hard times we're havin' an' no mistake—"

"Shut up, Mick!" The gun dug into Denny's ribs. "And stay shut!"

"Shure an' I'll not say another word," Dennis O'Toole agreed cheerfully.

And then the loyal old chauffeur's eyes moved up to the rear vision mirror. He wanted not only to see that all was well in the rear of the car, but also to wink assuringly to the children if they were looking toward him.

What he saw made his heart stand still, then begin to race as if it would leave his faithful body.

Three men were in the closed-in portion of the limousine. Denny could not see what manner of men they were at all, but he could see that they were binding and gagging the horrified children. His wrinkled face growing gray, he watched both of the Peckham girls as they were covered with blankets and pushed to the floor of the machine. Neither had been able to utter a sound. It took only fractions of a minute to complete the task.

The expensive engine made no more noise than the flutter of a butterfly's wing. Probably only Denny knew that the car was ready to leap forward.

"I'll be sittin' beside you, Mick," the man growled in O'Toole's ear. "If you ever expect to eat corned beef and cabbage again, do what I tell you, d'you hear? Otherwise..."

Denny said, "Kidnapin', is it?"

"Shut up!"

The Irishman glanced quietly at the man who covered him. "Shure, an' what do I care?" he grinned thinly.

"That's the old spirit," the man beside him sneered. "Take care of your hide."

"Shure," agreed Denny.

Not moving anything except his faded, keen blue eyes, Denny was missing nothing. There was the roadster which had beguiled him toward the side of the parkway—a roadster exactly like Mrs. Peckham's. A man was climbing into it and driving away. The service car with the automobile association emblem painted on the side was slowly moving forward. A hundred feet away it stopped and began to back toward the custom-built machine.

Denny knew that even if he yelled, should a machine pass, it would do little good. There was a man beside him. Three more in the rear of the car. A fifth in the service car. He supposed that all save the driver of the association machine had been in the roadster. And more than once Denny had driven through the parkway without meeting a single automobile. He certainly had no reason to hope for one now.

If he really wished anything, it was to hope that a mounted officer would come cantering down the bridle path.

The service car was only fifty feet away. In another moment, Denny was sure that the man beside him would relax his vigilance, knowing that the car could not go ahead. Denny wondered if the gangster realized that the engine was running. Probably not, or he would have shut it off. The racket of the towing car's big cyclinders completely covered the slight strumming of the Mercedes.

Denny's foot crept inch by inch toward the foot throttle as if it were a magnet. He saw the eyes of his captor waver away from him, and toward the towing car. One glance in the rear vision mirror showed him that the girls were out of sight on the floor, and that the three men were leaving the machine.

LIKE THE MOTION of a snake, old Denny's right hand flicked out. One sweep of his arm, and he released the hand brake and slid the gears into reverse, faster than the eye could follow. His foot jammed down on the gas. The limousine leaped backward in a sharp circle, and then stopped dead in its tracks, rubber burning, as O'Toole trod on the brake.

The man beside him was thrown first forward, then almost through the glass behind the driver's seat. His gun roared close to O'Toole, hitting only the steering post and screaming into the air.

Holding the wheel in his right hand, the chauffeur brought his bony left fist against the man's jaw with all the strength of his wiry shoulders. Fierce as the blow had been, O'Toole's position behind the wheel prevented it from being a knock-out.

Two of the three men were on their feet, guns out. The third, as he rose, cried, "No shooting!" and only that saved Denny's head from being blown off as the man beside him paused. He did the one thing O'Toole had hoped would not happen—yanked on the emergency just as Denny slid the car into second gear.

Why O'Toole had done all of these things, what made him think escape was possible, was his sense of love for the children and loyalty toward the Peckhams. It made him do more now. Possibly he should have thought that the kidnapers, whoever they were, would keep him, along with the youngsters, until ransom was paid. He did not think this at all.

Now, with three men less than a dozen feet away, with a man beside him holding a gun against him, Denny again did the last thing they expected. His fingers slipped the catch, well oiled, noiseless, of the door beside him. His right elbow hit the kidnaper's gun—and O'Toole scrambled from the Mercedes.

A gun cracked, once. Denny sprawled face forward, and even with the life welling from his veins tried to crawl away to summon help.

He was dead when the men hastily lifted him into the back of the car and shoved him under the blankets to further terrify the cowering children of Roger Peckham.

Not a moment was wasted now. The towing car was efficiently backed to the front of the limousine. The custom-built car, front wheels raised from the ground, was drawn so close to the association automobile that the name plate and insigne on the radiator could not be seen. One of the kidnapers, in mechanic's coveralls, got in beside the driver of the tow car. The other four lifted the big tool bag and spare parts compartment of the service car and slipped inside.

Two minutes later the Mercedes was driven out of the park into the jam of the morning traffic. At intersections, along with the lines of machines halted by the stoplight, it waited until the traffic officer set the east-west lanes moving again—the twenty thousand dollar automobile, in which a dead man grew stiff beside two bound, gagged, utterly terrified children.

2

SLIM CLEWS

ROGER PECKHAM TOOK his taxi downtown. Mrs. Peckham was at the eighth hole, and hitting the ball well; it looked as if she had found a way to stop slicing. The girls' school went about its morning work. Lois Peckham and Dorothy Peckham were absent, and the principal made a note to ring Mrs. Peckham later in the day and see if the girls were well. She hoped neither had contracted any contagious disease.

In the country, across the bay, Dennis O'Toole's son, Michael, hoped the old man would arrive in time for lunch, and not be detained in the Mercedes' garage. Old Denny liked chicken and dumplings. Only twice had Denny failed to appear on Fridays. Once the old chauffeur had written a line to explain his absence; the second time—although he had insisted he had written—no letter was received. Denny, feared his son, must be growing forgetful....

Not until three o'clock in the afternoon, six hours and a half later, did a call come to the Sunset District station.

The patrolman who was sent to examine the abandoned car found in the sand dunes south and west of the city, with a "drunken man" asleep in the back, found a great deal more than he expected.

There was the body of Dennis O'Toole, carefully placed to appear as if asleep. In death the old man was smiling, for all his failure to protect the children, even at the cost of his own life.

When the Mercedes, in perfect condition, was finally driven back to the Sunset District station, a search of O'Toole's clothing brought forth the following: a wallet, containing forty dollars in new bills, a check signed by Roger Peckham, two very fine cigars, keys, silver, chauffeur's license, bank book—and a note in O'Toole's handwriting.

The desk sergeant at the Sunset station read the letter.

"I am overcome by remorse. I cannot go through with this." O'Toole's name was at the end.

Seven hours had elapsed now since the custom-built car had been stopped in the park. The desk sergeant, perplexed, but not greatly excited, said, "Another suicide," and then called headquarters to report. Seven hours had elapsed—time enough for the kidnapers to have gone several hundred miles, time enough for them to have vanished with the Peckham children. The crime had been perfectly planned.

Seven hours is a long time.

ROGER PECKHAM, PRESIDENT of the Sierra-Pacific Bank, director in a dozen companies, financial genius, alternated between wild fear and rage. He was in Captain Dunand's office in the Hall of Justice. It was almost five o'clock.

"I tell you you've got to do something," he pleaded.

Dunand attempted to placate the frightened banker.

"We're doing what we can, sir," he said quietly. "I under-stand how you feel—"

"To hell with how I feel," the banker, a man who never swore, rasped. "Get me back my babies, and get them at once!"

Thinking, "After the thugs have a seven hours' start on us, and we don't know what sort of car they used, nor what they look like, nor who they are?" the gray-haired captain of detectives said:

"Every ferry is being watched. The State traffic officers are patrolling every highway and stopping every automo-bile containing any children. The sheriff's office in each county in the State has been notified. My best men are working on the case. I—just a minute—"

Dunand answered the summons of the telephone; to Peckham, while he waited, he said, "San Luis Obispo county is calling. The kidnapers might have driven that far by this time." Into the instrument he said, "Captain of detectives, San Francisco... hello, sheriff... two children..."

Mr. Peckham leaned forward pathetically, hands clenched.

Then Dunand said, "We'll supplement the telegraphed description tonight, sheriff. Yes, I'm sorry too. Both chil-dren were under five feet in height. Thanks anyhow. No, we don't know what make or type of car the kidnapers used."

His hands tight together, Peckham said, as Dunand turned toward him again, "I am a rich man, captain. Offer a reward for the children's return. Anything. Spare no expense." His face went white as he said, "Captain—you know some of these crimes lately. Do you think—"

"It'll be ransom," Dunand shot at him swiftly. "Don't

think about anything else, Mr. Peckham!" To make the banker stop shaking, he said soberly, "I hope it isn't going to inconvenience you, but I'm having your servants brought down here for questioning, to save time. Is Mrs. Peckham bearing up well? You've got to think of her, you know. Not let her break down."

"She feels that if she had not gone to play golf—"

"That this wouldn't have happened? Nonsense. Tell your wife so. This crime, Mr. Peckham, was carefully planned, and fiendishly executed. Now, we must learn one or two things, sir. Have you any enemies?"

"None, captain!"

Dunand knew Peckham's reputation for square dealing. He had asked the question as a matter of form, just as he asked the next:

"You have no idea who might have done this, nor why?"

"Absolutely not." Peckham swallowed and, controlling himself with difficulty, went on: "Only, I am positive that poor Dennis O'Toole had nothing to do with it. I don't care what the note said. I would have trusted O'Toole anywhere, and under any circumstances."

"So would I," Dunand agreed. "O'Toole, confession or no confession, was murdered. None of us believe O'Toole had anything to do with it. No man," Dunand said solemnly, "puts a muzzle at his back and shoots so that the bullet lodges in his breastbone. It couldn't be done. That is how O'Toole was shot."

"The confession—"

"Was intended to put us off the track still longer, and give the kidnapers more time to make their getaway. It is my opinion that they—whoever they are—really expected to have the car discovered only after we began to search for it, when your daughters were learned to be missing. The plan was diabolical, Mr. Peckham."

"The newspapers hint—my poor babies!—that this may be another case of a fiend in human form…"

"Forget the newspapers. If they 'hint' it is because they are just as much in the dark as we are. We are not passing up anything, sir. But first of all we must learn something to put us on the scent. Don't you see? All we know is that your daughters are missing. We have not another single fact at our disposal yet. Not a single clew, except—"

"Except what? Tell me, captain!"

"Two of my men have gone to get O'Toole's son. Whoever wrote that note must have forged Dennis O'Toole's signature, and imitated his handwriting."

"Young Michael O'Toole? Impossible!"

"In crime," Dunand said grimly, "that's a word we've learned not to use." He stopped as the door opened, and three men entered. "Well?" the gray-haired captain demanded. "This is Mr. Peckham, boys. Go ahead and talk."

DETECTIVE MATHEWS SAID, "Sweeney brought in the servants, chief. They are downstairs—"

"I know. Go on."

"Before he left the Peckham house with them, I asked about the way O'Toole took the children to school. Mrs. Peckham told me, and one of the maids had driven with them now and again—"

"I could have told you that," Peckham broke in. "O'Toole always followed the route I laid out for him. Down Fernando Street to Mission Avenue, along Mission to the Memorial Entrance to the parkway—"

"We followed the way he went," Mathews said quietly to Dunand. "Maybe it was accident, maybe it was Larkins' good eyesight, but we came to a place where rubber had been burned on the macadam. Like a car stopped in a hurry, or even swung around while the brakes were on. While Janeway"—the department's automotive expert—"was trying to identify the tracks, which was impossible because so many machines had passed over them, I found a dryish, sort of greasy place on the road. We scraped some of it up."

"Blood?" Dunand asked.

"Felt like it, chief. The chemist's got the sample now."

As he spoke a young man in patrolman's uniform knocked once and entered. Seeing the men with Dunand, he turned to go. The captain of detectives said, "Wait a few minutes, Wentworth. Sacramento wants a report on one of the tongs. See you about it in a few minutes. Sit down."

Jimmy Wentworth, sergeant of detectives in charge of the Chinatown detail, sat down. He supposed, and rightly, that the conference was about the Peckham kidnaping. He had heard the extras on the street.

He was glad to sit after his day of pacing a beat up and down the steep hills of Chinatown, where the Asiatics knew him only as the officer, young and foolish, who represented the white man's nonsensical laws. They did not know that Wentworth understood their habits, language, and customs as only a white man born in China could hope to know them.

"Reconstructing the crime," Mathews said, "O'Toole was stopped so suddenly that he jammed on his brakes.

Perhaps it was somebody with a gat. Or somebody faking to fall under the wheels."

"Or perhaps, which you couldn't know, by somebody grabbing the emergency," Dunand said. "The hand brake was wiped clean, Mathews, when we found the car. No fingerprints on it. The Sunset District boys were careful."

"Possibly that was it," the automotive expert, Janeway, agreed. "However, chief, don't forget that the car must have been driven out to the sand dunes, and the brakes used again. Er… Mr. Peckham, when was your Mercedes in an accident? It couldn't have been much. I couldn't even find where a fender had been replaced."

"It's never been in an accident," Peckham said briefly. "Never."

"The car has been towed recently," Janeway insisted. "I found the marks on the front axle—"

Peckham pleaded, "Gentlemen, is this all you're going to do? Tell me my car was towed? I want my children," and here the frightened father became the powerful figure of the Sierra-Pacific Bank, "and, gentlemen, I propose to have more than talk!"

DUNAND CLEARED THE air crisply. He knew what pressure the influential banker could bring to bear, but this was totally unnecessary. The department intended to find the children, as rapidly as possible if it could be done.

"Go ahead, Mathews," he said. "Give us your version of what took place."

The picture Detective Mathews painted was this: O'Toole, the trusted employee, had been driving the girls along the parkway, as always. He was halted. The kidnapers swarmed about the automobile. O'Toole, seeing the hopelessness of resistance, had leaped out to bring aid and to give a description of the attackers. He had been able to run not over fifteen feet before one of the gang had shot him in the back. It was Mathews's theory that the course of the bullet, from the base of the spine upward, proved that O'Toole might have knocked one of the kidnapers down in attempting to escape, and that the gangster had shot him while lying on the road. After this the chauffer's body was thrown in the Mercedes, and the children, perhaps transferred somewhere to another machine, were hurried away.

"The shot wasn't fired from the ground," Dunand said. "The bullet was deflected by bone, the autopsy surgeon says. It entered O'Toole's body about three and a half feet or so from the ground, and was fired almost parallel to the road. Funny way to shoot, Mathews. Possibly a quick shot, from the hip."

"They don't shoot that way any more," Larkins said. "The quick draw went out when gangsters came in. They've got to aim, and be close to the target.

"Don't forget that O'Toole fell face forward when shot. That takes away five feet or so of the fifteen foot distance. He must have been dropped when he was about ten feet away from the muzzle of the gun."

"Just the same, it was a shot made from the hip, Larkins."

Jimmy Wentworth's eyes were bright, but he said nothing.

"Have the servants in," Dunand ordered.

In order, Dunand questioned Mrs. Peckham's personal maid, the two housemaids, the gardener and his assistant, and the cook. All of them, except the cook, had been in the Peckham residence for a number of years. The cook had been employed a little under a month. None was able to shed any light, nor to suggest a reason why the children should have been kidnaped except for ransom. All insisted that they had seen no suspicious characters about the street, nor had any of them been asked by anybody concerning the time O'Toole drove the children to school, nor the route he took while doing it.

It was never the gray-haired captain's manner to browbeat any one. He ended by saying to them all, "You can see that these kidnapers knew just how to catch the girls. I don't suspect any of you. Neither does Mr. Peckham. We are only trying to find out something to help us. Anything—*anything*—any of you know, or think, or guess, will be of assistance."

MARY FLAHERTY, THE cook, leaned across Dunand's desk.

"Captain dear," she said, " 'tis ourselves that loved Denny O'Toole. Even meself, who knew him but a month. This mornin', captain, he says to me, 'Mary, 'tis a relief to have ye in th' kitchen. A woman in th' kitchen,' the blarneyer says, 'is the thing to give a man an appetite. Glad I am that Mr. Peckham rid himself of that dom Chink, no matter how good a cook he was!' And now him dead, and the children missin'!"

Dunand's expression never changed. "What Chinaman, Mary?"

"Shure, th' yella felly Mr. Peckham had as cook, captain. He—"

"If you are thinking of attaching suspicion to Yee Loung," Peckham said, "I'll tell you that he left only to return to China. He sailed on the T'aiping Shan a month ago." Bitterly he added, "After all this talk I suppose you'll suggest that my former cook kidnaped the children by means of thought waves!" He stood up. "I'm sick and disgusted of this nonsense," he said. "The lot of you here, talking like a parcel of old women! Getting nowhere! And in the meantime my children... dead, for all I know!... being taken farther and farther away! Nothing but talk!"

Dunand pleaded, "Mr. Peckham, we must find a clew. Every avenue of escape is guarded. Remember, sir, that seven hours elapsed before the kidnaping was discovered. No detail is too small to neglect. Did you discharge this cook, or did he leave freely?"

"Freely! I myself engaged his passage, and had his money transferred to China. He has a wife and family there."

Jimmy Wentworth spoke for the first time.

"He goes back to China every two years, Mr. Peckham?"

The banker said shortly, "All Chinese do."

"Was his two years up—his two years of residence in the States?"

Peckham saw who was speaking. His face became taut with rage. "Look here," he said to Dunand, "is every patrolman in San Francisco going to be called in to give opinions? By heaven, I will not stand for more delay! I—"

The captain was no longer suave. He said sharply, "Please answer the question, sir."

"I will," Peckham cried. "And then I'm going to get in touch with the governor! It's the last thing I'll tell you. Yee Loung left a little in advance of his customary two years— three months ahead. And if you want to know why, it was because his wife was ill and wrote him to come! And—"

"That's what I was hoping to hear," said Jimmy Wentworth. He said to Dunand, "It makes potential fact number two, chief! Or guess number two."

"What's the first one?" Dunand said softly.

"The hip shot, captain. The northern Chinese shoot that way with *jin-gals* and matchlocks. Always have, always will. Even with revolvers they'll do it every time if they're excited. Right from the hip, level with the earth. My dad said that in the Boxer outbreak you could tell every foreigner killed by the north Chinese. Shot through the middle, about three and a half feet above the ground."

"H-m," said Captain Dunand. He hesitated only an instant, and then said, "You've heard all there is to hear, Jim. Go down and have a look at the body, and talk to Dr. Murray, eh? Don't go off duty."

Wentworth left at once.

"Gentlemen," Peckham said, ready to leave also, "this is an outrage. Now you are going to attempt to fasten this kidnaping on some mysterious Chinese to cover your inaction! I can see how much help I can expect from the police! I'll secure private detectives, speak to the mayor, the chief, the governor… why, if you really intended to get me back my babies, you would have put your best man on this case, instead of listening to idiotic theories advanced by half-baked patrolmen!"

He made one more sobbing plea, his anger dissolved. "Captain, get me back my children, alive and well! Put a man like Wentworth on the case, captain! Won't you help me?"

Dunand said quietly, sorry for the unhappy man: "Sergeant Wentworth just left the room, Mr. Peckham. He is on the case now."

"That... that policeman? The young fellow who went out? He's Wentworth?" The banker's eyes were wide with astonishment. "Detective Sergeant Wentworth?"

"Give him whatever information he requests, sir," Dunand told Peckham. "No matter how personal, nor how trivial, it may seem. Yes, that was Jimmy Wentworth."

3

JIMMY WENTWORTH IS ATTACKED

THE SATURDAY MORNING papers, with no developments in the story since the extras of the previous evening, were able to give a fuller story of the abduction. Every similar crime was retold in gruesome detail. The administration supporting paper insisted that "the police expect an arrest hourly," intimating that this arrest would occur far from San Francisco. The anti-administration papers shrieked that the police were entirely at sea, and intimated that internal inefficiency had caused a fatal delay in starting work on the case. There were photographs of Roger Peckham and his family, of the servants, of Dennis O'Toole, of the note found on Denny's body. There was a diagram of the kidnaping.

Only one fact Captain Dunand concealed from the reporters. He said nothing of the course made by the fatal bullet. Nobody asked about it. Dennis O'Toole was dead; it was the Peckham children the newspapers and the public were concerned with.

Michael O'Toole had been brought to the Hall of Justice. He denied any knowledge of the note, proven to be a forgery of Dennis O'Toole's scrawl. He did say that one letter, which his father had written him, had never been received. This letter had been written something over a month ago.

During the night Jimmy Wentworth had little time for sleep. He spent a considerable time with the financial reporter of one of the newspapers, going over Peckham's connections and friends.

The newspaper man verified the fact that Peckham was a man without enemies, and that his conservative bank had never mixed with elements which might have the slightest cause for retaliation.

A Chinese named Yee Loung had sailed on the T'aiping Shan for Hongkong. Wentworth verified this beyond doubt.

In the morning, in plain clothes, he went to the Sierra-Pacific Bank, and with the cashier went over Peckham's personal account, looking vainly for any entry which might point toward payment of blackmail.

Wentworth realized how slim his clews were. A: O'Toole had been murdered by a bullet entering his body at an unusual angle. B: A Chinese cook had returned to his home across the Pacific three months before his two years were out. That was all. Nothing else to work on.

In the meantime, reports concerning the vanished children continued to pour into the Hall of Justice by telephone and by wire. A machine was seen rushing up the highway toward the Oregon line. A power boat was reported landing several people below the Point Arena Light, in an isolated cove; two of these seemed small, and might be children. A wrecked automobile was found on a mountain road. A car was stolen in Los Angeles, and found in San Diego with an empty milk bottle in the rear seat.

Every report was run down. The highway patrol was alert. Motorcycle officers, without relief, stopped every machine containing children, every machine going at a fast pace.

Stool pigeons and finks in the State prisons were set at work, to learn if any recently discharged prisoners had laid plans for the abduction while in jail. The parole office checked on paroled convicts. The police departments all over the State began rounding up parole violaters.

Not a single clew was obtained. Not a single report meant a thing. The Peckham children, after the murder of Dennis O'Toole, appeared to have utterly vanished. If there was a thing to do, except to watch, and wait until the demand for ransom was received, no one knew what it was.

AT HALF PAST nine, just as the bell on the old cathedral at the edge of Chinatown called attention to the gilt words on the tower:

Son, Observe the Time
And Flee from Evil.

Jimmy Wentworth, again in his blue patrolman's uniform, started to walk his beat. Chinatown was quiet. Wentworth's practiced eye caught no sign of excitement anywhere. The usual tourists gazing into the shop windows. The litchi nut seller. The guides on the corner of California Street. The blind beggar outside the church. Smell of incense, of dried shrimp, of squid, of lilies in blue pots. Scarlet placards on the "news-wall"... nothing there of importance. No brazenly-exhibited warning of tong warfare, painted in black on scarlet paper. No sinister, black-clad, lean Asiatics, hatchetmen and highbinders from North China, loitering in dark doorways and disappearing when the blue-clad officer marched along the street.

Wentworth stopped at the bowl shop owned by the Wangs. Old Wang Yu was a wizard at the lore of the Chinese; young Wang Chen-p'o, the son, was a friend of Jimmy's, and had been of assistance more than once.

"*Ni kam yat, hola,*" old Wang sang out nasally, his wrinkled face smiling at the sight of the detective. After the greeting, he added, "*Ni kam chiu hü, pin ch'ü loi ni?* Where have you been this morning? You are a few minutes late in passing."

Still in fluent Cantonese, Wentworth said, "Every one in the police department is trying to learn about the children who have been stolen, Wang Yu."

"For once," young Wang grinned, speaking in English as he entered the shop from the rear, "the Chinese are in the clear, eh, James?"

"You didn't do it," Wentworth retorted. "You're too lazy, Chen-p'o."

The ancient father, huddled on a teakwood stool behind his counter, continued smiling impassively a moment, and then said, "Has every one in the police been working, my white son?"

Jimmy nodded.

"Is it so?" old Wang said, as if to himself. "And now you have come to ask me what I know of Yee Loung, cook at the house of the banker?"

Wentworth was startled, but nodded a second time.

"I thought you would learn the cook had left for the Celestial Land Across the Sea in advance of his proper time. A letter came from his wife. She was sick. Yee Loung was very excited."

"Very excited?" Jimmy demanded.

"More excited than a sick wife makes necessary," said Wang Yu. "It was spoken of in Chinatown. But I am sure Yee Loung departed for China—"

"After telling some one all about the habits of the Peckham family!"

"Perhaps," Wang Yu agreed.

"Whom did he tell?" Wentworth asked quietly.

Wang looked at the bare counter before him. "The stars," he said. "The moon and the sun and the earthdragons. I do not know."

Wentworth said, "He was bribed, of course."

"Of course. Or—threatened. I have told you that he was very excited when he received the letter from… his wife." Gently, Wang continued, "The letter must have been from his wife. Every one saw it."

"Does a man show intimate letters?"

Old Wang smiled. "You know our customs too well to need an answer, my son."

Wentworth turned to the younger Chinese. "D'you mind giving me the names of Yee Loung's friends, Chen-p'o, as many as you can learn? Did he smoke opium?"

"He did. And"—Wang Chen-p'o's voice lowered—"I have heard it said that he smoked the opium of… Kong Gai."

THE NAME OF the Evil One of Chinatown was barely audible. Jimmy Wentworth had more than once thwarted the vengeful, powerful Kong Gai, whose symbol was a king cobra, and who more than once had killed by using cobra poison. Kong Gai hated the white detective, and Wentworth knew that Kong Gai only waited for a time when the sergeant might be off guard, in order to capture and torture him. A knife, a swift death, would never satisfy the fiendish Chinese who controlled the Oriental underworld.

"Yee Loung, Kong Gai, abduction," Wentworth said slowly. "It's far-fetched, Chen-p'o."

"Has Kong Gai ever missed a chance to obtain gold?"

"There hasn't been any request for ransom yet."

"The longer Peckham waits, the more willingly he will pay many thousands, James!"

Wentworth, lips tight, said, "And where do I look for Kong Gai?"

"In the stars," old Wang said again. "In the moon and the sun. No man knows. Only this I know, my son; Kong Gai is too careful to have the children taken to his lair! They will never be there—*if* the King Cobra has stolen them."

The son promised, "I'll see if I can pick up anything, Jimmy. We've got a lot of the Wang family in Chinatown. Maybe somebody's heard something—"

"Be careful," Wentworth cautioned him. "Warn any one you talk to not to say a word, Chen-p'o! If this is true, and it's all hunch so far, what a place Chinatown would be to hide the girls! We're scouring the country, stopping machines, wirelessing boats, and all the time the Peckham children may be… fifty feet from here!"

His head was working rapidly now. If the demand for ransom were made, and Kong Gai were behind the scheme, whoever would come for the gold or currency would undoubtedly be a Chinese. Let him get the money, follow him. In the meantime young Wang would perhaps pick up a scrap or two of information.

Then, shortly, the detective sergeant laughed.

"It sounds too much like a fairy tale," he said. "Just the same, I'm going to report it to my chief. Can I use your phone, please?"

In the rear room, Wentworth called headquarters.

"I've stumbled on something which may get us somewhere," he told Captain Dunand. "Knew you'd want to know, chief. It seems—"

"It seems," Dunand's voice came harshly over the wire, "that I let myself be fooled by all this foolishness of yours about North China and cockeyed shooting from the hip. Forget it, Jim. Peckham's just received the demand for ransom. Two hundred thousand dollars in bills. To be taken by Peckham himself to Reno, Nevada. If the ransom is not paid by noon on Monday, the girls are to be killed. It's diabolical, Jim. And in view of some cases I've seen, if the money isn't paid, the girls *will* be killed!

"The money is to be taken to a location out in the desert, and if there is more than Peckham and a man to drive the automobile to the appointed spot, or if another automobile with men in it is seen on the road to it, the girls are to be killed instantly. Which means that the kidnapers got through the cordon, and that they have the children with them.

"Peckham will pay the ransom! What else is there to do? We haven't one single clew, one hint, one anything… and now you want to tell me a bedtime story at ten in the morning! Go on out and walk your beat and maybe pick up a few lottery-ticket sellers! That's how much your *clews* mean!"

Dunand hung up before Wentworth could say a word.

When he walked back into the bowl shop, shrewd old Wang said at once, *"Mi chau cho'u…* all did not go well, my son?"

"Pretty badly," Jimmy Wentworth admitted wryly. "I'm just all wrong."

Wang said politely, "That is too bad. When you leave the shop, I advise that you use your eyes. Two men have arrived in the doorway opposite. They are very lean, and very ugly, and they are dressed in black."

"Thanks. I'll watch 'em. But if Kong Gai tries to get me, he won't do it with a knife, Wang Yu. That isn't his way of killing, except by accident."

Wentworth didn't want to talk more. Dunand was right. He had been led up a blind alley merely because, like every one else, he was trying to find some straw on which to fasten the crime. The ransom demand, sent from Reno probably, ended his usefulness in the matter. He only hoped that the girls were returned alive and uninjured.

He stepped out of the shop, caught a glimpse of the two dark figures lurking in the opposite doorway.

The moment he was in plain sight a gun spat. Only the reflection of the glass window of the shop saved Wentworth's life; the hatchetmen must have been dazzled by light.

JIMMY WENTWORTH'S OWN gun leaped out even while he swerved to the shelter of Wang's entrance. He fired once, blindly, to disconcert the hatchetman's aim. When a second and third bullet thudded into the wooden building near him, Jimmy Wentworth brought his gun up deliberately until the sights were on the black-clad figure opposite, and then pulled the trigger.

A scream echoed along a street deserted as if by magic. Only a few tourists remained in sight, not at all disturbed, believing that the sounds came from some back-firing automobile.

The second assassin had already vanished. Wentworth, gun ready, raced across the street. He hoped fervently that young Wang did not telephone the Hall of Justice for the riot squad; he would finish this himself. Without pausing he actually took several steps into the dark interior of the hallway, and then, remembering Kong Gai, at once turned and retreated. A man didn't go alone after a king cobra, into the cobra's own hole—not and come out alive.

Kong Gai, trying to trap him. The hatchetman had aimed to miss, of course. Vigilantly watchful, Jimmy Wentworth opened the Asiatic's silk coat. On the dead man's breast was the mark of Kong Gai, the cobra, the dreaded hooded serpent of the East.

Wentworth thought, "I'll be hanged if I think Kong Gai sent these men to lure me into the building. He knows the Wangs would telephone headquarters if I didn't come out. These two fellows were on their own, trying to curry favor with Kong Gai by getting me out of the way. That first shot was too close for comfort."

As he crossed the street again, dragging the Oriental's body after him and into Wang's shop, he wondered when the day would come when Kong Gai would strike out beyond Chinatown for richer plunder.

"Sorry to bring this hatchetman into your shop," Jimmy

apologized to young Wang. "Kong Gai knows that we're friendly; so it shouldn't do you any harm."

Chen-p'o said soberly, "Behind that cupboard, Jim, with the imitation bowls on the shelves, are four peepholes. Behind each peephole is a Wang hatchetman, and in each man's hand is a gun. We will protect ourselves the best we can. The point now is—"

"Why murder was attempted," said old Wang. "For every death, the Ninth Book says, there is a reason. Is it because Kong Gai hates you… or fears you?"

"He isn't afraid of me," said Jimmy, getting ready to call the dead wagon.

"Is he now?" Wang insisted.

"Why should he be? He hasn't any way of knowing I'm interested—or was, until a little while ago!—in catching the kidnapers. He doesn't know I had a theory which was all wet. He doesn't know—"

Impatiently, old Wang asked, "Enough of this 'he does not know!' What *does* he know? Where have you been this morning, my son, which might tell him anything?"

Jimmy said alertly, "I was in the Sierra-Pacific Bank—"

"Ah!" said the impassive old Chinese.

4

THE SUSPICIOUS PHONE CALL

WHEN THE MORGUE automobile drove up, and the body of Kong Gai's follower was placed inside, Wentworth said, for the benefit of the blind beggar huddled against the wall:

"I'll go along and make out a report." He remained on the seat beside the driver only until the car was out of Chinatown, and then walked rapidly to the nearest taxi. "Sierra-Pacific Bank," he said.

"Been a holdup?" the driver asked, starting his car quickly.

"There will be if I don't get in there soon, because I'm overdrawn," Jimmy told him. "Step on it. I don't want to be broken."

"Sure, officer. Say, I got a ticket f'r parkin' too long—"

"Hurry it up and I'll see what can be done," Wentworth promised.

They were in front of the Sierra-Pacific very rapidly. "I've got to get back to my beat," Jimmy said. "Park her right in front here, and wait for me."

"That's where the officers of the bank park," the other said. "I'll get kicked out."

"No you won't. Just sit there and make believe you're a millionaire, buddy."

"I wouldn't want to be Peckham, officer! I betcha his kids is cut up in pieces by now, huh? I—"

But Jimmy Wentworth was already inside the bank.

He walked swiftly to the cashier's private office. It took a moment for him to be admitted, and his first words to the bank official were: "Will you call your switchboard operator at once, and have her make a record of every outgoing call, by whom made in the bank, and what the number asked for is? If she can overhear any conversations, that will help. Don't waste a second!"

The official repeated Wentworth's order, and then said, "You can be sure Miss Fleming will not fail, officer. But might I ask why? I assume it is in connection with the unfortunate kidnaping?"

"That's it," said Jimmy. "You don't remember me, sir. I was here earlier. Wentworth."

The cashier chuckled. "I never heard of a detective disguised as a policeman," he said. "That's a new one on me!"

"Please keep it to yourself," said Jimmy. Hopefully, he continued: "Have you any Chinese employed in the bank? In the foreign exchange department? Anywhere?"

"Not a one, detective."

Jimmy said, "Too bad. I'm going now, sir. I'll call you in a few minutes, and then you can give me whatever your operator has learned—the calls, and numbers, you know."

He decided that about the safest place to get out of the cab would be at headquarters; he wanted to see the ransom note anyway. Going straight to Dunand's office, he found his chief alone, and frowning as he stared out of the window.

"Got another bedtime story?" Dunand asked.

"Not yet," Jimmy Wentworth grinned. "Don't be disgusted, chief. It may not be as silly as you think—"

"No. Maybe it's sillier."

Wentworth called the Sierra-Pacific Bank. Dunand's ears pricked up as he heard the number, although he said nothing. To the cashier Jimmy said, "This is Sergeant Wentworth. Can you get me the information now?" He waited while the bank official secured it on another telephone.

Then Jimmy listened to names and numbers; each time, after the name, the cashier either gave the man's bank title, or a word or two concerning the call. The operator had indeed been on the job.

Wentworth, listening, was silent so long that Dunand became restless. He stood up and began to pace the floor.

And then Jimmy Wentworth heard what set his heart to beating rapidly. "George Chidister," came the cashier's steady voice, uninterested in the information which meant nothing to him. "Calling China Exchange, 00711. Miss Fleming said the conversation was very short. Just a word, and then Mr. Chidister hung up. She didn't hear what it might be."

"Thanks," Jimmy said, after permitting the cashier to continue, lest his suspicion be directed to the China number. "I'm sorry. We had a clew, but it hasn't worked out." The instant he hung up the telephone, he took it from the hook again. To the officer at the headquarters switchboard he said, "China 00711, Jerry. This's Jim Wentworth. Find out the name it's listed under, the address, and all the rest, please."

DUNAND COULD CONTAIN himself no longer.

"Still chasing Chinese shadows?" he blurted. "Read this ransom letter, and see exactly where we stand!"

He handed the letter to his detective. Wentworth read it rapidly. The note said: "You are to be at the Ferry Building at five forty Sunday evening. Stand at the *Exit* sign next to the candy stand. Then take the Silver State Express to Reno. Bring two hundred thousand dollars in bills. Register at the Inter-Mountain Hotel in Reno. A letter will be waiting for you, addressed to A.O. Kennedy, the name under which you are to register. In this letter will be a marked road map. Watch the speedometer of your automobile. When it reads 41.8 miles from the hotel, you will see a clump of trees. Stop. In the trees you will find a large tin can. Place the bills in the can. Drive back to Reno.

"If police are with you at the Ferry, on the train, in the hotel; if detectives precede or follow you, in the automobile, or if there is any investigation in Reno, you will never see your daughters again, except dismembered.

"Noon, Monday, is the last moment you have to bring the two hundred thousand dollars. If you are a sensible man, have nothing to do with the police."

The message was unsigned.

There were maps on Dunand's desk. Every road leading out of the Nevada city was already marked, indicating approximately forty-two miles from the site of the hotel. In moderate tones, the captain of detectives said, "Peckham has been as good as his word. He has used influence everywhere. We are under orders, Jim, to do absolutely nothing which might hinder Peckham in taking the money to the rendezvous. I don't want the children killed, but I do want to be able to get the kidnapers!"

"An educated man wrote the ransom demand," Wentworth said. "The word 'dismembered' proves that. And the time—five forty on Sunday—shows how much thought has been given this plot, chief. The Sunday traffic, returning from across the bay, will make it impossible to spot any one watching for Peckham. What gets me is how any one managed to get across the Sierra roads with the youngsters!"

"Maybe I haven't thought about that," Dunand muttered. "The State traffic office reports that every machine had been stopped, every truck searched, on all of the roads into Nevada. But there are planes now, Jim. Private planes. Or the kidnapers may have gone north or south and then cut east. They'd have time to do it by noon Monday."

The ransom note in his hand, Wentworth said suddenly, "Will you have Kingdon up here, chief?" naming the department's expert on handwriting and typewriters.

"If it'll do you any good," Dunand told him wearily, "we've already learned that the note was typed on a new Super-Speed, and here's the list of purchasers within the past three months. Eleven hundred deliveries." He shoved the list to Wentworth. "Go call on 'em all, Jim. And then find out that the typewriter may have been bought in Oakland, or in Los Angeles, or in Portland…"

The young Chinatown detective read name after name, never finding the one he hoped to see. There were, at the end, a number of cash sales, in which the purchaser had taken the typewriter with him.

Dunand's phone was ringing. The captain, answering

it, said to Wentworth, "The China exchange number is at 966A Waverley Place," and hung up the instrument abruptly.

"Is it?" Jimmy said softly. "I've had my eye on 966A. Too many Chinese going there. Hop joint. And, chief, what would you say if I told you that a man in Peckham's bank called that number a little while ago?"

"That you've got ants in your pants," Dunand said inelegantly.

"Mmm. Maybe I have. But suppose, for the sake of argument, that I told you I went to the Sierra-Pacific Bank earlier this morning, and after I left there and went back to my beat, a couple of highbinders took a shot at me? What then?"

"If they'd hit you in your stubborn head, you wouldn't even get a headache."

Grinning, Jimmy Wentworth went on, "And these hatchetmen—the one I plugged, anyhow—wore Kong Gai's cobra mark on his chest. *And* they came after me only when it was reported back to Chinatown that I'd been in Peckham's bank!"

Dunand stared at his detective. "There are lots of Chinks in Reno," he admitted. "Do we dare go against orders"—he was talking almost to himself—"and send you up there? If anything happened to the girls, I wouldn't forgive myself. Being broken means nothing. D'you think you could get to Reno without being seen?"

"Not if Kong Gai's spies are watching me, chief. The fact that I wouldn't be on my beat Monday would probably finish the children, if Kong Gai is mixed up in this mess. The Wangs think he is. They hinted as much. They think

Yee Loung, the Peckham cook, gave the information, and then was shipped out of the country. Go to Reno, chief? No!"

"Well?"

"I think the place for me, if I do any good, is right here in Chinatown!"

"You... Jimmy, you don't think those children are here in San Francisco?"

"I do."

"And this Reno thing is a stall?"

"That's it."

Dunand snapped, "Try and find 'em, Jimmy! You know Chinatown—"

"Where?" Wentworth said briefly. "In what tunnel are they hidden? All I can do, chief, is keep my eyes open, and my ears open. I'd like only one thing."

"Shoot! I'm not convinced, Jimmy, but I won't pass up a single angle of this case. What d'you want, boy?"

"Half a dozen men from the riot squad, armed as if they were going to stop a regiment, as if they had to break down barricades. Rifles, the new machine gun, pineapples, a sledge hammer—the whole works, chief. Send them one by one, to-night, into the Wangs' shop by the back way. You know the place—the fence next to the old cathedral. They are to eat and sleep at Wangs', out of sight—"

"For how long?"

"Until Monday noon."

Dunand said, "I'll do it. It's grasping at a straw. D'you think there's anything in it, Jimmy?"

"No Chinaman," said Jimmy Wentworth, "ever changes his plans unless there is a good reason. Yee Loung, sick wife or no sick wife, didn't intend to return to China until his two years were up. When he got this letter telling of her illness—a real letter, he showed it to everybody—he was all excited. And I learned one thing which even Mr. Peckham didn't know, or didn't understand. When Yee Loung sailed, he took all of his money with him. Which meant he wasn't coming back. Why? Only one reason: he had made enough to keep him and his three or four families in comfort until he died. And where did he get his money? Not from Peckham. From Kong Gai in payment for the information."

"I don't know," Dunand muttered. "But it won't do any harm to try. Why, it's the only clew we have, Jim!" He said suddenly, "How are you going to find the girls, Jimmy? Have the Wangs ask? What else?"

"They're at work already. But that isn't what I'm counting on. Chief, after a crime what do crooks do, when there's something to be split?"

"Get together," Dunand said. "What good'll that do? You've got to find the girls before Peckham deposits the money. I'm not fool enough to expect to see them alive after that—that doesn't happen very often, and the odds are all against it—"

"That's what I'm counting on," Jimmy Wentworth said again. "When everything seems to be going right the crooks may get together! And that's when I'm going to be watching 966A Waverley!"

5

THE RIOT SQUAD RAIDS

TROUBLES FOR ROGER Peckham did not come singly, although the financier, leaving the hotel in Reno at nine in the morning did not know, and would not have cared, about the second happening. In San Francisco things were beginning to take place in the stock market. Conservative Sierra-Pacific Bank stock, which had withheld all assaults, began to slide, due to persistent hammering. Rumors of insolvency were heard. There was a terrific bear movement. A dozen brokers—acting on orders they insisted were secret—continued the terrific onslaught. From 188, Sierra-Pacific was smashed, in less than a half hour, to a bare 120. The market had never seen such a crash. In vain the bank officials sought to stem the tide.

Newspapers, brokers, investors insisted on some statement from the president—Roger Peckham. And Peckham was on the desert.

In another fifteen minutes it was stated by some one that Peckham had fled and that the entire kidnaping affair was a hoax to cover his departing! It was said that the Sierra-Pacific was going on the rocks—and down went the stock another twenty points!

What the Street would have liked to have known was

where the bear movement in Sierra-Pacific started, and who was behind it—who was, at every drop, becoming richer and richer. For it was learned that somebody, somewhere, was short in Sierra-Pacific. The bear operators all denied having begun the cataclysm. Other banks insisted that they were not interested in beating down the S-P price, and rightly, for their own stocks began to drop also, slowly, but definitely.

Every one cried for Roger Peckham, who alone could have stemmed the financial tide—and Roger Peckham was somewhere far in the desert! He had told none where he was going, lest harm—through a leak—come to his vanished children. The police knew, but no one else. Dunand knew, and knew what was taking place in the stock market. Wentworth knew nothing about it at all.

IN THE REAR of the Wangs' bowl shop were seven officers, lean men in perfect condition. Old Wang, sitting at his counter, absorbed apparently in nothing, knowing that the shop was being spied on from across the street, nevertheless managed to watch up the cross street, a half block up the hill. During the night a white man had crept carefully across the roofs, starting from the top floor rooms of a Wang relative, until, crouched down behind the parapet, he was able to see Waverley Place below him and the house marked as 966A.

Old Wang could not see this white man. If, however, he saw a square of newspaper held above the parapet he would know that Jimmy Wentworth was telling him that the riot squad was to obey the orders already issued.

Up on the roof, with Chinatown spread out below him, Jimmy Wentworth's doubts grew as the time advanced. Ten o'clock. Ten fifteen. Ten thirty! All quiet below. The blind beggar had moved until he was able to *watch* any one who entered 966A. Wentworth knew that the "blind" man was a Kong Gai spy. Some day he would arrest him, but only when he had a crime to pin on the hatchetman.

Wentworth, more and more nervous, wondered if the rule that "when crooks split all the crooks are present" would fail to work. His chain of circumstances was a slim one. Nine-tenths of it was guesswork. Yet how else, in Chinatown, could a man get anywhere? Yee Loung had been bribed. A man named Chidister had telephoned China 00711—966A Waverley Place. Chidister worked in Peckham's bank. Wentworth himself had been shot at by the Cobra Men... it wasn't enough. If Jimmy had known what was taking place in the market—Sierra-Pacific, by eleven thirty, had been hammered down to under a hundred—he would have felt differently.

The great clock on the cathedral boomed the noon hour in twelve long strokes. Noon! Were the Peckham children delivered to their father? Or was Roger Peckham lying dead in the desert? And the children dead also?

Jimmy Wentworth thought, "I'm trying to be too subtle. Like the Chinese themselves"—and then, as he saw a white man arrive in a cab, get out, and pay the driver, he stared at him once, and then at the photograph he had been given at the bank. It was the man Chidister!

"Coming for the pay off," Wentworth said, his lips lifting in a grim smile. He held up his square of newspaper, and instantly unrolled the rope ladder between the two three-story buildings, clambering down like a sailor.

In a moment he was peering into the street, through a crack in the high board gate. Chidister had disappeared.

The blind beggar sat in the sun. All was—for one instant—as quiet as ever.

THEN THERE WAS the rush of pounding feet. Racing up the hill came four of the riot squad, the sun glinting off the steel of Mulcahey's sledge hammer. Wentworth knew that the other three were tearing along the street behind Waverley Place, if escape was planned in that way.

The blind beggar instantly began to sing a shrill, mournful song. Inside, some one answered him, and Wentworth could hear the thud as the bars were dropped behind some solid door. Mulcahey would take care of that!

Wentworth remained motionless until the four officers rushed into the building. So did the blind beggar. Almost at once there came the cry, "Open in the name of the law!" and, obliterating the final words, the crashing of Mulcahey's sledge.

The blind beggar stood up—none of the officers had so much as looked at him, having been warned—and began to shuffle crabwise up the street. Once only he looked behind him. When he paused in turning, Jimmy Wentworth was in a dark doorway.

Chinatown, from every window, was watching the blind beggar. None thought to look at the stooped man slipping along in the shadow of the buildings after him—and the man was Jimmy Wentworth.

From 966A came shrill nasal cries, the roar of automatics, and, suddenly, the rapid drumbeat of the machine gun. Then dead silence!

The blind beggar began to run.

Jimmy Wentworth's heart was ice in his breast. One slip, one mistake, and—if his theory was correct—the Peckham children would never be seen alive again. Nearer and nearer he approached the Cobra spy. When the Chinese turned the corner, Wentworth was in the next doorway. When the Chinese stopped, looked up and down the street rapidly, the white detective was in a stairway leading to a cellar.

Wentworth thought, "If he isn't at the place now, if this is only part of the way, heaven help those children!"

The time had come to act. The Chinese, by his caution, must be at the hiding-place. As the "blind beggar" placed a key to the lock of a basement door, Wentworth was on him. Arms and legs wound about the unsuspecting yellow man's body. The detective's fingers pressed fiercely around the Chinese's throat. Save one little scuffle in the shadow, all was silent.

Wentworth's ears were tuned for any sound of warning. None came. In a moment he had cuffed and gagged the limp Chinese, and then he himself turned the key.

Inside, it was dark as the pit. Jimmy Wentworth did not dare use his torch, lest the beam of light alarm whoever was inside. He crept along, arms outstretched, until another door blocked the way. Noiselessly he passed his hands up and down the heavy wood, looking for a lock. There was none. Did some secret button open the door? Or... there was only one thing to try. Wentworth, knowing Chinese customs, believed it would work.

He raised his voice in the self-same nasal chant that he had heard the beggar-hatchetman use, a song he had heard more than once in China:

"O serpent!

O king of all snakes!

O deadly messenger of the Cobra King!

O beautiful evil one—"

The door swung open.

ALTHOUGH LIGHT HALF blinded him, Wentworth's gun roared twice, once at each of the black-clad figures rising from the floor. One fell; the other leaped forward, shooting from the hip as he advanced. Wentworth felt the sear of a bullet scorching his thigh. He fired a third time, point blank, and the highbinder, screaming horribly, sprawled to the floor.

A woman's thin voice screamed in Chinese, "What is wrong? Shall I kill the little ones?"

In the same language, Wentworth called, "All is now well!" and, without a moment's hesitation, rushed, shoulder low, at the one ordinary door, from which the question had come. He smashed through with the first attempt, falling with the flimsy barrier. Before he could get to his feet the old hag in the second room darted at him, and only by twisting his body did Wentworth avert the wild knife thrust. Had the crone come at him a second time the white man could not have avoided death.

As she whirled, her tattered trousers brushing against Wentworth's outstretched hand, he saw what she intended. Without the waste of a second, without attempting to fire, Wentworth grasped the scrawny ankle, and felled the witch-like Chinese woman. She slashed at him murderously. Once the knife ripped into Jimmy's shoulder, and then he had her knife-wrist pinioned. After that, it took no time at all to bind her securely.

In the corner, cowering together, Wentworth saw what appeared to be two Chinese children, in gay coats and trousers.

"It's all right now," he said in English. "Come along, girls. We don't want to waste a second."

The two terrified children were beyond tears. Not until they saw Wentworth's shield did they really understand that they had been rescued.

The blind beggar lay where Wentworth had bound him. Chinatown—nothing is unseen—supposed that Kong Gai had decided to do away with a servant who had outworn his usefulness. When it was seen that two children, dressed like high-caste Oriental girls, were being taken away by a poorly dressed white man with a cap covering his face, the Chinese felt that whatever was taking place, the less they knew about it the better.

Kong Gai had erred! To better cover the place of concealment, he had not told his own Cobra Men, and the place was not guarded from the outside. Jimmy Wentworth, taking off the handcuffs, left the blind beggar where he lay. Kong Gai would take care of him, and to take him along would excite too much suspicion. He held the shaking little hand of Lois in his own; his right hand was deep in his old coat pocket. But it was not necessary to draw his gun again.

The Peckham children were found!

CAPTAIN DUNAND'S OFFICE was in an uproar at one o'clock. Six Chinese, two of them wounded, were snarling together in a corner. A white man, very angry, was arguing with the detective captain.

"I don't care if it was a hop joint," he was saying as Wentworth entered. "I had business there. We have Chinese clients at the bank. This is an outrage!"

"Is it?" said Jimmy, keeping the two children behind him. "Did you get your share in the two hundred thousand, Chidister? What was the agreement? Were you to get your split at noon?"

"I don't know what you're talking about," Chidister cried. "We've got bank customers who have some of our stock, I tell you. One of my superiors wanted me to get in touch with them, and tell them not to get excited about the market—"

"What's the matter with it?" Jimmy demanded.

"Gone to hell," said Dunand briefly. "And we've just had a call from Reno. Peckham put the money out in the desert. He's O.K. But he hasn't heard a word about his daughters. And, Jim, what's the idea of bringing a couple of slave girls here? Get 'em in the raid?"

Wentworth stepped aside. "Take a close look, chief," he said.

"Jim! You've got 'em!"

"Safe and sound," said Jimmy Wentworth. He turned to Chidister. "You are under arrest," he said quietly, "as an accessory to the murder of Dennis O'Toole, and for an attempt to kidnap Lois and Dorothy Peckham."

Chidister snapped, "Don't be a fool, officer!"

"It's clear now," said Jimmy. "Got Peckham out of the way so you could run down the bank stock, eh? Hired Kong Gai to kidnap the children? I believe, Mr. Chidister, that you will be found involved in the orders to hammer Sierra-Pacific—"

The bank man broke. "I was acting under orders," he pleaded. "I didn't know all this was involved. I—"

"Take him away," said Dunand. "That's enough."

Wentworth said softly, "Chidister, one thing! Did your orders come from a white man?"

"You're a devil," Chidister groaned.

"How much do you know?"

Wentworth turned to the gray-haired captain. "I told you the day would come when Kong Gai would reach outside Chinatown, chief. It's come. We've got to get him! Kong Gai wasn't very careful this time. He was too sure his plot would work. When he begins to use white men entirely—and he can, with his money—we're going to be in for a siege of trouble."

The captain's shoulders sagged momentarily, and then he said, "You've been giving him a run for his money, Jimmy. We're proud of you. Finding the Peckham children… are you all right, girls? Not hurt?"

"No, sir," Dorothy Peckham said. "We were sure we were going to be killed. And then all of a sudden this nice man came—he's a real detective, isn't he?—and everything was fine. We didn't cry very much." She began to cry now, and Jimmy Wentworth patted her hand.

While Dunand called hastily for the matron, the girl lifted her face, put her arm about Wentworth's head, and kissed him shyly.

The matron was in the room; when she said, "Come along, girls," both protested.

"Can we go straight home?" they demanded. "We want to take the detective home with us and show him to mother, and maybe stop at school and show him to the girls. A real detective! I've been rescued, and kissed by a detective!"

"I haven't," the younger girl giggled. "But I'm going to be."

Captain Dunand watched Jimmy Wentworth, one child holding either hand, leave his office. Into the telephone he said, "Inter-Mountain Hotel? Give me Mr. Peckham, please," and then, to the men of the riot squad who were guarding the hatchetmen of King Cobra, the Evil One of Chinatown, he said softly, "On one hand, a fiendish devil, with money, with spies, with tunnels and underground dens and opium and a secret organization of murderers… and on the other, Jimmy Wentworth!"

The giant Mulcahey scratched his chin, "An' 'tis on our Jimmy I'd be bettin'," he said. "Shure and the saints are helpin' him."

"If I were a betting man, I'd take that," said Dunand. "The odds are a hundred to one against Wentworth. However, I'm not a betting man, and even so, I've heard of hundred-to-one shots coming home!"

"He's a great lad," agreed Mulcahey, as he helped herd the hatchetmen out of the office and to the cell-block below. "A great lad is Sergeant Jimmy!"

THE JADE SERPENT

*Something Evil Was Brewing in Chinatown
to Bring Kong Gai's Warning—"If the
Woman Tells, She Dies Horribly"*

1

THE RED ANT

DOWN ON THE waterfront a thousand men and women pressed as near the landing stages as the line of police and marines dared permit. Only the broadly smiling countenance of old Sergeant O'Shea, in charge of Pier 14 this sweltering afternoon, kept the crowd in anything like good humor.

Again and again the veteran officer, having handled impatient throngs before, would announce as he marched about, "Ye'll all get out to th' fleet! Only don't shove, or ye'll have them in front swimmin', instead of goin' out in th' nice boats. 'Tis all one to me, friends. I wouldn't mind at all jumpin' in after somebody meself this kind of weather!" The crowd would laugh, and settle down to wait their turn more amiably.

The Pacific Fleet was in San Francisco Harbor. Since early morning, every trim naval cutter which arrived at the landing stages to disgorge sailors with shore leave, had returned to the battleships and airplane carriers with a gunwale-deep load of visitors.

The harbor was gay with welcome. The buildings along the Embarcadero, where crimps once held forth—men not above putting chloral in a sailor's first drink and shanghai-

*Jimmy saw two
Chinese slip up
to the couple*

ing him for another long voyage instead of showing him
the promised joys of Barbary Coast—were to-day hung
with red, white and blue bunting. Docked vessels were
all bright with flags. Market Street had banners on every
electrolier. Even the merchants of Chinatown, waiting to
sell Oriental trinkets to sailors and marines, had placed
crossed flags above their doors.

Here and there on Pier 14 sailors wishful to return to
their ships tried to work their way through the packed mass
of people. Some of the returning seamen were in pairs.
Some were bringing girls who wanted to see the wonders

*The woman turned white
at the hatchetman's words*

of the fleet. Almost all carried some sort of parcel, containing purchases made ashore.

The impatient crowd eyed the immaculate officers'
launches, flashing back and forth from ship to shore, with
envious faces. A hot, perspiring woman holding a pepper-
mint-eating youngster on each side called out to a youthful
ensign, "Hey, admiral! How about taking me along with
you?"

The naval officer, fresh from Annapolis, turned his head
rigidly, his features set coldly according to regulations.
Something of the way the waiting crowd must feel moved
him, for suddenly he grinned and waved his hand, shouting boyishly, "I can't do it, honey! My girl's too jealous!"

The crowd felt better after that. Why, these stiffly
starched officers were regular fellows!

At intervals a boatswain's mate would call, "Idaho boat! Any one for the Idaho?" or, "Saratoga! Any one for the airplane carrier Saratoga?" and the people would squeeze and jam forward, until the lucky ones had scrambled down the gangplank and into the cutter bobbing against the landing stage. No matter how swiftly the tenders swirled against the docks, the crowd did not seem to diminish in numbers. It continued to gather. Ten minutes after a Filipino mess-boy, in blue coat and blue and white cap, arrived to return to the airplane carrier Monmouth, sister ship of the Saratoga, there were several hundred people behind him.

The Filipino, all apologies, did his best to work through the crowd, but it was impossible. Men and women seemed wedged and unable to move. Like the others, the mess-boy from the Monmouth settled down to wait his turn to get out to his ship.

Like many of the other men of the fleet, he carried his white canvas ditty bag with him. Instead of lugging it over a shoulder, he carried it, perhaps because of the crowd, hugged against his chest.

FIFTEEN MINUTES AFTER the uniformed Filipino mess-boy named Fascio Martinez arrived at Pier 14, the door of Captain Dunand's office at the Hall of Justice was flung open, and a young man in the dark blue of a patrolman rushed inside. The instant he banged the door behind him, he began to jerk off his coat feverishly, hurling it to the floor.

"Here, here," Dunand boomed in amazement. "What d'ye think this is? Have you gone crazy, Jim?"

"I'll be crazy in another ten seconds," Jimmy Wentworth

almost shouted. Without wasting time in additional explanation he ripped off his shirt and singlet.

"What's the idea?" the gray-haired captain of detectives demanded. "This isn't the locker room! What's the matter with you, Jimmy? Been drinkin' Chinee firewater?"

"My back," groaned the detective sergeant of Chinatown. "It's on fire! Take a look at it!"

Dunand rose ponderously from his chair, brows drawn together. As Wentworth showed his bared shoulders, Dunand exclaimed, "You're all bloody, lad!" and followed the words by seizing the telephone and asking for the department physician to be sent at once to his office.

"Take it off," Wentworth Begged.

"Take what off? Easy does it, Jimmy! The doctor'll be here in a minute—"

"Take it off," repeated Jimmy Wentworth. "I felt the thing biting when I was crossing Waverley Place to see what was going on there… afterward, I tried to scratch it off, but I couldn't get at it. It's a bug, chief! It—"

"I don't see anything except blood."

"Use your eyes," Wentworth cried. "I'm not joking, captain! I'm being eaten alive!"

Dunand stepped closer.

Again he said, "All I see is blood," and then, excitedly, "By golly, you're right! There it is! I see it now! Hold still, Jimmy! I'll get it… don't wriggle… there! Got it! Look at th' damn' thing, boy!"

Wentworth saw what Dunand had torn from his flesh—a gigantic red ant. It was fully an inch long, and shaped like a small scorpion, but without any tail-stinger.

The Chinatown detective, born in China, knew exactly what the horrible insect was the moment he saw it.

"That's an Annamese ant," he said. "They're terrible things, chief. Come from south China. When a column of 'em reach a village, the natives run. Why, if these ants come upon some animal asleep in the woods, a half hour later there isn't anything left except a skeleton! That's how voracious they are. I saw a village where they'd been. A horse had been staked outside of the village, and when the natives ran away they forgot about it. The ants ate that horse alive. And—"

"Ouch!" Dunand roared. "Th' confounded thing bit me!"

Hastily, Jimmy Wentworth took the first handy object, an envelope, from Dunand's desk, and placed the red ant inside. Almost instantly the insect had ripped its way through the paper, but not before the two detectives had imprisoned envelope and contents in a tin box.

"Go ahead and suffocate!" Dunand bellowed. "Look at the blood it brought from my finger, Jimmy! And it feels like the sting of a wasp." His face red, Dunand began to suck his finger tip.

The headquarters physician, entering, said, "What's going on here? Who's my patient?"

"He bit me on the finger," growled the gray-haired captain.

"Wentworth did?"

"No," roared Dunand. "The ant!" The doctor began to laugh.

"Look at the sergeant's back," Dunand said grimly. "See if that's funny."

AFTER ONE LOOK, the doctor, whistling noiselessly,

reached for his bag. He said, as he went to work efficiently with cotton and disinfectant, "Training to be a Spartan, sergeant? I don't see how you stood the pain. Why, you're lacerated, man!"

"I'll live," Jimmy Wentworth managed to grin. "Long enough, I hope, to find out why south China red ants have come to our Chinatown... and maybe to find just what that woman was going to tell me, and didn't."

"What woman?" Captain Dunand asked.

Wentworth sighed with relief as the physician began to spread a soothing salve over his fiery back.

"I was walking along Waverley Place," he said. "Couple of Chinese slipped along the street, and one of 'em said something to a woman and her escort. He was a naval officer. I saw the woman turn white. It was just then I felt the first bite of the ant.

"The Chinese—hatchetmen, if I ever saw any—vanished into a shop when I came along. I asked the officer what happened. The woman said, 'They told me I'd better not say anything about—' and then the man, who might have been her husband, broke in and told her to say nothing. And that was that."

"Mean anything?" Dunand wanted to know.

"Not yet," Jimmy Wentworth said. "But, in Chinatown, everything has some meaning. We'll wait and see what happens. If necessary, we can find the officer. I'd know him again. Like the woman, he seemed disturbed."

"Trouble always comes fast enough," the captain of detectives remarked. "Well, I hope you can take it easy, with that back. Why not get along home now—"

"He'll stay here an hour more," the physician said firmly.

"I want to change that dressing. We don't want any infection setting in, captain."

While Wentworth made himself as comfortable as possible at headquarters, old Sergeant O'Shea, watching the crowd at the pier with a fatherly eye, heard a sudden wild scream. He saw a twisting, swirling movement in the crowd, and without hesitation hammered his way toward it. Perhaps it was only an argument. O'Shea hoped it would be nothing worse. If that was the trouble, he'd soon have the two boys, whoever they were, shaking hands and ashamed of themselves....

On the planks of Pier 14 lay Fascio Martinez, the Filipino mess-boy, very dead, with the coat of his uniform sticky with blood.

The rip in the mess-boy's coat told O'Shea the story. "Knifed," he thought. "And done under me very eye!" Of the circle of people he demanded coolly, "Well? Who seen it done? Speak up! What happened?"

Nobody had seen anything.

One man said that the Filipino had been directly in back of him, and that the mess-boy had been holding a canvas ditty bag. The man knew this because the bag had been jammed against his spine. In proof of this, the ditty bag was found on the floor of the pier.

Another man said that somebody had been shoving through the crowd just before the Filipino cried out in agony. Others verified this, although no one was able to describe the possible murderer in the slightest way, and no one was even positive that any person had slipped in, or out, through the throng. It might all have been the pressure of the mass, first trying to get an inch nearer the landing stages, next jerking to see what had caused the bloodcurdling cry.

Seeing he was getting nowhere, O'Shea raised his voice again. "Nobody leave th' pier," he called. "Hendricks! O'Connor! Blake! Close th' street gate, Vanning! Every one see that nobody goes off th' dock, boys!"

Up came the boatswain's mate in charge of the nearest landing stage, fighting his way to the dead mess-boy's side. His whistle went instantly to his lips, and the shrill blasts rose above the noise of the excited people. Sailors and marines arrived, and were joined in another moment by two officers. Swift, crisp orders followed. The navy took charge. In no time at all the dead body of the Filipino, together with his ditty bag, was carried to a waiting officers' gig of the Monmouth, which careened instantly into open water, its bell beating furiously and demanding right of way, toward the giant airplane carrier.

Under O'Shea's practiced eye, the crowd passed in single file through the gate. A thousand citizens cannot be searched. A knife, as O'Shea knew, can easily be thrown into the bay. Here and there the veteran officer picked out people who failed to pass his grim inspection—a racetrack tout, several vagrants, a runner for the Tenderloin, a fellow with downcast eyes and round San Quentin haircut—ordering them held for questioning at the Hall of Justice. The man who had observed the mess-boy was also requested to report to headquarters. O'Shea felt that he was doing whatever was possible, but knew that it would be utterly useless.

No more perfect place could have been selected for a murder.

2

THE WARNING

THERE WAS BITTERNESS in Captain Dunand's voice as he said, "That's the way it goes, Jimmy! You heard what the reporters said? 'Thanks for telling us, cap, but all we'll use is a line!' But if that poor Filipino had been a banker's son, it'd be all over the front pages! And the newspapers don't care if we catch the murderer or not... what d'you make of it, Jim? Probably a quarrel between this Martinez and some other Filipino?"

"Looks like it," Wentworth said. "Or—"

"Or what?"

Knowing what Dunand would say, nevertheless Wentworth answered honestly, "Or there might be some connection between Martinez and the warning given those two this afternoon in Chinatown."

Dunand said exactly what Jimmy Wentworth expected. "Boloney," the captain of detectives grunted. "I suppose," he went on heavily, "you're going to find out if this naval officer whose wife was warned—heaven knows why!—if he's an officer on the Monmouth, and then we'll have a fine clew, won't we?"

"I am not," the Chinatown detective sergeant grinned. "I'm going to stick around here and let everybody wait on the poor invalid. It's clews we want, chief, and not coincidences. And anyhow it isn't my case."

"What reason have you to think that there could be a connection?" Dunand insisted.

"I don't," Jimmy told him. "You're probably right, chief. But it's the 'or' we always have to look for, so the obvious solution doesn't blind us to the truth. I was just talking. Forget it, sir."

"Hmm," growled Dunand. "I'll send somebody out to the ship, of course. If it was a sailors' fight, the naval authorities'll want to handle it themselves, which will suit us. Anyhow—"

Both men turned at a knock at the door.

A well-dressed woman, in her early thirties, and a man in a uniform of the navy entered.

"Captain Dunand?" the officer asked. When the head of the detective bureau, rising, bowed, the officer continued, "I'm Lieutenant Hughson. This is Mrs. Hughson, captain. We've something to tell you."

Dunand said nothing about what had taken place in Chinatown. He had already looked questioningly at Wentworth, and his sergeant had nodded.

"This note was placed in my wife's hand just as she was stepping into a taxi," Hughson said. "After due consideration, we decided to hand it to you. May I ask, captain, that you say nothing about it to the newspapers? The department does not take kindly to publicity or notoriety attained by an officer."

Dunand read the printed letter, and then handed it to Wentworth. "It seems to mean what it says," he commented.

"That's what I fear," Lieutenant Hughson admitted.

Jimmy Wentworth examined the note. It read:

> We advise you to keep your information to yourself. It will
> do you no good to say anything. It will do you a great deal of
> harm. Remain silent for one week. After that, you may say
> whatever you will. For your silence you will receive $1000 in
> cash at the end of the week. If you tell any one of what you
> know you will die horribly.

The message was unsigned.

The Chinatown detective sergeant said calmly, "The first thing, Mrs. Hughson, is to tell us what this information is, of course."

They exchanged glances.

"Better talk, Jane," the officer said.

Nodding, Mrs. Hughson began: "This morning, my husband took me to the museum. I have always been interested in fine jades. My father was a student of mineralogy. When we were stationed in China, I wrote several papers on jade. Anyhow, when we were looking over the exhibit, I said to my husband that I was very disappointed, and that it seemed a shame to deceive the public. Because all of the really fine jades in the museum were imitations, and not really jade at all."

"Some one must have overheard her," Lieutenant Hughson said. "We decided against saying anything to the museum people, firstly because we didn't want to take the time—my wife had some shopping to do in Chinatown—and secondly because it really wasn't any of our business. Then—"

The woman took up the tale. "When we were in Chinatown, two Chinese came up to us, and threatened me if I didn't keep still. Some police officer came up, and they ran away—"

"*Ni ying in kiu Ink I po fu ni'a,*" Jimmy Wentworth broke in.

Mrs. Hughson's eyes opened wide. "That's Cantonese, isn't it?" she asked. "I understand a few words, but—"

WENTWORTH REPEATED THE singsong words in English: "You should have appealed to me at once for protection." He added, "I was the patrolman who came up, Mrs. Hughson. Now, please, tell me what the hatchet-men said when they spoke to you."

"Just that I must remain silent."

"I see. They didn't mention any name?"

"Name?"

Dunand, listening, knew what his sergeant was driving at. Wentworth must think that Kong Gai, the sinister Evil One of Chinatown, was back of the affair of the imitation jades.

"Is there any other information you can give us?" Wentworth asked quietly.

"None," Lieutenant Hughson said. "Do you really believe my wife is in danger, or are we unduly alarmed?"

"I believe that your wife is in extreme peril," Wentworth told the naval officer. "Where is she living, please?"

"We are staying at the Pacific. My wife came here to see me. We sail for the Philippines, as you know. She will join me in Manila—"

Wentworth said to Dunand, "We'll assign two men. They'll use the room opposite the Hughsons, and keep Mrs. Hughson in sight whenever she leaves the hotel."

Dunand nodded.

The lieutenant demanded, "What does it all mean, sergeant?"

"I wish I knew," Jimmy Wentworth said. "Now, if you'd worn wings on your uniform, and were a flying officer from the Monmouth, it might make it a good deal easier."

"I am on the Monmouth! I'm a navigating officer, however, and not a flier. Why, sergeant?"

"Because a man—a Filipino mess-boy named Fascio Martinez—was killed on Pier 14, and it might give us something to work on. He was murdered with a knife. That's the Asiatic way of killing. Of course, some other boy may have done it, or… It might have been a Chinese. It is all the long arm of coincidence, Lieutenant Hughson, and yet there may be some connection."

"If any one would steal fine jades," the woman suggested, "it would be apt to be a Chinese."

"That's what I was thinking," Wentworth smiled. "And only Orientals would take the time to have imitations made, so perfect that they would fool any one except a student."

"Hadn't we better ring the Museum?" Dunand asked. "To verify this."

"No," demurred Jimmy thoughtfully. "Make just that many more people who know about it, and we'll have talk. Let's say nothing for a little, and see what I can pick up first."

Wentworth stepped to the window and stared out at the steep street leading up from the Hall of Justice to China-town. At last he saw what he looked for, and then asked Dunand and the Hughsons to come and look also.

"The fourth shop up the street," Wentworth pointed out. "See two men sitting on the basement stairs? Picking over a basket of dried shrimp? Not doing anything except work, are they? Now, wait a minute... see one of 'em turn so he can see the door of the Hall of Justice here? Hatchetmen. Watching to see what happens. They must have seen you come here."

"I don't think so," Hughson said. "Just as our cab drove up, a trolley car stopped on the corner. We must have been concealed from view."

"Good," Jimmy Wentworth snapped. "You'll be concealed from view when you leave, too! We'll take care of that. Now, lieutenant, if you can arrange it for me, I'd like to go out to your ship, and see if I can learn anything about the habits of the Filipino mess-boy. We'll take good care of Mrs. Hughson for you—"

"Won't you be seen in my company going out to the Monmouth?"

Jimmy Wentworth grinned.

"There'll be somebody see me go, I hope," he said. "You can count on that. And somebody will be waiting for me to return. Is the commanding officer the sort who will listen to argument, lieutenant, or would it be useless to ask a favor of him?"

"Captain Farling is a fine man, sergeant. Aside from that, we are very close friends."

"Then let's go," Jimmy Wentworth suggested.

"What're you up to?" Captain Dunand rumbled. "You're a sick man, Jimmy! I'm not going to have you working to-day! I'll have the doctor order you on sick leave. I'll—"

"We can talk that over when I get back, sir. Do you think

I've been bitten and don't intend to do something about it? Well, I do! My back feels fine… come on, lieutenant, before my superior officer changes his mind!"

"Ants," muttered Dunand. "Ants!"

It sounded more like cursing than the name of an insect.

Wentworth's eyes dropped to the note of warning. Somehow, the word "torture" seemed to leap out of the sheet.

"You may be correct, chief," the Chinatown detective said soberly.

"Oh, go ahead," the captain growled. "Missing jades. Warning. A dead Filipino killed Chink-fashion with a knife. Maybe there is a connection. It's worth trying. But don't try to run ants in on it, Jimmy Wentworth!"

"Red ants," Wentworth said softly, "come from south China. The finest workmen in jade come from south China. The largest factory for making imitation jade is in south China… I'll report to you later, captain!"

3

THE SECOND MESSAGE

TWO SAILORS REACHED down to grasp Wentworth's arm as the launch bobbed against the shining gray sides of the airplane carrier Monmouth, but the Chinatown detective leaped easily to the ladder, and climbed aboard. He had stopped on the way to change to civilian clothes, and, on the deck of the strange craft, looked more like a youthful sightseer than a sergeant of detectives.

Wentworth gazed with real interest at the smooth surface of the Monmouth's curious deck, on which bombers and scouts, for the inspection of visitors, were arrayed in two long lines. Across the deck, and flush with it, were the chains to check the progress of landing planes. In the center of the craft was an enormous elevator, by means of which planes were lowered into the ship to be stowed away. The runway extended from bow to stern. The aircraft took off from the front of the gigantic boat, and landed at the rear.

With Hughson guiding him, shoulders erect, the detective sergeant walked down a steep companionway and into the steel interior of the Monmouth. Past lettered compartments, past concealed gun ports armed with anti-aircraft guns or quick-firers to repel destroyer attacks, the two men walked rapidly, sailors snapping to attention as they passed.

Wentworth had already asked to talk with some one who had known the dead mess-boy, and Hughson had wisely suggested a countryman and fellow workman of Martinez. The lieutenant led the way to a small gymnasium deep in the ship, where two brown-skinned, well built Filipino lads were skipping rope. They were naked to the skin. Their muscles rippled under the artificial light. An old sailor, the ship's trainer, watched them. Other sailors lounged about, reading, talking or playing backgammon.

All saluted as the two men entered. The old trainer must have thought that Wentworth was merely being shown about the ship, for, standing at attention, he said, "The lieutenant can see that we've got a couple of good boys in trainin'. Th' Monmouth'll be a cinch to win th' flyweight championship of th' fleet. Only the lieutenant might tell th' boys they got to forget about… well, about poor Fascio Martinez, sir."

Hughson said crisply, "Glad to tell them, Donohue. Did you know Martinez?"

"I did, sir."

"Well?"

"Not as well as I know some of th' other boys, sir."

"Who did know him?"

Donohue indicated one of the rope-jumpers. "Jose knew him, lieutenant."

"Good. I want to talk to Jose. And you also, Donohue." Sharply, "Clear the room!"

Every one except the trainer and the Filipino boy in

blue trunks left immediately. Hughson slid the door closed behind them.

"Now, tell this gentleman whatever he asks," Hughson commanded.

Wentworth said gravely, "You know Martinez has been killed. Has he acted as if he feared any one?"

"No, sir," the Filipino said, too slowly.

Wentworth let it pass. He continued: "I see. Has he acted unusual lately? About anything?"

The dark-skinned boy muttered a word or two in Spanish, and then said, "No, sir."

Hughson broke in: "The truth," he snapped.

"*Sí*, lieutenant," Jose agreed, standing straighter. Then he said, "It is of a truth… that Fascio Martinez acted strangely."

"That's better," applauded Wentworth. "Now, explain what you mean."

"He said yesterday, 'I am of the Navy tired. Soon will I be a man of wealth.' We ask him when this would be, but answer he did not. Then he say, 'Honolulu, we have big time!' We ask, 'Hombre, you get money Honolulu?' and he say, 'Where and when I get money I not tell.'" Jose shivered. "Instead of money," he concluded, "he get knife."

"Did he say why he was going to get this money, Jose?"

The Filipino shrugged. "We guess, so we not ask, *señor*. Fascio Martinez, may his soul rest in peace, make money sometimes selling opium."

Wentworth's eyes were shining now. Here was a direct clew, traceable and important. It could lead directly to Chinatown.

"I'd like to see Martinez's bag and belongings," Wentworth requested.

The ditty bag and the mess-boy's clothing, at Hughson's order, were brought to the ship's gymnasium. Donohue and Jose were sent from the place.

Even before Jimmy Wentworth opened the canvas bag, he pointed to a slit in the fabric. Hughson said promptly, "That bag was cut ashore, sergeant. It wouldn't pass inspection here."

Clew number two! Somebody had wanted something in the ditty bag.

SWIFTLY WENTWORTH UNROLLED the canvas, and with practiced fingers went through the contents. If he hoped for opium, he found none, although a uniform pocket in the bag smelled slightly of burned chocolate—the odor of opium. Efficiently he continued his search, until, in a pocket of the blue dress coat, his fingers encountered something hard and cold. And heavy.

Something told Jimmy Wentworth what it would be even before he withdrew his hand. Quietly, for Hughson to see, he held up a serpent carved in finest kingfisher blue jade.

"I think," Hughson said softly, "that my wife remarked that one of the gems of the Museum collection was a jade serpent. It's supposed to be worth something like fifty thousand dollars. Is that it? Or another imitation?"

"I'm not an expert, but this isn't the kind you can buy for a few dollars Mex. It's real. Therefore, Martinez was killed because of this piece of priceless jade. Whoever knifed him on Pier 14 didn't have time to search the bag and recover the jade, but the murderer must have tried. That's why the bag is slashed. In cramped quarters, and in a hurry, nothing else was possible."

A loud speaker began to announce: "Lieutenant Hughson! Lieutenant Hughson! Will the lieutenant report to the quarter-deck at once? Lieutenant Hughson!"

"That's the way we do it now," Hughson smiled. "I'll be forced to run, sergeant. The Old Man himself must want me. Care to come along?"

"I want to get off the ship and ashore as soon as I can," Wentworth said. "I was seen coming out, of course, by some spy. I don't want to be seen landing. Can I be put ashore—this's what I was going to ask of your captain—at a different pier somewhere?"

"We can do better than that if you're in a hurry," Hughson responded. "Come with me. This may be something. It isn't usual for an officer of my rating to be summoned this way."

The jade serpent in his pocket, Wentworth accompanied the naval lieutenant. As they mounted the ladder leading to the bridge, a fellow officer of Hughson's, coming down, said, "The Old Man's so mad he can't sit down, Charley. De la Cruz, another Filipino, went ashore with Martinez, and hasn't come back. God knows what's happened, but the Old Man wants blood!"

Captain Farling's gaunt, weatherbeaten face, showed his anger.

"A fine state of affairs," he said severely, after Wentworth had been introduced to him. "Can't you keep your city safe for my men, sergeant? Here, take this!" He handed Wentworth a brass button, marked U.S.N. "Nobody knows who

brought it aboard. If I could find the man who did it, I'd…
I'd… here! You two read the note!"

Wentworth and Hughson read it together:

> "Send ashore Martinez's bag. Check it at the ferry. Leave
> the check with the newsboy near the cigar stand. Do not
> open the bag. If it is not sent ashore in one half hour, or if
> it is opened, Mrs. Hughson will die horribly, as de la Cruz
> died. She is already in my hands. The police can do nothing
> for you or for her. We took her away from them so easily that
> you will realize our power.
>
> "Deliver the ditty bag within a half hour or the white
> woman will receive the vengeance of
>
> > "Kong Gai."

Under the signature was drawn, in green ink, a coiled
king cobra, ready to strike.

HUGHSON SAID FIERCELY, "Get the damned bag ashore!
They've kidnaped Jane! In the hands of Chinese! Why—"

Soberly, Wentworth said, "You can radio ashore, in code,
can't you, captain? Good! Send a message to someone telling them to get in touch with police headquarters, so that
we can be reassured that this is only bluff!"

A junior officer was told what to do, and hurried away
to the wireless room. Hughson was useless now. He stared
out toward the skyline of San Francisco, as if he could see
through the buildings of concrete and stone. With the
button in the palm of his hand, Wentworth's thoughts
went first to his aching back, and then to what the button
meant—to him. He knew the horrible custom, in south

China, of sending what remained of a dead man in order to show that vengeance had been fulfilled.

Kong Gai! At last it was clear. The Evil One was back of it all. The pieces of the puzzle did not dovetail yet, but certainly Fascio Martinez was mixed in the affair of the stolen jades, and had died for keeping one of the valuable stones. Where, however, did this second Filipino enter the picture?

Wentworth asked, "Captain, of course de la Cruz and Martinez were friends?"

Captain Farling's ire rose. "What d'you think I am?" he asked coldly. "The social mentor of all of the men on my ship? Perhaps they were. Probably they went ashore together. I can find out, if you wish. What I want," he snapped, "is to get my hands on the fellow who brought that intimidating note out to the Monmouth! I'll show him something! Threaten the wife of one of my officers! I'll threaten him!"

"It isn't possible to do it," Wentworth said. "I wouldn't mind placing the man under arrest myself, sir, but it would be a waste of time to look for him. He may have left the ship already, although it is more possible that he's keeping an eye on me to see what I'm going to do."

"And in the meantime my wife is being held by these fiends," Hughson groaned. "While we do nothing."

The junior officer returned.

Tonelessly, he said, "According to the captain's instructions, we have communicated with the shore station. They advise"—he looked at the sheet of paper from the wireless room—"that 'San Francisco Police Department report

Mrs. Hughson having tea with friends in the Palm Court of the Pacific Hotel.'"

Hughson said, "Thank God!"

"There was too much talk in that note," Wentworth smiled. "It looked like a bluff. Just the same, I'm glad all is well with your wife. You needn't worry. The detective bureau will see that she comes to no harm." Wentworth got down to business. "We were given half an hour to get the bag ashore—the time it takes for a launch to land at Pier 14. I want to get ashore more quickly than that, so I can be in the city while Kong Gai is waiting to see if the bluff works."

"My gig is waiting," Hughson suggested promptly. "It can beat a cutter by ten minutes, if a spy intends to follow you. Isn't that what you mean?"

Before Wentworth could reply, the keen-minded captain said, "We'll hold all cutters and all shore-going visitors until Wentworth has time to land. That's even better, eh?"

"It would help," Jimmy admitted. He grinned suddenly. "Or you could give me a good twenty minutes before any one could land with the bag by putting me ashore in a plane, sir."

"Land you two hundred feet from the Ferry Building," agreed Farling. "Glad to do it, if you'll get your man, sergeant."

"I won't get him," Wentworth said, thinking of Kong Gai. "But I ought to make a few arrests."

"How?" Hughson asked curiously. "I know almost as much as you do, Wentworth, and I don't see where you have a single clew."

"I have one only," Jimmy told him. "The note Captain

Farling received gives it to me stronger than ever. It is all in the word 'torture.' I'll explain later, lieutenant. Now, I must get ashore."

A minute later, in jumper and leather jacket; with face concealed by goggles and helmet, Wentworth clambered into a seaplane moored beside the Monmouth. There was a spatter of foam, and then the plane lifted into the blue light of evening, speeding Jimmy Wentworth back to the city.

4

THE TERRIBLE DEATH

MEN SLIPPED SWIFTLY from the Hall of Justice; detectives off duty were given instructions at their homes. The curator of the museum himself was called away from his evening's engagement, and, not long after, his telephone call was received in Captain Dunand's office. Secrecy was no longer necessary, Wentworth felt.

"It is a fact," the museum head said excitedly. "The entire collection has vanished! In its place are imitations of the original jades! Diabolically done, captain. The imitations are carved like the real jades, and are made of jasper and nephrite—inexpensive materials. The collection was priceless! The Imperial Beads! The *han-yu*—a rare amulet from an emperor's tomb. Butterfly jades in yellow and brown. The total will run into hundreds of thousands! Have you caught the thief, captain?"

"We're doing our best. You are positive your jades are all imitations now?"

"Of course. It must have taken months to make the copies. Why, even I was almost fooled. One jade serpent is so like the original that it almost needs an expert to know the difference. And, by George, I can tell you who made the imitations!"

"Good! Who was it?"

"Some Chinese. A student interested in Oriental art."

But when Dunand asked for a description of the Asiatic, the curator was unable to say more than the man was a Chinese—black hair, dark clothing, medium height. He might have been any of the thousands of dwellers in Chinatown.

Hard on this verifying information Detective Sloan entered Dunand's office, and placed a heavy paper parcel on the desk. To Dunand and Wentworth he said hastily, "Got it in the second place I went. Honest Louie Peters's pawnshop, on the edge of the Coast. Louie was glad to get rid of 'em. He seemed scared to death."

In the package were the missing jades, some shining green, some blue like a kingfisher's wing. Picking up a brown jade, Jimmy said:

"For centuries this stone has been in a great man's tomb. The color comes from the decomposition of the body; minerals are absorbed by the jade. It is called *han-yu*. Mouth jade. If it is placed in the mouth of a dead man, it assures protection in after life, no matter how evil the man may have been when alive—"

"Kong Gai!" Dunand said.

"Exactly." Wentworth looked at his watch. He still had over ten minutes of the half hour. Leaning forward in his chair, he said earnestly, "Here is my theory, sir, built on Chinese superstitions and customs, and on what has already happened.

"Firstly, Kong Gai had the imitations made, exact copies of the priceless collection.

"Secondly, the theft was actually made by Fascio Martinez, at the instigation of Kong Gai. Fascio was a dope user, or seller anyhow. It's logical that he knew Kong Gai. Fascio Martinez was to deliver the jades to Kong Gai's hatchet-men, and the Evil One intended to keep some of the jades, and have Martinez turn the rest of them over to a Cobra hatchetman in Honolulu, where the sale could be made. Martinez, on shipboard, would never be suspected as the thief, and would be perfectly safe. Kong Gai wanted the jade serpent, and the mouth jade, as talismen. Martinez must have thought it the most valuable of the jades, and so kept it to sell himself.

"Thirdly, Mrs. Hughson had the good fortune—or almost the bad luck!—to see the imitation jades, and a Kong Gai spy hanging around rushed to the Evil One with the news.

"Fourthly, another Filipino mess-boy has disappeared in Chinatown, and Kong Gai says he was tortured. Kong Gai knew that this de la Cruz was a friend of Martinez's, and wanted to make him talk when Martinez didn't show up with the jades. Exactly what happened we'll never know.

"Fifthly—"

"The moon is made of green cheese," Dunand suggested.

"Sure," Jimmy grinned, again looking at his watch. "I know how it sounds, sir. You've got to take into account the workings of the strange Oriental mind. Kong Gai would not see anything ridiculous in stealing the jades, in prof-iting by the robbery, in killing a couple of Filipinos, and then retaining a sacred jade to get him through the gates of heaven. He wants to be buried like an emperor."

"All of which catches nobody," Dunand remarked.

"I'm on my way now," Jimmy said.

"Here goes for a try at it."

"Your clews? What are they?"

"The fact that imitation jades are made by south-Chinese, that red ants come from south China, that de la Cruz may have been tortured, and that there is a new moon to-morrow."

"Made of green cheese?"

"Don't laugh, chief! I know how it sounds. But the propitious time, according to Chinese, to remove bones is only when there is a new moon!"

"Going to a boneyard, Jimmy?" Detective Sloan asked warily.

"Sure. Coming with me?"

"I've never been lucky with the bones, Jimmy."

"Maybe you will this time, Sloan." Wentworth glanced at his watch. "Got to go," he said. "Time's nearly up. It's a good thing I had enough of it to come here first, chief. O.K., Sloan. It's twelve minutes to eight. Bring four or five men. Leave the Hall of Justice before eight. Leave one by one, in case you're watched. I don't think you will be, because Kong Gai's spy, or spies—for some will be on Pier 14—still think I'm on the Monmouth.

"Walk to California Street. Hang around. Take a cable car up the hill. Get off at Chinatown. Be there a minute or so after eight. After that, you'll know what to do!"

"Where do I do it, Jimmy?"

"The doorway opposite a wicker shop. You'll see."

A FEW MINUTES later, in civilian clothes, Wentworth swung from the rear of the cable car. He looked a long way from being the Chinatown patrolman as he gazed into an apothecary's lighted shop, where an old Chinese doctor was taking a patient's pulse on both wrists. Over the man's head were leaves and roots for weak people, swallows' nests for consumptives, the jaw bone of a tiger ready for some wealthy patient.

Farther down the street the heroine of a Chinese play screeched, stopping only to gulp tea to enable her voice to reach higher and more awful notes. In a restaurant where Americans were not admitted, the moon-violin squawked, cymbals clashed, and a drum thundered. Wentworth knew that a banquet was in progress; sharks' fins, fish-bladders stuffed with boneless pigeons, mushrooms and crabs, all in blue Canton dishes.

How clearly he remembered everything. The exact place where he first felt the stinging bite of the red ant. The dark doorway between two shop windows, opposite the wicker shop. He had leaned against that doorway, watching the unloading of a truckload of wicker chairs, when the giant insect had crawled down his neck and gone to work on his flesh.

The dark doorway!

Without moving, Wentworth saw that the clock on the cathedral read a minute to eight. His hand went automatically to his belt; it, the holster and gun, were under his civilian coat. He walked quietly across the street, not missing the two loiterers near the doorway. Men in black. Hatchetmen of Kong Gai, on guard.

Wentworth walked sedately until he was at the doorway, and then whirled like a flash. Shoulder low, he made no effort to open the door, but crashed against the flimsy barrier, and was inside. Without hesitation, with the roar of a gun to hurry him, he leaped up the dark stairs, flash

light in hand. A row of doors opened off the hall. As Wentworth's torch lit them one after another, he heard a second
shot, nearer, and then the more muffled cracks of heavy
department Colts. Sloan and his men had known what to
do when they saw Chinese shots blazing.

Door after door Wentworth examined hastily. At the
end of the hallway he came to a lateral corridor, and as
his light flashed to the door at the end—where he saw a
faint glow as of white paint, the color of death in south
China—a nearer door opened, and two tongmen sprang
out.

The Chinatown detective, alert and prepared, stepped
back one pace, shifting his flash light, and drew his gun.
He fired, Chinese-fashion, from the hip, and his first bullet
took the nearest hatchetman under the striking arm. With
a hideous scream the servant of the King Cobra fell, so that
his companion sprawled over him in his anxiety to get at
the white man with a knife.

Wentworth put a bullet through the fleshy part of the
hatchetman's shoulder, kicked the heavy killing-knife out
of reach, and then ran to the door at the end of the dim
hallway. Behind him Sloan was pounding.

None save a person knowing the devious ways of the
Orient would have placed any interpretation on the little
streak of white paint on the door, but it said to Wentworth,
"Here is a dead man."

The door was locked. Wentworth smashed it down
fiercely as he heard the feet of his brother officers on the
stairs.

In the room one feeble light burned—the Lamp of the
Dead Spirits. There was illumination sufficient to show

Wentworth what he expected to see. On the floor gleamed the skeleton of a man—a man of small stature—and the bones were picked clean.

Turning, Jimmy Wentworth said grimly, "Here the Filipino, de la Cruz, was tortured. Kong Gai must have supposed de la Cruz knew what Martinez was doing."

Sloan said hoarsely, "That Filipino was alive only yesterday, Jimmy! And look at him now! What did it?"

Wentworth pointed to scratches on the dust of the floor. Then he sent the beam of his flash around the walls and ceiling, and pointed to a corner.

"There's one of 'em left," he said quietly. "The others, almost all, were swept back into some container again. Annamese ants did it, fellows. Red ants from south China. They can eat their way through a village in a night. De la Cruz was bound, and the ants loosed on him."

Sloan muttered, "What a way to die! What next?"

"Ask Kong Gai," said Jimmy Wentworth grimly.

YELLOW YEGGS

Beneath the City, Wentworth Crept Through Kong Gai's Sinister Tunnel—and Behind Him the King Cobra Himself Was Coming....

1

WENTWORTH DISCOVERS SOMETHING

A SEVEN TON dump truck moved slowly over the cobbled streets of San Francisco's Chinatown, heavily laden with excavated earth. The driver glanced at the clock on the old brick cathedral as he drove past, and decided that this load would be the last for the day.

At the southerly border of the Oriental district he swung the truck off the thoroughfare. It was a nuisance, being forced to circle the shopping district, and go several blocks westward, rather than risk argument with traffic officers who did not take kindly to ponderous trucks on congested streets. Although the westward course forced Joe Masterson to drive his truck up steep streets, it was a shorter route than swinging around the banking section to the east.

The excavating for the basement of the building in Chinatown was taking longer than Masterson had expected. He was glad that he was doing the job on day wages instead of by estimate. A lot of sand was coming out of the excavation. But that was none of Joe Masterson's business.

Two blocks from Stockton street, at the top of the rise, a policeman stepped from the sidewalk and hailed him. The

*Limply the men in
the vault collapsed*

truck had been crawling up the hill, and the driver pulled
his brake at the level intersection.

His first words showed his guilt. "Have a heart, officer,"
Joe Masterson said. "It's my last load before quittin' tonight.
Maybe th' truck's a trifle overweight, but there's a lot o' dirt
comin' out of this hole I'm workin' on."

"Sure there is," Jimmy Wentworth admitted. "I'll just
hop up with you, and you tell me about it while you're
driving."

The truckman looked his surprise, but slid his gears
into low.

When Jimmy Wentworth was settled on the gunny-sack
covered seat he slipped a hand into his pocket and showed
Joe Masterson his shield.

"Keep your mouth shut," the Chinatown detective

commanded. "If anyone—a Chinese, for example—saw me stop you, and says anything about it tomorrow, tell 'em you were arrested for overloading. I'll give you a ticket you can show to prove it."

Masterson thought wearily that this cop was being funny with him. "Sure," he said. "Have your little joke,

Up poured Kong Gai's hatchetmen

officer. Where do you want me to drive this load? Down to th' scales to be weighed?"

"I don't care how much you're overloaded," Detective Sergeant Wentworth said placidly, "and I don't care where you're driving. I just want to ask you a few questions."

"You mean it?"

"Do you think the Detective Bureau's running around stopping trucks?" Jimmy asked, grinning.

"Say," the driver retorted, "when a guy sees a dick disguised as a cop, he can expect anything!"

Jimmy wanted to get down to business. He said quietly, "You've taken a lot of dirt out of that excavation. Any idea why?"

Masterson shook his head.

"You run your own truck," Wentworth said, having found this out for himself. "Who hired you on the job?"

"The contractor. Welbing & O'Meara."

"You're handling the job on subcontract?"

Masterson shook his head. "I give an estimate," he said, "but th' owner must've butted in, for old man O'Meara comes to me and says, 'How 'bout payin' you by th' day on this job, Joe?' and I says it's O.K. by me. I asks O'Meara how come, and he tells me it's a crazy notion of th' owner. That's all I know about it."

The dump truck rumbled around a corner.

"Where are you taking the dirt?" Jimmy Wentworth asked.

"A fill out in th' Sunset district, off'cer."

"I'll ride out with you."

JOE MASTERSON CLEARED his throat, and then slid lower in his seat. For several blocks the men rode in silence. The young Chinatown detective knew that sooner or later Masterson would be forced to satisfy his curiosity, and at last the truck driver said, "Say, what's it all about, anyhow?"

"I happened to walk past the excavation early this morning," Jimmy Wentworth said quietly. "The sand you were having scooped into the truck looked lighter in color than the sand in the hole. Was it?"

"Yeah," Masterson grunted.

"Because it was wet by fog during the night?"

"Sand gets darker when it's wet," the driver said.

"That's what I thought. Any idea why the morning load should be a different color from the other loads?"

Masterson swerved the truck to let an automobile pass him, and then spat over the side. He said laconically, "It's different sand, off'cer."

Which was what Jimmy Wentworth had thought himself. "Can you show me some of it where you've been dumping?"

"I'll try," Joe Masterson promised. "What's up, off'cer? I can keep my mouth shut!"

Wentworth looked at the eager, honest face of the truck driver. Masterson might have been truculent, instead of open. There was no real reason for not telling him, provided the man would remain silent. Even if Masterson did say something about Wentworth's discovery, it would do no damage. There was nothing new about the affair.

Smiling, Jimmy Wentworth said, "I'm not solving a crime, old man. I'm just curious. That's straight! The reason there's a difference in the color of the sand, of course, is because the Chinese are digging another tunnel under Chinatown, and you're taking away the dirt from it."

"I thought these tunnels were a lot of baloney!"

Wentworth shook his head.

"You can go from almost any shop in Chinatown to the owner's house without going above ground," Jimmy informed the incredulous driver. "There must be a couple of hundred tunnels in the district."

"Seen any of 'em?" Masterson demanded.

"I've been through a lot of them," Wentworth told him.

The truck driver snorted. "You keep your job; I'll keep mine," he said. "Go through a tunnel and get a Chink knife in the back? Not Joe Masterson! But say, detective, if there're a hundred tunnels already, why get excited about one more? Who cares if th' Chinks like to play rabbit under th' ground?"

Wentworth said only, "It's part of my job to see what's going on, even if it doesn't mean anything."

He did not tell Masterson that the frame building next to the excavation was believed to house an opium joint, and that it was his opinion that the tunnel was being made to give Chinese a hidden way of reaching the joint. Nor did he add that Kong Gai, the Evil One of Chinatown, was in control of the drug industry of the Asiatic section.

In this fact was Wentworth's real interest. He never passed up any way to get on Kong Gai's well-concealed trail, never neglected a chance which might draw him closer to the horrible King Cobra, who was already responsible for a score of awful crimes, and who had never been brought to justice.

MASTERSON BEGAN TO laugh. His awe of the young fellow in patrolman's blue was vanishing. So he said, chuckling, "An' I suppose you'll try an' get some of this sand, huh? It'll tell you where th' tunnel's bein' made?"

"It won't tell me anything," Wentworth admitted. "I'll show it to a geologist, and he can tell just about which part of the city the sand comes from."

"Applesauce!" Joe Masterson decided that this dick dressed in a policeman's uniform was just a kid trying to act like a detective. It would be a good yarn to tell over a glass of beer at the speakeasy. So he said, "Say, bud, what's your name, in case I need a dick some day?"

Jimmy knew what his companion must be thinking, although it didn't bother him in the least.

"Wentworth," he said, grinning again.

The driver turned to stare at him, and almost ran down a pedestrian.

"You?" he demanded. "Detective Sergeant Wentworth?"

"Sure," Jimmy laughed. "What of it?"

"Well, I'll be darned," the big driver exploded. "I thought you was… say, sergeant, after we go to th' fill, d'ye mind stoppin' a minute at my house, so th' missus can shake your hand? She read about how you got all them Chinks up in th' Sierras, an' how you—"

"Nothing doing," Jimmy said, flushing. "You tell your wife I was lucky, and let it go at that."

"Anything you say, sergeant! An'… I won't say a word about this here sand an' tunnel, an' all. Not a word, sergeant!"

"The less a fellow says about Chinese, the better off he is," Jimmy Wentworth said cryptically.

"You mean—"

"I mean that you've got a nice broad back, Joe, and a hatchetman couldn't miss you with a knife."

"You take that chance every minute of the day!"

"It's my job," Jimmy Wentworth explained simply. "Now, let's forget about it, and go have a look-see at this sand."

2

THE MYSTERIOUS GIFT

TWO HOURS LATER, Wentworth was back at the gray Hall of Justice, in Captain Dunand's office facing the hills and tiled roofs of Chinatown.

He had stopped on the way to Headquarters to leave two samples of sand with an eminent geologist, and while he apologized to Dr. Risdon for calling at his home on business, Wentworth explained that the Detective Bureau would appreciate an opinion being telephoned them just as soon as possible. Dr. Risdon said he believed he could venture an analysis of the yellowish-gray and gray samples in a short space of time, and promised to do as the sergeant of detectives requested.

Wentworth reported all this to Captain Dunand.

"I like curiosity in a man," the gray-haired captain admitted. "But why all the haste, Jimmy?"

"Just want to find out, chief. Doesn't it seem strange to you that the Chinese would make a tunnel long enough to reach clear out of Chinatown? I hate to let any grass grow under my feet."

"Or have tunnels built under 'em, boy? Well, what do you make of it?"

Jimmy Wentworth said exactly what he thought. "The

excavation is next to an opium den. I haven't made an arrest there, because it would only mean that Kong Gai would start the place up somewhere else. Matter of fact, I know of five other hop joints right now, but what good does it do to go after 'em? And they are good spots to go after hatchetmen when we want them, so I leave them alone.

"My opinion, sir, is that Kong Gai has decided to have an underground passage to an opium joint, to throw us completely off the track. I don't really think it is to this den at all, because Kong Gai probably realizes I'm wise to it. He may be organizing a superjoint, well concealed, and this tunnel is the connecting link to it. The new place may not even be in Chinatown! It may be somewhere else, and will be reached by this tunnel. That's all a guess, sir. But it is the only thing I have been able to figure out."

"Sounds logical, Jimmy. What can we do about it?"

"Not very much. Perhaps show that we are up to the scheme, and perhaps Kong Gai will abandon his idea."

Dunand rubbed his chin, and stared out at the winking lights of Chinatown.

"If he has this smoking joint outside of Chinatown, it might be his own hangout," the captain of detectives remarked. "Be a great thing if we could catch him, Jimmy!"

Nodding, Wentworth said, "Then you think we'd better try and see where this tunnel goes? It's a long chance, sir. I don't honestly believe we can do it. I don't know how to go about it."

"Neither do I. But we'd spoil everything by being in a hurry, eh? No sense in going to the excavation and nosing around?"

Wentworth said, "None in the world. Merely put 'em

on guard. The excavation may not be an end of the tunnel at all, but just the place where the dirt is brought to the surface." Hatred of the venomous Kong Gai welled up in the Chinatown detective, and he blurted, "Let's forget all about the future, and the right way to do things, chief, and go down to the excavation tomorrow morning! There's a steam shovel on the job, and we'll find the tunnel. I'm afraid of what Kong Gai is up to! We can stop the building of the tunnel right now—"

"And have it built somewhere else," Dunand said logically. He saw how wrought up his sergeant was, and went on soothingly, "It may not be as bad as you fear, lad. I'll admit Kong Gai is a devil, but if he's poisonin' Chinks with opium smoking, he may leave other crimes alone for awhile."

"That's true," Jimmy said as sober as before. "I wish we could drive him out of the country, chief—"

"I want to see how he'd look at the end of a rope!"

"Don't think I don't want him caught," Wentworth agreed. "I do. He's not only a menace to Americans, but he has Chinatown completely terrorized. The decent, honorable Chinese look to us for protection against his hatchetmen. There is nothing finer than a respectable Oriental—"

"Which reminds me," the gray-haired captain smiled, "that a package came for you this evening, Jimmy. There it is. Over there on the table. It was brought by a Chink youngster. Always some present! The old merchants certainly think you're a fine cop, boy. I don't object to the presents, but don't let 'em wreck your digestion! I know you took the day off after Chinese New Year!"

WENTWORTH CROSSED THE room, and picked up a long

paper parcel. He carefully determined its weight, and then pressed slowly on it, finding the contents soft and yielding. Next, with a finger, he poked a hole in the paper, sniffing gingerly to see if any odor of anything escaped.

Dunand did not blame Wentworth. He knew the diabolical ways which Kong Gai used to slay.

The parcel bore the name, in Chinese and English, of one of the great Oriental bazaars. Below the name, stamped in red, was the bazaar trademark; a bird with folded wings. From the beak of the bird came a little streak of flame.

Satisfied that the parcel was not dangerous, Wentworth returned to what Dunand had been saying: "New Year! I never ate so many sweetened pork dumplings in all my life! Nor drank so much ceremonial tea. There's a funny thing," Wentworth went on, as he undid the string, "no matter what a Chinese gives you, it is bad form to thank him in any way. You mustn't even mention receiving the present. Twenty days later, you give him a gift in return, and he doesn't dare mention receiving it, either. That's the way high class Chinese always do."

"I wouldn't care how it was done," Dunand remarked, as Wentworth brought the contents of the parcel to light, "if somebody'd give me a present like that!"

Revealed on Dunand's flat topped desk were several pairs of magnificent silk pyjamas, pure white, of heavy crepe silk. The sleeping garments were in excellent taste, and not at all effeminate.

Tucked in the jacket pocket of the uppermost coat was a slip of paper, and Wentworth immediately took it out and read it aloud; "May your sleep be filled with pleasing dreams, and may you think happily of the house of the Fire Bird." The words were written in English.

"What's this fire bird thing?" the gray-haired captain of detectives asked.

"The emblem of the firm of Ho Y'aung Mi." Jimmy said. "Something like our trademarks, but intended to bring good luck. The Fire Bird is called Pi Fang in Chinese. Originally, it was considered an omen portending fire, or death by fire, to any house where it appeared. Now, it means merely, 'May you be warm in body and comfortable in spirit.'"

"Good idea for pyjamas," Dunand laughed. "Keep you warm during the winter. Now you've got to figure on a return gift... what're you examining 'em for, Jimmy? Anything wrong?"

Wentworth was looking intently at the silken garment in his hand, rubbing his finger over the crepe doubtfully.

At last he said thoughtfully, "I've seen a lot of silk manufactured, chief, in China. From the time Chinese girls spend days wrapped tightly in padded gowns, with layers of cotton between the gown and body, and the cotton filled with worms not big enough to eat mulberry leaves; from that time until the cocoons are dumped into the vats I've seen what happened. I've seen the long strands ready for spinning and weaving.

"Look at this cloth. It's very heavy. Probably a dozen threads of reeled silk, representing as many cocoons, have been spun together to make each thread of silk. The secret of crepe is that the woof threads are tightly twisted, half to the right and half to the left; woven together alternately, and when the web is dipped this reverse twisting makes the crinkle we call crepe. Next—"

"I wear me a flannel nightgown," Dunand chuckled. "It's all very fine, Jimmy, but it's been a long day, and—"

"Wait a minute, sir," Wentworth pleaded. "In China, the dipping is done in water mixed with ashes made from millet straw, which gives the crepe a slightly yellow color. What color are these pyjamas?"

"Pure white. What of it?"

"In Japan," Jimmy Wentworth went on, "the dip is water mixed with rice-straw ash, and after the fabric is stretched and rolled, it is absolutely white. This is Japanese silk, chief, and... well, the firm of Ho Y'aung Mi would be shot before they would sell a Japanese product in these days."

"Somebody gyped 'em?"

"No! They've got real silk experts. I don't believe Ho Y'aung Mi sent me these pyjamas at all. I'm going to risk it by asking them right now! It looks funny to me." Before Dunand could ask another question Wentworth had the telephone off the stand and was calling his number at the China exchange. Dunand realized how seriously his Chinatown detective must have studied the directory, to be able to call a number without asking for the book.

"*Ni kam yat, hola!*" Wentworth said in Chinese, before he remembered that it was wiser to speak in English. "This is Wentworth, the policeman."

HO Y'AUNG CHANG, son of the head of the establishment—open, like many of the bazaars, at night, for the tourist trade, said in perfect English, "Good evening, officer. So you are trying to learn our terrible language? To what do we owe the honor of this call?"

Wentworth said at once, "My apologies. Mr. Y'aung. I've received a package wrapped in your store paper, containing silk pyjamas. There isn't any note saying who sent them. Can you tell me?"

Thus Jimmy was "saving face" in case the pyjamas were really a gift.

"Pyjamas from our store? I will go and see if any were sold recently."

So the Y'aung family were not making the present to the white officer! Wentworth said, "Wait a minute, please. Have you ever carried Japanese crepe silk in stock, either in the roll or made up in pyjamas?"

"Never," the Chinese said instantly. "These pyjamas are of Japanese silk, sergeant? Then they did not come from this shop! My honorable and august father would not permit Japanese wares within our doors. Someone is... playing a trick on you."

"Thank you," Wentworth said softly. "And say nothing about it, please."

"My health is an important thing to me," young Y'aung agreed. "I will say no word."

3

DANGEROUS PLANS

THE DETECTIVE SERGEANT thanked him, replaced the instrument a moment, and then asked the station operator for the Headquarters chemist. Dr. Washburn had gone home, but his assistant answered. To him Wentworth said, "This's Wentworth. I'm in Dunand's office." In his excitement he forgot the captain's title. "Come up, won't you, and have a look at some cloth? It may be impregnated with poison; bring your testing chemicals."

Dunand growled, "Now what? I've heard of not lookin' gift horses in the mouth, and not putting gift cigars there, either, but this's the darnedest thing I ever heard of." He reached for the pile of pyjamas.

"Put 'em down," Jimmy snapped. "Heaven knows what's wrong with them!"

While the two detectives watched, the assistant chemist expertly daubed the silk with liquids from different bottles. He watched the wet spots closely, until one of them slowly began to darken and change color. Then without a second's hesitation he dipped the darkening place on the pyjama coat-sleeve into a saucer, and filled the flat porcelain container with more liquid. The liquid was colorless as water, but the pyjama-cloth resting in the saucer became stained until there was a black spot, gleaming and lustrous as the pupil of an Oriental eye, on the originally white fabric.

The assistant looked up. "There you are," he said.

"There you are... there you are what?" Dunand grunted. "What's all the hocus-pocus?"

Wentworth's question was to the chemist: "Lead salt?" he asked.

"Mercury," said the chemist. "A hell of a lot worse, sergeant. Have you worn the pyjamas at all? If so—"

Jimmy shook his head.

"You're lucky," the chemist said briefly. "Otherwise, you'd be in for a few weeks at the hospital. I can't tell you anything, exactly, without a complete analysis. However, some mercury compound has been worked into the silk. Can't say which one. If you'd worn the pyjamas a night or so, the mercury would have worked into the pores—a fellow always sweats a little at night—and that would have been that!"

Dunand's eyes were clouding with rage.

"What a damnable way to commit murder," he growled. "Killin' a man in his sleep! Nobody but Kong Gai would kill in that manner."

The chemist was packing his test tubes and bottles into their containers. He said to the captain and sergeant, "I hardly think the mercury with which the silk is impregnated would kill."

"What would it do?" demanded Dunand.

"What difference does it make? Wentworth was suspicious and didn't wear the poisoned silk—"

"Go ahead," Wentworth insisted. "You can't shock me."

"If you had worn the pyjamas, sergeant, I can tell you exactly what would have happened. First, a slight skin eruption, difficult to diagnose. In a day or so—without anyone being able to do anything about it!—tremors and twitching, affecting your arms and hands, and, before night, probably your entire body. Lastly—"

Again the chemist paused.

Dunand said sharply "Don't you think the sergeant realizes he would have died? Don't you think he's faced death before?"

"He wouldn't die," the assistant chemist said slowly. "He would only be an imbecile for the rest of his life!"

DUNAND CALLED ON his Maker, not in irreverence, but in sheer desperate search for courage. Wentworth's own face was gray, although his lips were tightly drawn together.

At the door the chemist turned. "You asked for it, remember," he said grimly. "Now you know!"

With that he departed.

For a long time the two detectives, captain and young sergeant, sat in silence. Once Wentworth lit a cigarette, and only with effort managed to control the shaking of his fingers.

At last, his voice very low, he said, "So the tunnel means more than we supposed. One of Kong Gai's spies saw me stop the dump truck. Kong Gai wants me out of the way. Badly enough, I believe, to have a hatchetman drop me right on my beat. I sort of sense this, sir. To return to Chinatown would be suicide. I'm going back just once more, and then we'll rip the tunnel apart and put an immediate end to what it means. We don't dare waste time. We're completely in the dark. We've got to act at once!"

"You mean now? Tonight?"

Wentworth lit another cigarette from the glowing end of the first. He wanted to say, "Yes! Let's get a steam shovelman, and shoot the riot squad out into Chinatown, and wreck the whole damned excavation. Blow up the tunnel!" Yet that wasn't the thing to do. He knew that, despite the honest fear in his heart. Fear of the terrible Venomous One.

And so Jimmy Wentworth said, "At four in the morning—tomorrow morning—every murderer and tongman and hatchetman in Chinatown will be bowed down at the Altar of the Snake. When anything desperately criminal is planned, the killers spend a full hour *ko'u-to'uing* to the Snake God. Where do they do this? If I knew, I could wipe 'em out! I don't know. No white man does. More than once I've verified this by wandering down the streets between four and five. There's never a spy in sight. Not even the old chestnut seller, and Kong Gai owns him, body and soul, for a few pinches of opium.

"At four, playing safe, I can be dropped from the night-hawk cab right at the excavation, and crawl into the hole. If, as I guess, the dirt from the tunnel is brought out during the night, I ought to be able to find the opening some-how—"

"How about whoever's working in the tunnel?"

"I've got to take a chance that the workers are killers, and that they'll be at the Snake Altar! I've got to see where that tunnel goes, if I can!"

"How'll you do it, in the dark?"

"Pedometer for distance, compass for direction. I'll put down every change of direction, although the tunnel is probably in a straight line, shortest distance between the two points. I'll be safe, chief. I'll report to you what I find, and then we can act."

"I will not let you go alone, boy!"

"Every added man would make detection that much easier. You know that, sir. I must go alone."

Dunand looked suddenly older. He could not keep his eyes from the heap of poisoned silk. When he spoke, his words were cold and measured: "It's my job to stay here, in charge of the Bureau," he said grimly. "It's your job to prevent murder and death, and to keep on the trail of this fiend Kong Gai. I have no plan to offer as a substitute for your own. As you say, we are completely in the dark. Intuition and your knowledge of the Chinese makes you feel something is imminent, something which must be connected with this tunnel. And so all I can say"—Dunand's harsh voice softened—"all I can say is… lad, be careful!"

"I'll be careful," Jimmy Wentworth said, with a cheerfulness he did not feel. Venturing into a tunnel, the end of which might be Kong Gai's secret lair! Careful! Wouldn't it be just as well to take a squad of men, heavily armed with choppers, and be prepared for whatever might be encountered? No! The proper thing to do was to find what Kong Gai intended, and, instead of warning the Evil One, and permitting him to change his plans, to finally stop whatever diabolical plot was in the wind at the time of its attempted execution. That was the real way to accomplish something worth while.

"If you go in at four, you've got to be out before five," Dunand worried. "Call me up before five, Jimmy. Otherwise I'll have the whole department down in Chinatown, and we'll tear it apart for you!"

"I'll check in by nine," Wentworth said, hoping to alleviate his chief's anxiety. "At five I'll be in the tub, washing off dirt from the tunnel, and at five-thirty I'll be grabbing a little sleep! Stop worrying, sir! I won't see a soul in the tunnel, and even if I do I can always sneak out again. See you at nine tomorrow, chief. If I'm lucky, I'll have some information. If I'm not, no harm will be done. I promise to be careful, and even if I run across something, I won't try to follow it up without reporting."

"Well…"

"See you in the morning," Jimmy said softly, and left before Dunand could protest further.

4

BENEATH THE CITY

THE BRAZEN BELL in the tower of the old brick church sang out the hour of four. The dead, silent hour of the Snake, worshipped by Asiatic murderers and hatchetmen, by those terrible disciples and slaves of Kong Gai which the Evil One held to him by fear, by promise, or through use of the poppy drug.

Boom… boom… boom… boom….

The street below the cathedral was deserted. Street lights, made in imitation of green and gold Chinese lanterns, had already been dimmed of all their globes except one: they cast sickly and grotesque shadows on the sidewalk. A heavy fog had swept in from the Pacific. It clung to the supporting dragons of the tiled roofs as if the strange monsters were actually alive and breathing.

The door of every honest Chinese household was barred and double-barred against the awful ghosts—the headless ape, the tiger with the face of a woman, the fish which can walk like a man, and which lives on the liquor about human eye-balls—against the fearful Things of the Fourth Hell which are able to come to earth during the hour of the Snake. If any honest Oriental heard the fatal four booms of the great bell, he said a prayer hastily, reached out beyond his quilts and lit a sacred taper, and then buried his head more deeply in the covers.

Here and there, before the sweet voice of the old bell sang four times, black-clad figures slipped noiselessly, ominously, through the fog, and disappeared into different black doorways, seeking an underground passage leading to the dread Place of the Snake. Hatchetmen. Brothers of the Cobra, as venomous as the serpent itself, but less horrible than their leader, the feared King Cobra, Kong Gai.

But before the bell had sent its long solemn notes echoing over the Oriental district for the last of the four beats, the streets were empty.

Hardly had the final hum of the great bell ceased than a taxi swung around a corner into Chinatown, and, in second gear, started up the steep street where the excavation was being made. Voices were raised from the cab in raucous singing of drunken melodies.

The cab, in climbing the hill, avoided the center of the street, where cable-slot and car tracks on either side presented a slippery silver ribbon of steel in the fog. Close to the curb the taxi was driven. Directly opposite the excavation, while the passengers were singing lustily and making no pretense at silence, a dark figure slid from the driver's compartment to the cobbles.

On hands and knees, noiseless and swift as a snake, Jimmy Wentworth, in a suit as gray as the fog, crossed the sand-covered pavement, and let himself down into the sand-pit. He dropped without a sound. The soft, fog-wet sand broke his fall. It would have been easier to have crept down the truck runway of timbers, but Wentworth wanted to keep completely in shadow.

Gun in hand, he lay perfectly still for a full two minutes. Then he began to creep around the edge of the excavation.

The building just east of the excavation was owned by one of the honorable Six Companies. Wentworth circled it swiftly and without interest; crossed the rear of the great depression, and reached the westward building, higher up the hill. This, for all the deed showed honest men owned the shop and rooms above, was one of Kong Gai's opium dens.

More, being higher than the excavation, it would be the logical way to pass dirt from under the building into the hole.

The concrete foundation of the westward building was almost entirely exposed.

Against it were secured braces, heavy timbers anchored in the sand by short piles, and then angled against the concrete, lest the building slip down the hill and into the pit.

Wentworth knew how the Chinese mined. Many times his father, formerly himself a San Francisco patrolman, had explained how the Chinese Boxers operated during the famous rebellion in China.

With this in mind Jimmy Wentworth thrust his heavy night stick into the sand, close to foundation-bottom, between the supporting timbers, as he crept along. Again and again the wood went deep into the sand. Not until the detective was almost back to the pavement-line did wood meet something which did not give an inch.

The Chinatown detective wasted not an instant. If he were being observed, the hatchetmen would swarm down when they saw that he had discovered the concealed mouth of the tunnel. One glance about him proved that attack could only come from the street. The building behind him was a blank wall; so was the shop on the opposite side of the excavation.

Placing his gun conveniently close, Wentworth knelt with his back to the opium den. Then, like a dog, he began to scratch out the sand, scooping it away rapidly and sending it back against the concrete. Nothing happened. No one attacked. No shrill cry of *"Sha! Sha!* Kill!" curdled the silent, foggy air.

In moments Wentworth's fingers reached smooth metal. In another minute—now bending over the small place he had scraped, with disregard of any attack—the young detective had cleared away a four-foot-square piece of metal, and, with particles of sand between his fingernails, lifted the sheet of thin steel.

A black hole yawned below him.

Wentworth, gun replaced in holster, night stick fastened again to his belt, quietly let himself down until his feet touched bottom. His head and shoulders were still out of the hole. Then he went about a curious business. Holding the steel at an angle, he covered as much of it as he could reach with sand, and then slid completely into the hole, still trying to keep the steel square pointed down hill, so sand banked against the concrete foundation would continue to run down over it.

Wentworth did not believe that any Kong Gai hatchet-man would come to the excavation during the dread Hour of the Snake, but he was taking no chance at being caught in the tunnel.

The weight of the steel, as sand dribbled down to it from

above, grew more than even Wentworth's lithely muscled arms could support. He let the square down as far as it would go, to its original position, and, again very silent, waited. There was not a sound in the tunnel.

Gun in right hand, Jimmy Wentworth pressed the button of his flashlight, and blinked as the walls of the tunnel sprang into being.

The tunnel only ran in one way—south. Due south. This was Jimmy's guess, even before he verified it with the compass. South! Away from Chinatown! Why?

There was no time to be lost. Wentworth meant to be completely out of the tunnel long before five o'clock. With the light of the torch blazing before him, he began to advance.

The sides of the tunnel, and the top, were made of rough timbers, all short lengths. Before he had gone fifty feet Wentworth realized the care, and time, that had gone into the making of this tunnel.

None save Asiatics would have attempted such a seemingly impossible task—and why had they done it?

At the end of his first fifty feet, Wentworth came to a chamber made in the earth, in a place where the soil was clay, hard, firm, and sticky. Here were more timbers, wheelbarrows, spades and picks and shovels. Here, also, were unmarked boxes and barrels. Obviously the engineering headquarters for the tunnel.

Wentworth did not dare pause to examine the materials. He pressed cautiously onward, aware that his flash would betray him to any watcher, but positive that there was no one in the tunnel.

FOR SEVERAL MINUTES the course continued due south,

toward the shopping district, and then for an instant Wentworth thought he had come to the end of the underground passage. No, not the end. He had reached a place where the tunnel dipped suddenly and turned, according to his compass, almost at right angles eastward. Wentworth guessed that he must be just about beneath the old cathedral, on the southern extremity of Chinatown. If this were so, it seemed to him that he ought to be able to hear the rumbling clack-clack of the California Street cable.

Standing erect, Wentworth pressed his ear to the timbers. He was rewarded by hearing a muffled "click-click, clack-clack"—the cable which pulled the street-cars up and down hill, making contact with the supporting rollers.

So he was under California Street! And the tunnel had turned eastward. Squarely east!

It was almost easier to slide than to walk now. Wentworth could imagine the toiling, hop-excited coolies and hatchetmen, bringing up their barrows of earth in the stupendous undertaking… and then, as the floor of the tunnel levelled off again, and he came to a large chamber in the earth, his heart almost stopped, and then began to race until he almost panted with excitement.

This was the true end of the tunnel! Here, again, were picks and shovels and boxes; here, also, was a crude stairway reaching upward. And the end of the stairway, Wentworth saw, was a mass of concrete and steel. In one place the massive material had been mined and cut away, until only a shell of the floor of the building above remained.

Wentworth mounted the stairway, and with his hand first, and night stick next, beat heavily against the exposed concrete. Only in one place did it give out a hollow sound—the place where the concrete had been scraped away.

Standing on the rough stairway, Wentworth swiftly reviewed his course. First, through Chinatown, as far as the cathedral and the California Streetcars. Next, down hill, following the course of the cable-cars—the natural place to tunnel, where no obstructions such as foundations would be met. Downhill, to a level spot again—Kearny street, or Montgomery. Probably the latter, for he had walked about a block on the level.

And so Jimmy Wentworth knew where he must be. Not exactly, but that made little difference! For here, along California street, was bank after bank, the powerful financial institutions of San Francisco! Elbow to elbow they stood. The Bank of Northern California. The Canadian Commercial. The British-Liverpool-Havre National Bank. The American-Pacific. In their vaults were the wealth of the Coast; gold, currency, negotiable securities....

And Kong Gai, the Evil One, was after it!

Wentworth glanced at his watch. This was certainly not the time to stand around wondering what ought to be done. For a split second he thought of attempting to drive a pick into the shell Of the floor above him, to show someone in the bank-basement that much was wrong. Then, the pick actually in hand, he realized that his job was not only to warn the bank authorities, but also to attempt to catch the criminals—perhaps red-handed.

The watch said four twenty-two. Plenty of time to get out of the tunnel, and reach Dunand's home. Wentworth knew that there was no time to waste. Why, even this morning, if they desired, the Chinese might burst into one of the great banks! Although Jimmy supposed that their plan must be to attempt opening a vault. A smile broke over his face at the thought. Let'em try! White men's inventions would foil yellow devils' ingenuity!

In better spirits, but still carrying the pick—being deep in thought—Jimmy Wentworth began to retrace his steps. He went swiftly for a few minutes, and then started the steep climb following the street above. Again he reassured himself of the rumble of the cable overhead; once, with the flashlight against the roof of the tunnel, he saw a telephone conduit projecting through the crude timbers—double proof that he was under a street.

Wentworth was halfway up the steep tunnel when his flashlight revealed something against the wall which made him pause and stare.

Pinned to a timber was a painting, facing east, so he had not seen it while coming down. A painting of a curious bird, something like a crane with only one leg and one wing, with green and red plumage and a white beak. In its beak was something giving forth fire. The talons of the single foot were clutched about painted gold coins.

The Fire Bird!

WHAT WAS THE emblem doing here? What connection did it have with the poisoned silk? Could it mean that the responsible, supposedly honorable Y'aung family were really a part of Kong Gai's terrible clan? Wentworth refused to believe this.

As he stared closer, his very heart constricted. The "something" in the Fire Bird's pale beak was a crude likeness of his own face! Smoke was painted as issuing from his eyes, and from his mouth, in tiny red letters, was written in Chinese characters: "Soon I will burn!"

So that was what Kong Gai intended for him! Wentworth believed that it must mean the burning caused by the mercury poison of the silk garment at first; he must ask the chemist exactly what the action of mercury felt like. Or was there some other, and deeper, meaning? Unless the poisoned silk had been intended for some time—and the painting of the Fire Bird looked as if it had been hanging for weeks in the tunnel—the dreadful symbol must have a hidden meaning, related, naturally, to death by fire!

Wentworth had spent several minutes examining the Fire Bird. He began to walk up the tunnel now with greater rapidity. Coming down, he had half slid along. The return was more difficult. Here and there, attached to the side timbers, were handholds; pieces of rope by means of which the opium-crazed and tireless coolies could pull themselves along with their burdens.

Several times Jimmy Wentworth grasped these ropes as he advanced hastily. Almost at the top of the incline, where the tunnel turned northward toward Chinatown, near the old cathedral, the detective saw a paper sign on the wall. The Chinese characters were almost indecipherable. Wentworth, grasping the rope beneath the sign, pulled himself closer to have a better look. For an instant the rope held his weight, and then it gave suddenly, so that he stumbled backward. An immediate sense of giddiness overcame him.

The young detective sergeant tried terribly to fight off the nausea, the blindness and failing reason. Instinctively, even while he strove for recovery of senses and balance, he knew that the rope must have released some odorless and deadly gas. Then he felt himself going completely out of control.

Only once did Jimmy Wentworth attempt to thrust out his pick and hold it against a timber. It was a terrible sensation, like being between life and death. His mind was becoming more and more lax, but his muscles remained as tense as before. His grip on the pickhandle was as if the hickory haft had become a part of his very hand.

Wentworth felt, with the last remaining particle of reason, that he was sliding, tumbling, falling down the steep tunnel, and then everything, to him, became black.

In another minute James Wentworth, detective sergeant in charge of the Chinatown detail, lay in a crumpled heap at the foot of the tunnel. The pick-handle was still clenched in his unconscious right hand, and the flashlight in his left. For several minutes the torch burned steadily, cutting a swath of brightness, and then, the filament jarred by the long fall, the light began to wink, and soon vanished.

The tunnel leading from Chinatown to the heart of the financial district became as silent and ominous as death.

5

THE ATTACK ON THE VAULT

AT TWENTY-ONE MINUTES to nine, on every banking day of the year, the time lock of the great vault of the Bank of Northern California clicks. At twenty-one minutes to nine, without the variation of more than three or four seconds, the fourth assistant cashier, George A. Hobson, watches several men operate the levers and knobs which make it possible for the outer armor-plate steel door to be opened. In the vault-room with Hobson and the other bank men are armed guards, three of them. One watches the safe, one lets his eyes roam about the concrete-and-steel chamber; the third observes the barred grille separating the vault-room from the rest of the bank basement.

Out of the vault, each morning, are taken trays of gold and packets of currency for the day's business. The floor of the vault is piled high with the million dollars in gold which the bank must always keep on hand to satisfy the demands of the Federal Banking authorities; in addition, there are steel boxes of currency to keep the bank's reserve up to the total insisted upon by the State officials. In inner compartments, all doubly locked and bolted, are millions of dollars of negotiable securities, held in the Bank of Northern California for the various correspondent banks all over the West. These cannot be touched save by order from one of the executive officers, and are never opened in the early morning.

Nevertheless, at this hour before nine, several million dollars are exposed. To protect this wealth, the stairway leading to the basement is well guarded. There is but one staircase, where a guard stands, his finger not an inch from the buzzer leading directly to the Bankers' Protective Association. Not even a shot through the heart could prevent the spasmodic pressing of the button. However, this is merely a formality. During the ten minutes that the great vault is open, no one can enter the bank without passing the scrutiny of the guard at the outer door, who will unlock his portal only for the employees of the bank.

On this morning everything proceeded as usual, Hobson watched and checked the packets of currency and trays of gold and rolls of silver as they were taken from the vault and placed on the little cart to be conveyed up to the banking floor. For a good many years Hobson had done this. His work was almost automatic. When the task was completed, and the money for the day's business had been removed, Hobson would step to the telephone leading directly to the Protective Association, and say only, "All O.K." after which the vault would be shut. Even with the time lock off, it would take hours for the most skilled powdermen to get through the ponderous outer barrier.

If, however, more than ten minutes elapsed before Hobson put in his call, the Protective Association would be wanting to know what was wrong—not only from Hobson in the vault-room, but from officials upstairs in the bank.

Hobson was starting to check the first tray of twenty-dollar gold pieces, destined for shipment to Alaska to pay off salmon fishers in hard cash, when he thought, "I'm in for a cold. It's this icy room that does it. I'll go home early."

He was able to think that much coherently.

Then, without even being able to scream nor cry out, he suddenly gasped for breath and began to tear at his throat with his fingers. His eyes were blinded, and his chest felt as if being squeezed in a gigantic, terrible vise. Green slime appeared instantly at his lips, and he made an agonized effort to breathe, still clutching at his throat.

The vault-room whirled before his eyes. He may or may not have seen his fellow workers already choking and gasping on the floor. The guards had dropped their weapons in their complete collapse, and were fighting desperately for life.

Up from a small hole in the three-foot thick concrete floor (Hobson could not see this, nor had anyone else) came puffing a steady stream of grayish-green vapor, thick, odorless, deadly.

THE WORKERS AND guards writhed on the concrete floor. Death was close at hand. At one moment, face leaden-hued, froth escaping from mouth and nose, the white men would attempt to draw air into their tortured lungs, and the next, exhausted, they would again lower their heads to the cold floor.

For three minutes the fiendish gas jetted into the vault-room.

No one was in the bank basement to see what was taking place. The guard at the stairway was not only a full two hundred feet away, but also protected from detecting the gas by the many turns in the corridor.

Three minutes—making in all five minutes of the ten before which the Protective Association would not think of inquiring—elapsed. The only sound in the vault was the infinitesimal puff-puff of the liberated gas, and the chokings of the stricken men.

George Hobson's agony was the worst. He was partially conscious. Again and again, even with death facing him, he tried to pull his body toward the telephone. He could not move an inch. Between efforts were moments of deadly stupor, growing longer each time.

Hobson's dulled ears did not hear the sudden crash of crowbars and picks against the concrete shell through which the gas had been emerging, but his eyes, in one of his times of consciousness, saw a sight almost as terrible as the dying men about him.

Up from beneath the floor of the basement came an apparition. There were two shining eyes—goggles treated with cellulose acetate; there was, in place of a nose, a long piece of rubber like an elephant's trunk. Hobson's weary brain, sick to death and utterly confused, seemed to tell the man that these were monsters of hell....

Then his senses left him completely.

Man after man followed the first Chinese in the gas mask. Without wasting an instant of time, the gold and currency was swept into canvas sacks. While one of the masked men examined the inner compartments of the vault, finding them impenetrable, his fellows, one at each end, began moving the boxes toward the mouth of the tunnel, dragging their heavy burdens across the concrete floor.

In less than two minutes—eight minutes of the ten had by now been consumed—the Chinese were leaving the vault-room with their spoil.

One of the dying men moaned and tried feebly to tear at his throat. A hatchetman bent down, and thrust his short-bladed knife deep into the white man's chest. Red blood began to bubble forth, to spread in a growing pool on the floor. From one of the masked faces came a sound—a muffled laugh.

Nine minutes of the ten had passed as the last of the Chinese slid through the hole in the concrete.

Almost one full minute more all was quiet, and then there was a soft, gentle roar, and a tiny shake, like a miniature earthquake. Sand sifted up through the hole. The men of the King Cobra had set off a small charge at the end of the tunnel, and the sand must have immediately closed in, blocking any possible pursuit through the tunnel itself.

In ten seconds more a bell rang in the vault-room, with no one able to answer it. Bells rang on the banking floor. Men turned toward one another in amazement. The guards from the Association, weapons drawn, raced down to the basement... and found only death! Worse, they also, partially gassed, were only able to stagger away, hands to their throats, and were barely managing to tell the officials of the bank what they had seen in the vault-room.

To the Protective Association came the feverish words: "The vault's been rifled! Men dead! Poison gas!"

WHILE GRAY-CLAD OPERATIVES tore for the powerful black limousine used by the Association, the operative in charge of the office was frantically communicating with Headquarters.

"Bank of Northern California," he shouted to Mallory, the desk sergeant. "Robbed! Poison gas!"

Before he could say another word, the gong was frantically howling its summons. The riot car swung out in seconds from under the Hall of Justice. Detectives and the picked men of the squad leaped to the running board. As the car roared along Kearny street, guns were jerked out. Beside the driver, Sergeant O'Rourke wet his finger once, and took the least particle of dust from the sight of the blue-barreled chopper.

No sooner had the riot car's siren loosed its first blast than Headquarters was springing into action. Officers off duty rushed to the desk. Doors were slammed open. Reporters in the Police Room phoned their city desks: "Something's up! Let you know soon's I get something!"

Captain Dunand's own bell was ringing as the desk sergeant called him, but while the gray-haired chief of detectives waited, Mallory was sending his command to the Harbor Hospital: "Bank North Cal," he was saying fearfully. "Gas! Get going! Hell's broken loose!"

Then Mallory was able to speak with Dunand.

"Protective Association report that the Bank of Northern California has been robbed, sir, by means of poisoned gas. Riot squad has already left. Orders, sir?"

Dunand snapped, "Call the bank. Get descriptions. Have first officer arriving telephone me. Find out what sort of car was used. Send out warning all officers. Inform ferries. Inform State Police. Call me again. Keep in touch with Protective Association."

"Right, sir."

"As soon as you can, get Sergeant Wentworth. Send him up to me."

"Very well, captain."

"The moment you've done this, get me a wire to the bank for myself."

The riot car, siren hooting fiercely for right-of-way, raced up to the front of the magnificent edifice. Officers with drawn guns tore to the entrance. A bank official, waiting there, shouted, "In the basement, men!" and all of the squad save O'Rourke, in charge, rushed inside.

A crowd was already gathering. The traffic officer on the corner was attempting to keep them in check, and at the same time to hammer his way through the press of excited people. To him O'Rourke cried, "Madison! Why ain't you inside?"

"Just was called this second," Officer Madison said, fighting closer. "What's up?"

"Up? Up?" blazed O'Rourke. "The bank's been cleaned, and I suppose you never seen 'em get away? What're your eyes for?" Of the crowd he pleaded, "Who saw a car drive away in a hurry after th' hold-up? Who seen it?"

"There was no car," the bank official said softly.

"Eh?"

"Done from the inside, sergeant. Tunnel. It's been blown up—"

"The safe?"

"The tunnel!"

O'Rourke's blue eyes snapped wider open. "A telephone," he whispered. "I got to report that!"

As he followed the bank official into the sobered atmosphere of the cool building, O'Rourke heard the siren of the Harbor Hospital ambulance. White-clad doctors and internes swarmed across the banking floor while O'Rourke gave Headquarters' number. Some of the men were carrying heavy oxygen tanks.

O'Rourke was connected directly with Dunand, and the sergeant managed to control his voice as he said, "O'Rourke. At the bank. No details. I'm told a tunnel let th' robbers into th' bank. Tunnel under th' basement. I—"

"Get into the tunnel," Dunand ordered instantly. "Follow 'em, man! Don't let 'em get away!"

"Blown up," said O'Rourke. "Here comes one of th' boys—hold th' line—" In a moment O'Rourke was able to relay his information: "Vault cleaned. Vault-room is filled with gas. Harbor Hospital men are draggin' out th'… th' dead. They're all wearin' masks. Mulcahey reports 'tis bad, sir. He got a look where th' floor was broken open—through three foot of steel an' concrete!—and now th' hole's already all filled with sand again—"

"Sand?" said Dunand thinly. "Sand! Good God! Wentworth was right!"

O'Rourke, puzzled, could now hear his chief's voice using another telephone, demanding of the desk sergeant, "Have you raised Wentworth? No answer? Hasn't reported? Nobody's seen him?" And then, chill and cold, Dunand's words were again for O'Rourke's ears: "Tell the president of the bank that we had a hint of some disaster like this, although we only learned it last night. And you can tell him that somewhere in that tunnel one of the department's detectives met his death trying to stop the Chinese!"

"Eh? Chinese, sir? An' who tried t' stop 'em?"

"Wentworth! Alone, he met Kong Gai and his hatch-etmen!"

"I'll be tellin' th' boys, too," muttered O'Rourke. "Although from what Mulcahey says about what th' Chinks done to dyin' men, 'tis little needed to make us do our best, sir."

"Get on with it," Dunand growled.

Jimmy Wentworth might lie dead in the tunnel, but the work of detection must go on.

Almost a half hour from the time the first stream of gas jetted into the vault-room police cars roared up the hill into Chinatown, and blue-clad officers swarmed into the excavation. Kong Gai and his Slaves of the Snake had done their work well. There was no sign of any tunnel-mouth. Nor had the white men working in the deep pit seen or heard, at any time since starting work at eight, the slightest thing to have aroused their suspicions. The steam-shovel now gouged great bites of sand out of the sandy excavation—and revealed only more sand.

Seeing the frantic efforts which were being made by the police, a humpbacked lily vendor smiled to himself as he squatted eating watermelon seeds in the shadow of an opposite building. He did not know as yet what had happened, although he could guess that Kong Gai the Evil One was concerned with it. Nevertheless the performance amused him. These policemen in blue! Expecting to find Kong Gai, where Kong Gai might logically be expected to be found! What fools these white men were!

6

THE KING COBRA COMES

SLOWLY, PAINFULLY, JIMMY Wentworth managed to open his eyes. For a full minute he lay without moving, until he realized exactly what had happened, and where he was. Then, as he rose stiffly to an elbow, his hand unclenched from the handle of the pick.

The Chinatown detective was as much amazed by the fact that he had retained hold of the hickory haft as by the fact that he was somehow still alive. Every bone in his body felt as if it had been pounded by clubs. His muscles, still partially under the influence of the deadly gas, seemed stiff and rigid. It was with effort that he opened and closed the palms of his hands.

Now that he was conscious, the action of the mysterious gas began to wear off. Jimmy Wentworth felt his muscles become less tight and tense; he came to his knees, and then looked at his watch. In the pitchy blackness the radium-painted hands showed him the hour. Seventeen minutes to seven!

Were the Chinese already in the tunnel, already at work? Wentworth strained his senses listening, but heard nothing. No sound of pick, nor of hammer. Yet that might mean nothing. The place under one of the banks must be about ready for the final attack. Wentworth realized this not only from the fact that the concrete had been bared, and partly chiselled away, but because Kong Gai—learning that the detective was on the alert concerning the excavation—had attempted murder lest his plans go wrong.

The hatchetmen and opium-smoking coolies might well be under the bank. Right this moment. If this was the case, the far end of the tunnel would naturally be well guarded.

It was so dark that Wentworth was unable to tell where he was, although he knew he must have fallen to the level part of the tunnel, somewhere below Kearny street. There was only one thing to do, Jimmy decided swiftly. To remain in the tunnel, and attempt to escape during the Dead Hour the next morning, was ridiculous. Surprise was on his side. He would try to work his way, in the darkness, back to the mouth of the tunnel, and somehow overwhelm the guards.

Then he knew that the tunnel must still be empty. Otherwise, the Chinese, in walking to the cleared space beneath the bank, would have found him.

This sent the blood coursing through his veins. He could retrace his steps, even in the dark; he could perhaps get to Headquarters before anything happened. And heavily armed men from the force would filter into every bank in the financial district, to give the Evil One's men a deadly reception.

Jimmy stood up. His head spun round a moment, and then, except for a stiffness of his muscles and the soreness of his whole body, he felt as well as ever.

Three steps forward, a hand to the nearest side of the tunnel, the sergeant of detectives managed to take, and the next instant he stood as still as the timber against which his hand was resting.

Roaring and echoing in the black tunnel was the terrible music of Chinese trumpets. Blare, blare, blare in the blackness, sobbing tremulously on high notes. Then boom, boom, as the eery sound descended the scale and filled the underground passage with a noise like thunder.

The men of Kong Gai were in the tunnel!

WESTWARD, THERE WAS a little spray of light, growing brighter each instant as the Brothers of the Snake turned the corner and began to march down the incline under California Street. The trumpets were not sounded again, nor was there any sound except the shuff-shuff of many feet, descending toward Wentworth.

The tunnel was no longer in complete darkness. Wentworth did not think of flight. His gun out, he worked his body between two of the supporting timbers, and then managed to slide down so that he was entirely behind a barrel standing on the floor of the tunnel. Unless the barrel was moved, his place of concealment was safe enough. If the barrel was taken away, Jimmy meant to sell his life as dearly as possible. The last bullet in the clip—unless he had a shot with it at Kong Gai—would be for himself.

With measured tread the Chinese approached. The barrel was empty. When the light of their electric torches grew yellow and bright, Wentworth was able to glimpse the passing men through a space in the staves.

First came a hatchetman in blood red trousers, with a black tunic embroidered with a king cobra. The hatchetman swung a great two-handed sword. Across his back was slung a rifle. Next another Brother of the Snake carried a green banner, with the deadly snake emblem seemingly alive as the folds of the silk hissed together. Never in all Wentworth's life, even in China, had he seen such barbaric splendor. The hatchetmen in many-colored jackets—yellow and black, blue and silver, gold and crimson—passed him in never ending procession. Here was Kong Gai's inner strength; here was the King Cobra's real force—and it was a dozen times what Wentworth had ever estimated! What a force for evil the Evil One had!

And then Jimmy Wentworth's heart almost stopped. Blood pounded in his head, in his eyes.

For, with mincing steps, he saw at last the horrible Kong Gai himself! Horrible? Not in appearance! Kong Gai the Deadly was not large. His face was as beautiful as that of a Chinese flower-girl. Only the evil, greenish-black eyes betrayed the man for the fiend he really was. On Kong Gai's lips was a little smile.

Perfumed was the King Cobra. Attired in mauve and scarlet silks, he walked with a brawny Manchu guard before and behind him. A thin dagger, ornamented with a hand-loop of seed pearls and sapphires, swung at his side.

Jimmy made his decision.

He knew that the plans were about to be put into execution—and that there was nothing to be done about it. He could of course wait until the Chinese had all passed him, and were busy with their labors to break into the bank, but he realized also that the presence of Kong Gai in the tunnel meant that ten—twenty—perhaps more—hatchetmen and guards would be at the other end of the tunnel, protecting the person of their awful master. There was no possible chance of getting out and giving the alarm.

And so the young Chinatown detective, without a sound, slowly raised up from behind the barrel. Between the two supporting timbers, none saw him. Up came his heavy automatic. Wentworth's finger pressed firmly on the trigger....

THERE WAS NOT even the click which might have told of an imperfect shell in the firing chamber! The gun had been damaged when Wentworth had fallen down the length of the incline.

Cold, icy sweat began to drip along Wentworth's body. He was unable to move. Every particle of energy had been bent on a perfect shot, although he knew that he himself, immediately after, was to die.

Instinctively, he almost rushed out, to try and throttle Kong Gai with his bare hands, to wring the evil life out of the villainous Chinese... and then the cortege had passed him, and the tunnel slowly became black again.

Jimmy Wentworth's excited brain slowly sobered, and he took stock of his position and the situation. To attempt escape now was out of the question. In the dark he could do nothing about his gun. There were two possibilities, and two only. He might wait until the tunnel was finally emptied the next morning at the Dead Hour—provided the Chinese did not consummate their plans today, as he thought they would—or he could find the pick, which must be somewhere near on the floor of the tunnel, and when Kong Gai returned, with one blow remove the menace of San Francisco.

Whichever thing he did, it meant that he must wait. And so he settled down to see what was going to happen.

Time passed slowly, terribly slowly. Gradually his ears

became attuned to little sounds in the tunnel. A rat from Chinatown, gnawing at something. A constant, steady rumbling—the noise of the cable which propelled the California Street cars, probably directly above him. Sounds from the eastward end of the tunnel, where the men of Kong Gai were at work.

Once or twice a hatchetman, again in conventional killing costume of black silk, would hurry past him on some errand. Once a dozen coolies, eyes inflamed with drugs, rushed westward, and returned soon with iron and steel cylinders, looking like containers for gas. Boxes were carried to the place under the bank, some marked, in English, *Dangerous—Explosives.*

So the vaults of the bank were to be blown soon! And what could he do about it? Nothing! White men were undoubtedly about to die; he could do nothing about that, either. The best he could hope for would be that he might get some inkling of the future plans of the Chinese.

How close to them could he get? Anything, now, was better than remaining where he was. Wentworth glanced at his watch. Eight thirty! It had seemed like hours more. He was forced to wait while coolies hurried past him, following one of the armed hatchetmen who carried a flashlight; he waited until they returned, carrying more boxes, while almost a full fifteen minutes were consumed. Another hatchetman ran westward, toward the incline; this Brother of the Snake was in full gaudy costume. What his business might be Jimmy couldn't guess, but it kept him in concealment to see if the hatchetman would swiftly return.

By nine o'clock all seemed absolutely quiet, save for the little noises. Wentworth decided there would be no better time to work his way toward the bank: which one it was he had no way of knowing. He hoped to keep out of sight, should any more of the hatchetmen run along, by remaining pressed between the supporting side timbers; none of the tongmen would be expecting to see anyone in the tunnel. Before he started his precarious journey, he meant to secure again the pick lying on the floor of the tunnel.

Jimmy Wentworth was groping on hands and knees when he heard a fierce triumphant shout rock through the tunnel. Heart dead within him, the Chinatown sergeant of detectives knew that the Chinese must have rushed into the basement of the bank. The sound could mean no other possible thing. And yet he was wrong. Almost at once Chinese began to rush past him, swords swinging, rifles brandished.

Had the horde been repelled, discovered? Was it possible that the plot had been uncovered.

No. Coolies and hatchetmen began to hurry past him again, all headed westward. Some carried sacks over their shoulders. Others had heavy boxes suspended between long poles, and, grunting as they walked ahead with their heavy loads, shouted gleefully from man to man.

The bank had been looted.

7

TRAPPED!

PAST WENTWORTH, WALKING delicately, came Kong Gai. The white man's bare fist clenched, and, despite the result, he was about to leap out and, with one of the guard's weapons, try to hack the life out of the human fiend.

Only one thing stopped him—Kong Gai's own words. The Evil One, in lisping voice, said in Mandarin Chinese, *"Hai!* If this fool of a white policeman learns anything, and is able to visit me where I will be, what good will it do him? He will burn, brother, and you will see him die!"

And the other Chinese said. "If this Wentworth, whom we have ample cause to hate, is dead from the poison of the sleeping garments—"

"If he wore the silk, he dies," Kong Gai lisped. "But he may be saving the handsome sleeping garments. In that case, his death is merely delayed. Sooner or later, he will die horribly before your eyes, oh brother of the Cobra. I doubt it, but it might happen when we are at…"

The words fainted away; Wentworth barely heard "oh brother." The last word he did not hear at all.

So Kong Gai, having plotted his death once, through poison, was already figuring on other means of killing him. Good! Forewarned, he was doubly armed. "It might happen when we are at…" That would be the place they were going with their loot! If only he might have heard the final word! Perhaps, later, he would be able to get on the trail. If—if he could get out of the tunnel, all might yet be well.

And then to turn him to stone, he heard a dull reverberation, to eastward. Dust and sand made the air difficult to breathe until it settled. Wentworth knew that the Chinese must have blown up the tunnel with a charge placed somewhere near the bank end. A second boom rocked the floor of the tunnel, nearer.

His lips in a straight line, Jimmy knew that there was no time to waste. He began to move, as swiftly as he could in the dark, toward Chinatown, westward, toward the incline. A charge ahead of him exploded, almost throwing him flat, and filling his lungs with particles of sand, which also spattered against his face, bringing drops of blood.

Wentworth stood stock-still.

Now he knew the worst. The Chinese, in leaving the tunnel, had set several charges to destroy the passage. He himself had been caught between two of the explosions, and was hemmed in the death trap.

What a way to die!

To add to Jimmy Wentworth's horror, the rat began to scamper about, running between the white man's legs in its terror.

Wentworth knew only too well the impossibility of digging through the soft sand. It would merely keep sliding down, no matter how rapidly he used his pick. If there were a shovel, a barrow, even these would do him no good. Before long he would exhaust the air remaining in the tunnel, and that would be the end of him. Captain Dunand would know just about what had happened; would know that his sergeant had died performing his duty. But Jimmy wanted terribly to live. He wanted to live to catch Kong Gai. Above all, he wanted life! He was young… what a way to die!

There was no panic in Jimmy Wentworth's head. He leaned quietly back against the side of the tunnel, where he was standing, and was forced to bend a trifle to avoid hitting his head when he felt it touch his hair.

He stood there for several minutes. His case was hopeless. He would die, trapped, with only a rat for company. His throat began to ache from bits of sand; his lungs were beginning to feel tight, as if a steel cable were drawn around them. In sudden wild anger he drove his fist against a supporting timber of the side of the tunnel, and with a wild gesture ran his hand clear to the top of the heavy wood.

He touched something colder than wood, colder, smoother. Not sand! Not more wood! Steel.

At first the beating of his heart prevented him from hearing any other sound, and then again he heard the rumble-rumble-rumble of the cable above him as it passed over a roller. His heart raced still faster as, where he was now standing, he heard above him a duller rumble, and felt a little shaking of the earth. Where he had been hiding before must have been deeper beneath the street. Here, he was directly under the car-tracks, directly under the cable! Why, the supporting timbers might easily have been placed there originally by the streetcar company, and Kong

Gai had made use of them in advancing the course of his tunnel.

FIRST OF ALL, it was necessary to secure the pick. How slim his chances were he knew only too well, but it was something to do, and better than dying without making a fight for life. For a long, long time Jimmy Wentworth, on his knees, worked slowly eastward again, and was at last rewarded by finding the pick. He had counted, with one hand, the number of timbers he had passed, and retraced his way until he was again where he had so distinctly heard the sound of the cable and the muffled noise of the street-car it pulled along the thoroughfare above.

Wentworth's muscles writhed as he let the pick swing once before him, and then he drove it overhead. Against the steel beneath the cable-slot the steel of the pick shrilled, sending sparks into the tunnel, and numbing Wentworth's shoulders with the blow. He shifted his feet a little to the right. Again he swung the pick, this time against the concrete-and-rock bed of the track. Bits of loosened rock fell on him, but he did not feel the impact.

His breath coming with ever-increasing difficulty, Jimmy Wentworth continued his desperate assault. Swing—up with the pick—the impact. Pain in his shoulders. The work began to be automatic. His head was ringing now. Once he staggered, and kept from falling by reaching out, but he never changed his position. Up with the pick again! Another blow! One more! Oh... what was the use? He couldn't make one more blow! But he did, with the lessening power of his exhausted body, and while his lungs demanded air to maintain their pounding.

One more blow... another... another....

Blindly Jimmy Wentworth continued, only half conscious, to swing the mighty pick....

At first, with the rain of rock, broken concrete, sand into his upturned face, Wentworth thought that the little spot of light was a spark where his pick had struck rock or metal; then he supposed he was finished, and was becoming mad. Then, with a sigh, the Chinatown sergeant of detectives slid down in a heap on the floor of the tunnel. Even his elation could not keep him on his feet.

For there was a spot of daylight above, an inch or two round! And into the tunnel seeped life-giving air. Life!

Wentworth finally arose. Carefully he thrust the haft of the pick through the hole, and held it there, waiting. Just where the haft was protruding he had no way of knowing. Sooner or later, someone was certain to see it.

Two minutes passed, and then the head of the pick was knocked from his hands as the handle was shattered by the first street-car to crash against the hickory. The blow made Jimmy Wentworth's body tingle like an electric shock.

Had the gripman of the car seen the haft? Had he felt the car hit the protruding handle of the pick? Was he stopping his car to find out what had happened?

Jimmy Wentworth, worn out and exhausted, was no longer alert enough to tell. He raised his voice, crying, "I'm under the street! Under the street! The street!" but nothing seemed to happen. A minute passed, another.

And then Wentworth heard, muffled, a familiar voice, directly overhead: Dennis M'Carthy's powerful tones as the Kearny-California traffic officer said, " 'Tis th' work of some kids, belike—"

"Mac!" shouted Jimmy. "Mac! Mac!"

The remains of the hickory haft were jerked from the hole, for the bit of daylight appeared again.

"Mac!"

For an instant, silence, and next M'Carthy's furious, "And what is annyone doin' b'neath th' shtreet? What kind av funny business is goin' on here? Who are you?"

A third time Jimmy Wentworth pleaded, "Mac! M'Carthy! It's Wentworth!"

"What next?" bellowed Officer M'Carthy. "First th' bank... an' now Sergeant Wentworth playin' rabbit in th' street... and it's all right you are, Jimmy me lad? Nawthin' is wrong with ye?"

"O.K.," Jimmy said as crisply as he could. The words took the last atom of strength from him. As he swayed from side to side, with everything beginning to grow black, he managed to add, in a whisper which M'Carthy could never hear: "Only... there wasn't... very much... air... down here..."

"It's telephonin' Headquarters I'll be doin'," M'Carthy shouted. "Mebbe they'll dig ye out, seein' as how ye're a sergeant, Jimmy Wentworth, an' mebbe they'll be leavin' ye lay until all th' excitement is over at th' bank. Anny-how, rest easy. 'Tis a nice cool place ye're in. How'd ye get there, should th' desk sergeant ask it of me?"

Receiving no answer, M'Carthy, now and genuinely alarmed, hurried to the nearest call box.

8

JIMMY RECOVERS

JIMMY WENTWORTH'S EYES opened slowly. For a moment he expected to find himself in the deadly tunnel, and then he knew he was propped high in a hospital bed. Instantly an oxygen tank began to hiss, and Wentworth closed his eyes again, wearily but contentedly. He lay still for some time, thinking how wonderful it was to be alive, but wishing that the people in the room, doctors and nurses, would leave him alone.

Although it was warm in the bed, his hands and feet felt very cold, which was strange.

"He's all right?" a gruff, strained voice demanded.

"Unless his brain has been affected, yes," a doctor answered. "He's not only been gassed, captain, but he has suffered from lack of air and overexertion. But his marvelous physique and his youth are all in his favor in regaining his health."

This time, when Wentworth opened his eyes again, he saw Captain Dunand at the foot of the bed.

Jimmy Wentworth tried to grin, but the bandages covering most of his face prevented anyone seeing what he wanted to do. He said, in almost a natural voice: "Did you get any of them, chief?"

"You feel—pretty good?" asked the gray-haired captain of detectives.

"I feel pretty rotten," Jimmy said cheerfully. "They all got away?"

"Umm," admitted Dunand.

"Which bank?" Wentworth queried briefly.

"You know what happened?"

"I was there! But I didn't have a chance to do anything. You see, sir, I—"

A doctor broke in, "You must be quiet, sergeant. Now, captain—"

Wentworth brushed the order aside: "I'm not sick," he said. "Just a little tired. What took place at the bank, captain?"

"Men gassed," Dunand said shortly. "And men dead. All of them. Different gas from that you inhaled, the doctors say. And… it was Kong Gai, of course. Got away clean!"

Wentworth said, "I suppose a cigarette will kill me now?"

The captain of detectives knew at once that Wentworth must have learned something, but wisely he himself did not insist on being given the information. Of the doctor he asked, "When can the sergeant talk with me for a few minutes?"

"His one real danger was an affected brain, captain. If Sergeant Wentworth is willing to sleep quietly for an hour or two you can see him again."

IT WAS LATE in the afternoon when Captain Dunand returned to the hospital. This time he brought Lucille Carrington with him—the girl who had been rescued from Kong Gai by Wentworth.

Wentworth was feeling much better. His exhaustion had

been counteracted by sleep and food, and his eyes gleamed from under the many bandages.

"If you can find a spot anywhere," Jimmy suggested to the girl, "you can kiss me if you want."

She held his hand tightly.

"What did they do to you, Jimmy?" Lucille demanded.

"I did it all myself. Had to get out of the tunnel, and the only way I could do it was to break into the cable-slot and attract attention. A couple of rocks must have hit me on the head here and there. Honestly, I didn't feel them."

With the girl's hand in his, Wentworth explained quietly to Dunand what he had seen.

Dunand asked, "Why didn't we find the Chinatown end of the tunnel?"

"I've been thinking about that. Here is the answer: it wasn't the real end of the tunnel. The passage went further into Chinatown. The place at the excavation was only where the sand and dirt was taken out."

"You're positive?"

"Yes. The Brothers of the Snake arrived in costume, proving that they had come directly from Kong Gai's lair, and didn't enter at the excavation." Wentworth was silent, and then said, "The sample of sand, chief: it proved to be from the made land below Montgomery street, didn't it?"

"Yes, lad. The expert said he had quite a time identifying it. You see, originally the sand came from somewhere else, and therefore it was difficult to tell about it. If only the expert could have given us the information at once we'd have been ready for Kong Gai! As it is…"

"We've got to wait," Jimmy said gently. "Are the papers riding us, sir?"

"They're giving us a rough time! I'm doing all that can be done. The state men are watching the highways. We raided every opium joint we knew about, from your reports—"

"That'll prove to Kong Gai that he's under suspicion, although he'll never be willing to believe how much we actually know! It's a strange affair, chief! In some way I'm to be tempted, sooner or later, to my death... I wonder when! Well, when the time comes I'll go! It'll be some way connected with the picture I saw in the tunnel and the trade-mark on those pyjamas—a Fire Bird. Just what I couldn't guess. It's some subtle Oriental way of threatening me—a devilish warning in advance that of course I'm supposed to be too stupid to understand, thereby making Kong Gai's vengeance all the sweeter. It's the way he does these things— Well, we'll see."

9

CLEWS POINT NORTH

TWO DAYS LATER, Sergeant James Wentworth was again patrolling Chinatown. His face was still scarred from the sharp edges of rock; he still tired easily from the gassing and lack of air, but his head was as clear as ever. The first time he marched over his beat he saw, as he expected, that the black-clad, furtive figures of hatchetmen had almost entirely vanished. Kong Gai and his men were either in close hiding, or had vanished from the city.

Kong Gai's reasoning in the matter, Wentworth figured, must be that once the robbery was consummated the police would never link it with him, with Chinese. If this were so—and Kong Gai, for all his diabolical cleverness, believed himself infallible, after the manner of criminals—and if Kong Gai had left San Francisco, his trail might be easy to pick up, since the King Cobra would be positive he would never be connected with the crime.

Here and there, efficiently, Wentworth picked up clews. A merchant member of Six Companies vouchsafed the information that a supposed hatchetman in the employ of Kong Gai had bought various articles of clothing, announcing that "when one went north one might expect cold, despite everything a man was told." Another honorable merchant said that one of Kong Gai's many strange ventures had been the purchase of land some time back; where he did not know. The blind spinner in the black basement near the Wangs' bowl shop said, sorrowfully, that he had made a coat for someone out of fine wool, and that since all he had received was a kick, it was logical to believe that it must have been for Kong Gai or one of his Cobras.

With this much in hand, Jimmy Wentworth went to see young Wang Chen-p'o, enemy of Kong Gai, who had helped him in other cases. He told Chen-p'o what he knew, and was amazed with the ease with which the other gave him information.

"Is that all?" Chen-p'o laughed in excellent English. "Some time ago there was gossip in Chinatown about a land purchase. A sheep ranch, Jimmy. You know how we Chinese are; we never rest until we learn the truth. Although the purchase was made through many go-be-tweens, it is a cinch Kong Gai bought the ranch, and it is also pretty sure that's where he went. He 'went north'—well, the ranch is somewhere north. I'll ask my honorable father, if you'll excuse me a moment, and tell you."

When Chen-p'o returned he brought a map with him. Near the California-Oregon line a red circle had been drawn.

"That's where it is," he said. "My honorable father remarked when all Chinatown was discussing it—before you took over the job of making us behave—that some day Kong Gai'd duck up there, after he'd pulled an especially fine trick. Hmm… you think he robbed the bank, eh?"

"Forget all about my asking you," Jimmy grinned. "Kong Gai feels absolutely safe this time." He stared at the map.

"Caliore... that's the nearest town. Well, Chen-p'o, here's where I get some free transportation—"

"I trust," young Wang smiled, "that you do not take an unexpected journey to heaven!"

"Kong Gai won't expect visitors," Wentworth admitted, "but if anybody comes visiting him, I expect he'll be ready. It's up to me to be all set for his deviltry." Jimmy said nothing about the promised threat of the Fire-Bird. "Wish me luck, Chen-p'o."

"You will receive an elegant funeral. Firecrackers, dragons, paid mourners, and a big dinner," chuckled young Wang.

WHEN, LATER, WENTWORTH was in Captain Dunand's office, explaining what he wished to do, the gray-haired captain of detectives said, "D'you think you can slip out of town without Kong Gai knowin' it, lad?"

"Probably not," Wentworth admitted. "That's the chance I must take. When he learns I'm on my way, he'll prepare to match wits with me. That's the Chinese way, Kong Gai's way. Have someone get me a good map of the Caliore country, please. I have this in my favor: I know a little of what I'm up against, and Kong Gai doesn't realize I understand a little of the warning."

"What d'ye mean?"

"I'm to be killed, according to Kong-Gai, by fire. I've a notion he half expected I'd pick up the trail sooner or later, if he wasn't able to kill me before I got started. What he didn't expect would be that I'd learn anything at all. Well, I have, and now it's up to me to see what I can do about it."

That night, ten picked men from the department boarded the Northern Limited. Their bags bore things which would have startled the peaceful travelers. Machine guns, tear bombs, belts of cartridges. Many rifles in case of a long range fight. Before departing, Wentworth had spoken to the heads of the bank, and enlisted their support in case he needed assistance: the robbery had involved the Government, since it was a national bank. Wentworth laid his plans carefully, trying to overlook no detail.

Dunand was doubtful. He felt that Wentworth was not only periling his own life, but also the lives of ten other men. At the ferry he said, "Jim, we want Kong Gai for murder and robbery, true enough. If you have a real chance to get him, get him! Otherwise, I forbid you to waste a single life."

"Right," Jimmy said gently.

In the buffet car it was easy for Wentworth to draw fellow passengers into conversation. Before he turned in for the night he knew considerable about the Caliore country; enough so he was able to hand the porter a code telegram to be sent to Headquarters.

Wentworth had been looking for two pieces of information. Concerning, firstly, anything even vaguely about birds near Caliore, and, secondly, Chinese. He had asked the first question openly, explaining to a middle-aged passenger that he was interested in Pacific Coast birds of various varieties; the second bit of information had been given him without a hint.

This is what the passenger had said: "Birds? Yes, we have migratory birds up in the peat country. Funny thing, friend; there's a kind of bird that nests somewhere in the open, and every time there's a peat bed fire these birds fly over it. Matter of fact, that's the only way we can tell the peat's burning, you know. The peat catches fire—nobody ever knows how—and just smoulders under the surface. It'll burn for days, weeks, years, without anybody knowing it, until some poor devils of sheep break through the top crust… we used to blame the Chinks for it. We thought they tried to burn the grass to get a better growth the next spring, but I guess the fires are just accidents…"

Birds flying over hidden fires! Fire birds!

A chance to get Kong Gai, and the possibility of regaining the loot, provided it had been conveyed up to the Caliore sheep country, the barren land of little rain, of wide expanses of peat beds, of few springs and fewer inhabitants.

For appearance's sake Wentworth spent a half hour in the morning wandering about the town of Caliore, asking questions. If he saw a battered old car driven by a Chinese rumble and creak out of the town he said nothing of it. If he noticed that this car's engine was in excellent condition, and that the car moved at a far greater pace than seemed possible once it was on the road, he did not mention it, even to his men.

Here and there, Wentworth showed his shield to some of the reliable men in the town, asking always the question: had anyone seen birds flying over the barren waste of the sheep land? Wentworth knew how readily men's imaginations worked. He wanted if possible to get the exact location, without intimating that it might be near China Ranch, where he had speedily learned Kong Gai and his Cobras must be. That part hadn't been difficult to determine, but the fact about the birds was equally important.

It was a venerable sheepman who finally told him; "I've seen 'em west," he said. "That's it, pardner, west. Somewheres on th' China Camp road, 'bout four, five miles out o' town. Yes, sir, I've seen 'em."

"Four or five miles?"

"At a guess, stranger."

"Thanks, old man. Much obliged to you."

The old Californian bit off a chunk of tobacco, and mouthed a huge piece of it before replying. "Bad lot, them Chinks," he volunteered. "Heard they started a fire right on th' ranch, th' fools. Somebody went out t' see—peat fires is serious in this country—but it was all out by th' time we went. Couple o' weeks ago, that was. Not in th' place I told you about. Right on th' ranch."

"Thanks again," Jimmy smiled.

Birds! Wentworth was positive, as he had been on the train while making his investigations, that he had uncovered the secret hidden in the Fire Bird trademark. As he glanced at his watch now, his face was grim. In another hour, he would learn whether he had thought faster than Kong Gai. In another hour, his men would have a chance to recover the missing gold—or would be dead out on the peat beds!

10

THE TRAP OF FIRE

IN CALIORE'S MAIN garage, Wentworth had hired two touring cars. He made no secret of who he was, but said only that the police were after a criminal, without explaining the case. He promised the garage owner that any damage to the cars would be taken care of by the police.

And in a few minutes more Wentworth and his ten men were out of the dusty town and traveling swiftly westward. At first the road was excellent, but when it came to the third westward fork, the touring cars bounced over a bad road, an almost unused road—the road to the China sheep ranch. For five or ten minutes the road was hard and rutted, and then suddenly, all at once, it became perfectly smooth and level.

In the rear seat of each car detectives and police had unpacked choppers, had slipped the first cartridge of the belts into the chambers. Rifles were jointed together. Tear bombs lay ready on the floor.

Wentworth himself, sitting beside Officer Rainey in the first car, alone of the men, made no effort to prepare for attack. Again and again he kept an eye on his watch. This was a delicate affair. The element of time entered into it only in that nothing must happen before eleven o'clock. Otherwise, ten good men would be sacrificed, and he himself would meet death, probably after torture.

On every side the waste land stretched. The touring cars moved over the giant peat beds, fifty or more feet thick. The only proof of road were the ruts, deep and unmistakable, dug into the black earth by the wheels of machines. Far to the west a cloud hung over the distant Siskiyou Mountains. Somewhere on the barren land was China Ranch, in some depression near a live spring.

Several times Wentworth levelled powerful glasses, trying to see anything he might see. Once he saw a few sheep cropping the scanty grass northward; once he saw a vulture wheeling high in the air, waiting for carrion.

At five minutes past eleven he scanned the sky again, carefully, and saw a tiny speck far, far overhead. As he lowered the glasses toward the onward path of the cars, he observed what seemed to be two lines on the earth, one on either side of the road. Fissures in the peat bed? Or something else? Eyes staring, Wentworth looked above the fissures, and not at them at all!

At first he saw nothing. Then, as the car advanced, he seemed to have little black specks dancing in front of his eyes. Black specks? No! Birds! Birds high in the air!

Wentworth said, "Slow down, Rainey. That's better. We don't want to go too fast." Jimmy stared through his powerful glasses until his eyes ached, and was rewarded by seeing what must be a human head rise from the shelter of a hummock. This was the place; no doubt of it. The birds were flying above a spot where the peat was burning beneath the surface. Near this spot Kong Gai's hatchetmen were waiting, to see the white detective plunge to terrible death, to see him, as Kong Gai had promised, veritably burned alive!

While Rainey drove along steadily, Wentworth fastened straps about the steering wheel, so that it was immovable. Rainey took off his hands. The automobile moved in a straight line along the absolutely straight road.

Swiftly this time, Wentworth again looked through the glasses. There were the birds, circling above the road over the peat bed. Much closer. Tiny birds, darting this way and that.

Wentworth raised his voice: "Keep fifty feet behind us," he called. "Swerve a bit when I call, so there's a chance of keeping the Chinese from seeing us get out of this car!" To the men in his own car he said, "When you're out, down on your bellies! As the other car passes, get on the running-board, on this side, away from the mound on the left. Stoop down on the running board and keep as well out of sight as possible. Ready? O.K."

RAINEY SLOWED THE car's progress as the men slid out. Each obeyed Wentworth's order efficiently. Unless the Chinese were watching from some other spot save the hummock of earth, there was a good chance of their missing the performance. Wentworth would have given a good deal to have made the transfer earlier, but there had been the possibility of an attack on the cars, which would have made it dangerous to leave one unprotected.

Wentworth himself slipped out now. Rainey, a hand on the gas throttle, worked his way to the far side, and, as he jumped, jerked the throttle far down.

The driverless car leaped forward, as if on scouting duty,

toward the spot on the road beneath the circling little birds… nearer… nearer… almost there….

The following machine proceeded more sedately, with every officer alert.

The car without a driver was almost directly beneath the high wheeling birds; the pace slackened suddenly, as if the front wheels must be meeting some soft earth and therefore losing traction, and then, all at once, the big machine vanished! At the self-same instant there was a terrific roar. Flames sprang hundreds of feet into the air. Smoke, black, thick smoke, swirled after it.

Officer Hastings said unevenly, "If we'd been in that car… what a way to die!"

"Kong Gai's way," Wentworth said. "The peat bed was afire. Exploded the gasoline, of course. Keep ready, men! Get going faster now!"

On the edge of the black pall of smoke, rising higher every instant from the burning peat exposed now to the air, and burning freely, uncouth figures danced. Shots spat at the second of the cars as Chinese raced toward the second machine. Wild, uncouth figures of bloodthirsty hatchetmen. Some paused, despite the awful heat generated under the surface, to gesticulate horribly.

Had their companions been in the burning, exploded automobile, the remaining officers would have been disorganized. As it was, lips pressed together, they awaited Wentworth's word before returning the scattering, malicious fire of the Chinese. Wentworth said, "Let 'em have it, gang!" As he himself pressed trigger he glanced at his watch hastily. The appointed time! The arrival at the burning peat bed had been as closely calculated as had been possible. While guns roared, Wentworth grated, "Keep at it! We've got 'em! The odds may be a hundred to one, now, but... wait!"

That very instant there swept out of the sky a Fire Bird, as true a fire bird as the little ones which always circle above a concealed fire in the peat beds, which not even men can see—fires which burn unnoticed for years, although this fire had been set by Kong Gai to welcome and kill his enemy. A true Fire Bird! Down, down, in a steep vertical dive, roared the little pursuit plane. As it responded to the stick, its nose pointed upward slightly as it neared the earth, and then the machine-gunner in the forward cockpit pressed trigger, and the vicious gun chattered.

Banking, turning, twisting, the plane pursued the fleeing Chinese, and then sharply zoomed southward, and in another moment was bouncing over the level waste land and taxiing up to the police car.

"Now what?" demanded the helmeted army lieutenant.

"Know where this ranch is?" Jimmy demanded swiftly.

"Sure. West. Not far."

"Got room for me?"

"Let's go," grinned Lieutenant Morgan. "Climb in with East, up front."

Wentworth gave his men only a word: "Round 'em up," he said briefly. "I want to get to the ranch before Kong Gai knows what's happened. Drive after us as soon as you can—make it snappy!"

11

KONG GAI VANISHES

THE ENGINE ROARED. In an instant it was in the air, this Fire Bird of the white men. Lieutenant East scribbled on a pad, and handed the message to Wentworth, whose ears were already deafened by the motor roar: "Saw your signal. Nice work. How did you know what the Chinks intended?"

Jimmy wrote on the pad, "Got the dope from train passenger. Knew it had something to do with birds and with fire. Put two and two together. Hope we catch the man we are after."

"So do I," scrawled his companion in the cockpit.

Lieutenant Morgan rocked the plane and East reached back for Morgan's message. It read: "Now what? I can see plenty of men running around. Elevation only five hundred now. Attack again? If so, will go up to three thousand and drop."

Wentworth, wishing he could talk instead of this continual writing, reached around and handed his answer from cockpit to cockpit. "My party. Drop me and go up again. In case I'm attacked, do whatever you can."

The roar instantly stopped, and Wentworth had the sinking sensation as the swift plane's nose headed toward the earth.

As a sort of lesson, and not because of any order, Lieutenant East's gun began to whisper its deadly song again. The Chinese broke and ran, this way and that. By the time—only a minute—that the airplane touched ground and ran along to a stop, there was not a single black-clad figure in sight!

Wentworth's ears hummed; East shouted to him, "Let us stick around! Morgan'll keep the engine runnin', and if they come I can keep th' gun at 'em…"

Nodding, Jimmy clambered out of the plane, jerking out his gun.

China Ranch was deserted!

Here and there in the waste were scurrying figures, running from the white man's Fire Bird, running from death and the noose of the white man's justice.

Kong Gai?

When the police car, with eight of the officers, tore up to the squalid buildings, all stinking with the sweetish chocolatey odor of opium, no sign of the venomous Chinese was discovered. Had he escaped by running off? While Wentworth and the army men, together with three of the police, searched the buildings, the others started in pursuit of the fleeing hatchetmen, rounding up many of the Brothers of the Snake. But of Kong Gai nothing was found.

Every inch of the ranch house was searched, and then Wentworth said suddenly; "We're all wrong, men! Some time ago Kong Gai had a peat fire here; I'll just bet he hollowed out a place in the earth, and put the loot from the bank there. Gave him a chance to experiment against the day we might come after him, to see how the peat acted when it burned, and how much, and how thick a crust it left."

Over the earth the detectives went, carefully, thoroughly, looking for some trace of fire, or of earth different from the rest. They found exactly nothing. In sheer desperation Jimmy Wentworth himself joined them. Up and down he marched grimly, trying to make the only possibility stand up. It was a full hour before he came on the bodies of several of the little birds, some time dead.

Each had been killed by a blow from a stone or stick… Cantonese fashion. Each poor little neck, after death, had been carefully wrung.

Wentworth called his men together.

"Here's where the birds must have come, when Kong Gai started his little fire here. It's dangerous, although I'm positive the fire's completely out—there are no more birds flying, and Kong Gai tried to drive 'em away before by killing 'em out of pure cussedness—let's drive the car slowly up and down here. If we come to a softer spot, Rainey'll know it…"

EVEN JIMMY HIMSELF doubted the possibility of recovering the loot by this means, but he had nothing else to try. Rainey drove the machine toward the little dead birds, innocent victims of Kong Gai's ruthless ferocity.

Four dead birds. Why four? Had Kong Gai tired of the game, after killing so few? What twist in the Chinese' evil brain had made him kill four of the countless birds which had been circling in the air?

In Jimmy Wentworth's hand now was one of the feathered mites; unpleasant to hold, but this was not what made the Chinatown detective's eyes brighten. The body of the little creature was heavy! Far too heavy. In each of the birds, soon to be exposed to the elements, was a heavy rock or stone, of different color from the top of the peat beds. Four stones, left to mark... what?

Wentworth was about to say, "Dig here!" when he paused. Kong Gai would never be as obvious as that. What, then, did the birds mean? Was there any Chinese saying, or proverb, which might let light into the secret? Yes! "A bird can fly in one second equal to ten paces of a man!" Ten steps, multiply it by four, the number of birds! Forty paces. Where would that bring him?

Excitedly Wentworth stepped off the distance. Did it again. A third time and a fourth. Each time he marked the distance from the center. Each short journey away from the birds took him to an open peat bed, never to a building, for all were at a greater distance. Next Wentworth sent men after ropes; these, tied together, enabled him to make a crude circle, forty paces from the feathered bodies. Then he said:

"There's nothing to it but dig. We've got shovels here at the ranch. Let's go at it and see what happens."

" 'Tis a foine job for a Mulcahey who's earned his three stripes," groaned one of the officers, after an hour's work.

"It's the right kind of work for a Mulcahey," one of the other men laughed.

And, midway around the circle, buried five feet in black, burned peat soil, the missing treasure from the vaults of the Bank of Northern California was found! The surface above it was unburned; the scarred, blackened ground where the Chinese had made their first experimental fire was a long way distant, but the painstaking Chinese had somehow burrowed beneath the untouched surface to this point, where Kong Gai felt the wealth would be safe from anyone. And the four little harmless birds, killed by him wantonly to lend a touch of diabolical Orientalism to the stone markers, had betrayed him! That, and Wentworth's keenness and his deep knowledge of the ways of the East. The wily murderous King Cobra was foiled again.

Kong Gai himself? That was another matter. The head of the Cobra Clan had certainly been at the ranch, if the testimony of handsome quilts and teakwood stands could be trusted... but he had vanished utterly. Nor could Wentworth wring a word of his whereabouts from any of the captured hatchetmen.

Four of the officers remained a week at China Ranch, lest the King Cobra be in hiding nearby. Two detectives stayed at Caliore. Sheriffs were warned. But Kong Gai was not caught, nor was the slightest trace of him discovered.

The day the police left China Ranch, the lower part of a dipping vat opened, and the King Cobra stepped out. Above him had been the true vat, filled to the brim with creosote, smelling and black. Beneath this, in a hidden compartment, Kong Gai—who took no chances—had waited, supplied with food, water, and even oxygen, in case he was forced to replace the rivets on the side which gave him air.

Over the waste land Kong Gai wandered, his water bottle heavy at his side. To the north he could see, during the night, the glow of the burning peat bed, now exposed to air. Without air, it would have merely glowed beneath the surface, without smoke, without flame, eating, eating, into the peat on every side. How had Wentworth foreseen his deadly, perfect plan? High in the air the little birds circled, but Kong Gai gave no thought to them now. All he could do was to spit out words which promised little good to one Sergeant Wentworth.

But Jimmy Wentworth was not thinking of Kong Gai as the Venomous One crept back by devious routes to his lair deep in Chinatown. Dunand had given him a week off, and what Lucille was saying to him was as important to Jimmy as the words of praise from his beloved Chief.

For Lucille had just said, "That lovely ivory carving of the Fire Bird the merchant in Chinatown gave you, Jimmy… we'll have it in our living room pretty soon, won't we?"

Which was much more important than Kong Gai at that moment!

www.ingramcontent.com/pod-product-compliance
Lightning Source LLC
Chambersburg PA
CBHW031207020726
47499CB00002B/524